BECKIE WEINHEIMER

converting kate

VIKING

VIKING
Published by Penguin Group
Penguin Group (USA) Inc., 345 Hudson Street, New York, New York 10014, U.S.A.
Penguin Group (Canada), 90 Eglinton Avenue East, Suite 700, Toronto, Ontario,
Canada M4P 2Y3 (a division of Pearson Penguin Canada Inc.)
Penguin Books Ltd, 80 Strand, London WC2R 0RL, England
Penguin Ireland, 25 St Stephen's Green, Dublin 2, Ireland (a division of Penguin Books Ltd)
Penguin Group (Australia), 250 Camberwell Road, Camberwell, Victoria 3124, Australia
(a division of Pearson Australia Group Pty Ltd)
Penguin Books India Pvt Ltd, 11 Community Centre, Panchsheel Park, New Delhi – 110 017, India
Penguin Group (NZ), Cnr Airborne and Rosedale Roads, Albany, Auckland 1310, New Zealand
(a division of Pearson New Zealand Ltd)
Penguin Books (South Africa) (Pty) Ltd, 24 Sturdee Avenue, Rosebank, Johannesburg 2196,
South Africa

Penguin Books Ltd, Registered Offices: 80 Strand, London WC2R 0RL, England

First published in 2007 by Viking, a member of Penguin Group (USA) Inc.

10 9 8 7 6 5 4 3 2 1

LIBRARY OF CONGRESS CATALOGING-IN-PUBLICATION DATA
Weinheimer, Beckie.
Converting Kate / by Beckie Weinheimer. — 1st ed.
p. cm.
Summary: After moving from Arizona to Maine, sixteen-year-old Kate tries to recover
from her father's death as she resists her mother's dogmatic religious beliefs and
attempts to find a new direction to her life.

ISBN 978-0-670-06152-5 (hardcover)

[1. Self-perception—Fiction. 2. Family problems—Fiction. 3. Religion—Fiction. 4. Interpersonal
relations—Fiction. 5. High schools—Fiction. 6. Schools—Fiction. 7. Moving, Household—Fiction.
8. Maine—Fiction.] I. Title.
PZ7.W4334Con 2007
[Fic]—dc22
2006010200

Printed in the U.S.A.
Set in Sabon
Book design by Jim Hoover

To Alice, who once said,
"Maybe the peace comes in not knowing."

To Irene, who has been my own
Aunt Katherine in so many ways.

To my brother Eric, who first had the
courage to say, "I don't believe."

To Tony Hair, who has the integrity
and goodness of Pastor Browning.

To my mother, who gave me the gifts of hope,
of dreams, and of a great enthusiasm for life.

To Alan, my best friend, who read this
manuscript more times than I want to count,
and taught me that life has options.

acknowledgments

Thanks to the faculty and students at Vermont College, especially Karen Fisher-Baird. Also my thanks to Holly Kearl, Mary Kearl, Sheila Holsinger, Mark Hutchens, Cynthia Kolodny, Linda Ruble, Stephanie Barksdale, Malloree Jo Weinheimer, Russell Eric Weinheimer, Kyle Weinheimer, Tanya Weinheimer, Julie and Eric Allstrom, and the Shenandoah SCBWI retreat group.

Many thanks to Alan Stewart for his technical help with lobstering, and to Mike Staggs and his French fry oil fueled car. Additionally, my thanks to Steven Chudney, my agent, who took a chance on an unknown writer. To Catherine Frank for her insightful edits, for thinking up a title for my book, and for believing in Kate. And to Jim Hoover for his wonderful jacket design.

chapter one

"KATE?"

From where she stands on the back porch, Mom's voice is quieter than the early-morning sounds of chirping birds and scampering squirrels. Still, it pierces through me.

Listen children small and tall. Obey your parents. Heed their call. The words of the Sunday school hymn march uninvited through my head. I wish I could just wash my mind, scrub it clean, of all the rules, all the scriptures, and start over.

Instead of answering, I creep farther into the morning shadows, wheeling my bike toward the woods, where the scent of wild roses beckons. At the edge of Aunt Katherine's property, I heft the frame over a fallen tree, hoping for an escape route. But the sight ahead—a maze of sapling pines, thick ferns, and more fallen logs—is discouraging. It would take forever to plow my way through to the highway.

"Kate, is that you?" Mom calls again.

"No. It's a lunatic rapist, lurking in the woods, ready to attack a lone woman," I mutter as I drag my tires back over the tree and make my way toward the inn. When I'm within hearing distance, I use a low voice to keep from waking the guests. "I'm biking to school today."

"Your first day? It's seven miles and still dark out. Why aren't you taking the bus?" Mom whispers. She leans against the porch railing of the inn and reaches under her shoulder-length auburn hair to fasten her locket.

Above me, wisps of pink clouds like cotton candy are beginning to streak through the gray sky. After a week in Puffin Cove, I'm still in awe of the ever-changing Maine sky. If only I could evaporate and mix myself with the colorful clouds and reappear at school. That would freak Mom out. Even though our—her—church talks about visions and angels, I'm sure she's never actually seen anything mystic happen. But sadly, every particle of me is present and accounted for as I stand beside our guests' cars: a BMW convertible, a Ford Explorer, and a bright red Jeep Cherokee. And my personal interrogator, with hands on her hips, eyes zooming into me like telescopic lenses, won't be leaving me alone until I give her an answer.

"I taped a note on the fridge. All the clubs have sign-up tables before school today. I thought I might join cross-country."

"Cross-country? Why, that's wonderful. But I haven't made your lunch yet. If only you had told me yesterday, I

could have arranged for Aunt Katherine to cover for me."
She turns toward the cottage on the other side of the drive,
but the blinds of my great-aunt's windows are still shut and
everything is dark. "Do you even know the way?"

"Yes. I remember from when we went to register."

"Oh, Kate." Mom sighs. "Why don't you ask for my
help instead of trying to do everything yourself?"

I squint at the locket, her precious locket, the locket I
have grown to hate. My grip on the handlebars tightens.
Does she really want to know why? Hasn't she figured it
out during this endless year since Dad died? I glance at
my watch. "I've got to go, Mom. I already packed myself
a lunch."

"I hope it's got something healthy in it. And please tell
me you're changing out of those running shorts and into
one of your school skirts when you get there."

My shoulder muscles tense at the mention of school
skirts. Like I'd be caught wearing one of those ever again.

When I don't answer, Mom says, "Do you think cross-
country practice will start today?"

"Yes. That's what the papers we got at the school said."

"Well, don't be too late," her voice pleads, suddenly
soft and kind. "Remember the dinner at church? I was
thinking you could come with me."

I don't answer. I never do. Not anymore. Not about
church.

Mom's eyes shift focus when a light appears in one of

the guest bedrooms. Shadows stir behind the lace curtains. She smoothes her hair, pats at her skirt, and pastes on her charming innkeeper smile.

"All right, Kate. I can't do anything about driving you to school right now, but please be careful. The woods and back roads can be dangerous. That's where perverts hide, looking for prey."

"Right, like all the perverts in Maine are up at six a.m. just to catch me," I answer under my breath.

"What did you say?"

"Nothing. Bye, Mom."

"Good-bye, Kate. I'll be praying for you. Good luck with your first day at Rocky Point High. Remember, you are a witness for Christ."

Won't she ever get it? A witness for Christ? Me?

Despite her cheerful face, I notice her shoulders slump as she turns away. Her step is heavier than usual as she climbs the back-porch steps. Since we arrived last week, I've realized her life isn't easy. Mom has almost totally taken over running Aunt Katherine's bed-and-breakfast inn. She cooks, cleans, and shops for the guests every day and still manages to make me lunch and dinner. By nine p.m. she's yawning. Twice this past week she even fell asleep at the kitchen table, resting her head on top of menus and shopping lists. And she has no support group here, no one but Dad's aunt Katherine and me, her wayward daughter, her only child, who's headed for Hell. She left all her church friends, all her church committees, and her sister behind in Phoenix to run this inn. If my stomach wasn't spinning at the thought of starting at a brand-new high school—and if I didn't think about Dad—I could almost pity her.

But I do think about Dad.

chapter two

WANTING TO MELT into the tile floor, I slink past the mural of a gigantic red bird and the words GO CARDINALS painted on the cafeteria wall. How many years has it been here? Did Dad walk past it when he ate in this same lunchroom? Where did he sit? Did he have friends? Or, like me, did he have to scan the entire room for an empty table where he could hide?

At least in Phoenix we could eat outside. I found my own shaded palm tree after I quit going to church last year. I just couldn't face my religious friends with all their hopeful comments about my dead father. "It's not too late, Kate. You can still pray for the salvation of his soul. We have missionaries in Heaven who are trying to convert people in the spirit world every day." Hiding here will be much harder. I feel everyone's eyes on me. They seem to be whispering, "Oh, it's the new girl. She has no one to sit with." Is there some universal high-school code that says you're supposed to stare at and ignore the new kid? Even though I had sworn off prayer months ago, I find myself desperately begging any mystical force in the universe to deliver me from this misery, drop me into a dark hole or help me vanish.

And then I notice them. The girls in their long blue, black, and brown skirts walking straight in front of me like nuns on their way to Mass.

Modesty is a young woman's virtue. All skirts should be midcalf in length and of dark, subdued colors. It is our soul that should shine, not our outer clothing.

And sure enough the skirts all hit the girls at midcalf—school skirts. I don't breathe. Don't notice me, my head chants. Don't notice me. And they don't. They march to their table, right past me, just like I'm any generic person from the outside world! Despite the embarrassment of standing here alone, I can't help but smile. I look normal! I blend in!

It's not that I'm wearing anything that could even remotely be considered the height of style, even though I did see two other girls wearing Adidas running shorts just like mine. But unlike me, both girls had the waistband of their shorts rolled over so just the tiniest bit of their tan bellies was exposed, too little to get them kicked out of school, but enough to show off their flat stomachs. In place of a 10K T-shirt, they each wore matching Adidas tank tops, and platform flip-flops instead of serious running shoes. But still.

Against my will, my eyes stay glued to the church girls' table. One girl wears a *Keep the Faith* T-shirt. From here I can't read the tiny words underneath. But I know them by heart. *Be happy, be Christian.* I cringe. I have an identical yellow shirt, stuffed away with all my other church clothes in a box at the back of my closet. The Church of the Holy Divine seems to be plugging the same ideas here that it did back in Arizona. I got my shirt almost two years ago on my fourteenth birthday, like everyone at church does at that age. With it comes a special challenge to share the love of Jesus Christ with at least fourteen people throughout the year. They believe everyone in the world would be better off if they were members of the Church of the Holy Divine, because it is the only *true* church on the face of the earth. And to think I believed it, too. I make a vow to dig my T-shirt out of the bottom of my box and burn it.

Next I notice the six identical smiles and six sets of shining eyes. I always used to think people from our church were different because the spirit of Christ shone through us. But whatever is shining in their eyes feels more like something from a horror movie now. Did my eyes look like that? How far would I have followed our High Priest, Mom, and other church leaders if Dad hadn't died? If those girls knew who I was, they'd be all over me. They'd put *fellowship Kate* on their list of spiritual things to do. And then they could really beam, because they'd be fulfilling their true reason for being at Rocky Point High. Up until high school, kids who belong to the Church of the Holy Divine are homeschooled, but once you're fourteen, you're considered ready to go out into the world and bring others *the truth*. Yeah, right. Maybe the real reason they let us come to public high schools is that no stay-at-home moms know how to teach chemistry or calculus.

As they all bow their heads, I start to gag. Praying. In the school cafeteria. I did that, too. I turn away, not knowing how long I've been standing in this spot. I sigh and start searching for a place to sit again.

"Nice shirt."

A girl with short, curly dark hair grins up at me. I'm only five foot two and not used to looking down to talk to people, but she's at least two or three inches shorter than me. Her wrists and feet are so small they look elfish, but she's really stacked on top, even in her baggy T-shirt. "So I take it you run?" she asks, adjusting her backpack and armload of posters.

I nod.

"Didn't I see you stop in front of the cross-country table this morning?"

I nod again.

"But you didn't sign up for the team?"

"N-n-o," I stutter. I wanted to, I wanted to so badly, but I felt so scared, so shy.

"Why not?"

I shrug, too embarrassed to explain, and at the same time wonder if it's hard to run fast with big breasts. I'll never know. I'm almost flat.

"Well, come tell me about it at our table." She motions her shoulder toward a group of students near the far end of the cafeteria. "If I stand one more second, I'll drop something."

"Here, let me help." My voice suddenly comes to life as I take several of the posters out of her hands.

"Thanks. I'm Jamie, by the way."

"I'm Kate," I say, and follow her in a daze. Did some Heavenly being actually hear my prayer? Or do I just look that pathetic and alone?

"If you've run a 10K before, we could use you," Jamie says, turning her head back to me as she darts through clusters of students.

At the table, she drops posters, backpack, and several books as she introduces me to "the rest of the senior geeks." She points last to a tall guy who has cropped red hair, the thick kind that would be in tight curls if it grew an inch. "This is Douglas Riggs. We've been friends since preschool. We used to play on the teeter-totter together."

"Hey," they all seem to say in unison as I sit across from Douglas in a vacant spot. He's wearing this ugly tan sweater even though it's still warm out, a sweater you just know his mom picked out for him. He's twitching his leg so hard under the table that it vibrates.

Totally ignoring me, he stares at Jamie and asks, "So, what did you get on the review test today in calculus?"

Jamie takes the posters I'm holding and combines them with hers and tucks them all under the table. Her shirt says *Vegetarians have more fun.* She sits and pulls a banana out of her backpack before answering. "One hundred and four."

Douglas grins. "Me, too."

Jamie and Douglas high-five each other.

"You both got the bonus question, right?" one of the other girls asks.

Jamie shrugs as she peels the banana. "I got lucky and guessed the right formula to solve the extra-credit problem. How about you, Douglas?"

Douglas starts explaining the interval at which the tangent X approaches the limit of the function and the rest of the table have their eyes glued to him like he's revealing the secret answer to winning a million-dollar lottery ticket. They really are geeks.

I bite into my twelve-grain bagel and only half listen as Jamie chimes in with more about the derivatives. Okay, so they aren't exactly the cool group, but still . . . I shiver as I glance over at the table of long-skirted girls. Things could be worse.

"Now, Douglas, quit bugging me about calculus. I have work to do." She smiles and turns toward me. Between bites of her banana she says, "Kate, can I beg you to join the cross-country team?"

"Sure." My heart jumps. Did I just say that out loud?

"Sure? No fight? No 'I hate running in the heat'?"

"No," I say, and think, *Heat? Try running in Phoenix.*

"Can you start today after school?"

"Okay." I'm really doing this.

"Great! I always knew I was a born saleswoman!" She grins.

I smile back. So far this Jamie girl is making the hardest part of my day pretty painless.

"And speaking of cross-country, I gotta hang up these posters before lunch is over."

As she crouches under the table, I find my voice. "Would you like some help?"

Her eyes meet mine. "Sure."

I gather up some posters and follow her.

"I'm so glad you're going to do cross-country," she says as we make our way back through the throngs of students to the wall with the red cardinal. "We're going to do repeats this afternoon," she says as she tosses me the roll of tape. "Ever done those before?"

I nod and swallow a lump as I think of Dad and all our runs. He was on the cross-country team at Rocky Point High, too. He trained me just like I was on a team. With effort, I push him into the back of my mind and begin to worry about the more immediate problem. How am I ever going to do that huge workout and then bike all the way back home?

As I'm attaching one of Jamie's posters, which reads, *Cross-country. Run for health. Run for fun. Run for Rocky Point High. It's never too late to join. Practice starts today!* to the wall, a singsong voice echoes off the bricks. "Rich-ard." Both Jamie and I turn as Chelsea Riggs, a sophomore with thick red hair and a low-cut, tight-fitting blouse, zooms past us. She was in all my morning classes and made her presence well known every single hour. She sucked up to the teachers; flirted with the guys; and tried to gossip with the popular girls, the ones with the most stylish clothes.

"All I can say is those two deserve each other." Jamie rolls her eyes in disgust. "He pollutes the air with his Hummer and she pollutes it with her babbling and strong perfume."

I stifle a giggle. Chelsea even talked to me last period when she didn't seem to find any of her good friends in class. Or maybe, like me, she overheard three girls in the hallway: "Did you see Chelsea Riggs in those knockoff jeans? She thinks she's *hot.*" Then they all laughed.

But I'm not sure what knockoff jeans are, or a Hummer, although I think it must be some sort of car.

"Richard Penrose is new, too." Jamie nods at him as the two pass by us. At the mention of his full name, I turn and steal a good glance at him. He's this way-tall, blond-haired guy, and he seems to be working hard to ignore Chelsea as she jabbers away at his back.

"Did you say Penrose?"

Jamie chuckles. "Yup, the high-and-mighty Penrose family. Why, have you heard of them?"

I nod. "I only moved here last week, but my aunt Katherine owns the Whispering Woods Inn. She mentioned that a Penrose boy would be coming to our high school. She said his father and mine were friends growing up."

"So your dad's from here?"

"He was. When he married my mom, they moved out west."

Jamie nods. "I know the Whispering Woods Inn. Your aunt does a lot of recycling."

I chuckle. "She sure does, and it's driving my mom nuts. We didn't recycle at all in Phoenix."

"Really?" Jamie asks, like we must have moved here from Mars.

Then, at the sound of Chelsea's voice, she whispers, "Well, everyone wonders why Mr. Prep-School Star is here at Rocky Point." She pauses, looking around, and then leans in close to my ear. "I've heard that Mr. Penrose pulled Richard out of his fancy private school because he's afraid he'll turn out like his older brother, Phillip."

"What do you mean? What happened to his brother?"

"Oh, he's come out."

I look at her, puzzled.

"Gay," Jamie adds.

I try hard not to choke. I can't believe how casually she says *gay*, just like it's any word. She said it the same way she might say he's "tall."

Homosexuality is the modern plague, brought to the world by Satan and implemented by his true followers.

Jamie doesn't seem to notice me gasp. She says, "So rumor has it that Mr. Penrose has sentenced Richard to finish high school here in little old small-town Maine, where guys are either lumberjacks or lobstermen. You know, *real* men. You'd think a fancy lawyer from Boston like him would be smart enough to realize that homosexuality isn't a contagious disease."

I shrug, trying to act casual, while my mind races, trying to take all this information in. I know our church—Mom's church—thinks homosexuality is a huge sin, but I've never really given it much thought.

I follow Jamie to the next wall, and as I tape up another poster, I keep one eye on that Richard guy. He passes up the food line, swerving in and out of people like he's trying hard to escape from his redheaded shadow. He makes a beeline straight for the side cafeteria door, which I discovered earlier leads to only restrooms.

Chelsea's head jolts back as the swinging door slams shut very near her face. She glares at it for a few seconds, then stomps off.

"Oh dear, poor Chelsea," Jamie says.

When Jamie and I return to the table to finish lunch, Chelsea slides down on the bench beside me. "'S-up?" she says.

I shrug, not sure how to answer, and resist the urge to scratch my nose, which itches at the scent of her perfume.

Her eyes are glued to the cafeteria door like she is a fan waiting for Richard the Rock Star to make an appearance. She sucks in her stomach and takes tiny sips of her Diet Coke. Then she sets it on the table and begins to peel away some of the foil on a roll of Wint-O-Green Life Savers. "Want one?" She offers the roll to me.

"No, thanks."

Chelsea shrugs, pops the candy into her mouth, eyes the cafeteria door again, and then leans across the table and taps a senior guy's hand.

"Coach said the grass is dry enough for practice today after all." Chelsea had beamed last period when she told me that she is the manager of the golf team.

She turns back to me and asks, "So, what lame topic are they on today?" She nods her head toward Jamie and her friends, who are so serious and intense and debating numbers back and forth.

"They're talking about some calculus exam, I think."

"Pathetic! No wonder Richard thinks Rocky Point is full of losers." Her lips pout. She glares down the table.

"Did he actually tell you that?" Jamie asks.

"Well, no. But c'mon, the kids here are total hicks. No wonder he doesn't talk to anyone."

"He's only had half a day," Douglas, who's had his head in a calculus book, says. "Give him a chance."

Chelsea sticks her tongue out at him. And I realize he must be her big brother and probably both are Michelle Riggs's kids. Mom said her old friend had two students at Rocky Point High about my age.

I clear my throat, then ask Chelsea in a timid voice, "Is he your brother?"

"Sadly."

"I think our moms used to be friends. My mom worked here one summer when they were in college."

"Yeah," she says, and glances at my shorts, then tilts her head, puzzled. She shrugs, and turning away from me, she taps the table with her Diet Coke can. Everyone looks up, and their conversation, which is still on calculus, stops. "*Hello.* Real world here," she says, addressing the studious group of seniors. "Can't you people ever talk about anything more interesting than math?"

Why does she stay if it's so boring? As she fidgets, turning toward the bathroom, it hits me. She has a perfect watch-out point from here to the door.

"We're not talking about math," Douglas says. "It's cal-cu-lus." He emphasizes each syllable like he's introducing the word to a child.

"Whatever."

Jamie swivels around to face Chelsea. "Hmm. We could discuss alternative sources for fueling cars."

"Please!" Chelsea groans. "I don't want to hear any more about your revolting French-fry-oil-fueled car. It's like a McDonald's on wheels. I bet you could gain weight just from inhaling the fumes."

"I'm sorry if my alternative-fuel car bores you. But you know I don't get my used oil from McDonald's, I get it from Veggie World. Not a single piece of meat has hit my oil."

Chelsea sticks out her tongue like she is bored to death.

Jamie smiles. "Would you rather I talk about how much gas it takes to run that guzzling Hummer your friend Richard drives?"

Hummer? French-fry oil as fuel? I really have come from a different world.

"Oh my God, Jamie, just chill. Richard might hear you." She spins her head to check the bathroom door again.

"Chill?" Resting her elbow on the table, Jamie drums her fingers across her cheek. She wrinkles her forehead in mock concentration. "Hmm. Something Chelsea won't consider boring or too serious." She pauses. "Okay, I know. Here's a mystery for you to solve. When I got to my car last night at the grocery store, I discovered I've got secret friends. They left me a surprise."

"What?" Chelsea yawns.

"A religious pamphlet on the windshield."

"Really?" Chelsea leans across the table and pretends that she is so interested. "What did it say?"

"'Homosexuality is the modern plague, brought to the world by Satan and implemented by his true followers.'"

My cheeks grow warm. I stare at the tiny fiber flecks in my white paper napkin. I can't believe she memorized it word for word. I twist my juice-box straw back and forth and avoid everyone's eyes. I know the brochure Jamie's talking about. Mom probably has a stack at home. She carries a variety of church pamphlets in her purse, always ready for *golden chances* to share God's word. She loves missionary work. She believes every soul she saves adds another golden brick to her mansion in Heaven.

Use every opportunity to help our misguided brothers and sisters here on earth to find God's light and truth.

"Well, what do you expect when you drive around with a bumper sticker that says *I brake for gay rights?*" Chelsea replies.

"I expect to have equal rights for everyone," Jamie says in a calm, soft voice. She gazes past Chelsea, past us all like she's seeing something big and wonderful in her mind.

Douglas's leg, which had stopped twitching, begins again, fast, then faster until my juice box tips over. And he suddenly seems very interested in his Latin book. He opens it and starts mouthing verbs.

I manage to stand my juice upright before any liquid spills out.

Chelsea folds her arms and huffs. Then her eyes, shadowed in purple glitter, stretch wide. "Hey." She slaps the table. "I bet I know who put that flyer on your car." She waves to the table where I noticed the girls with the long, dark skirts. "You know, all of them go to that really freaky church. One of those girls told me they have all these totally strict rules. I think they're Amish or something." She glances at me like she's expecting some response.

I stare ahead like I'm fascinated with the top of Douglas's head.

"There are no Amish communities in this area," Douglas says, looking up from his Latin book, like he's an authority on the Amish.

"Besides," one of the girls at the table says, "I think the Amish wear some sort of prayer cap."

"Well, seriously, they dress like the Amish. I mean, what's with those ugly skirts all the time? They look like something my grandma would wear."

Douglas frowns.

Chelsea continues, "And they can't even drink Coke. They believe caffeinated drinks are a sin."

Tobacco, alcohol, and all drinks with caffeine destroy the spirit and body. They are temptations of the Devil designed to take his followers further from God.

In case anyone is looking my way, I open my eyes wide and pretend that hearing about the strange skirts and caffeine is all new to me. But her words, *like something my grandma would wear,* make my cheeks flush hot with embarrassment, and I shiver inwardly as I remember my navy blue, black, and brown calf-length skirts. How many people back in Phoenix had talked like this about me?

"I have to agree with them about Coke," Jamie says, grinning at Chelsea's Diet Coke can. "I mean, who would want to actually drink that sugary, bubbly stuff? It corrodes your teeth."

Douglas and several of the other seniors chuckle.

Chelsea puts both hands around the can like she can hide it. "Well, one a day can't hurt." She frowns. "Besides, mine is diet."

While she defends her Diet Coke, the bathroom door opens an inch at a time, and Richard slips out. Chelsea misses her golden chance. Richard glances at our table and our eyes lock. He quickly looks away and disappears into the hall.

"Okay, so I don't know everything about the skirt girls," Chelsea says, missing Richard completely. "But maybe Kate does." She turns to face me and eyes my shorts once more. "Don't you belong to their church, too?"

"What?" I squeeze my juice box, and it dribbles down my arm, onto the table.

"My mom said you did. She said you wouldn't be able to read our assigned book for English because of your family's religious beliefs. The skirt girls always get excused from reading the novels we have to read. I don't get it, I mean, it's just *To Kill a Mockingbird*. What can be wrong with that?"

No! Help! Rewind! The table is quiet, waiting for me to answer. I so want to escape, run and run until I'm at the ocean. Then I'd lie down and watch the sky and maybe this horrible shaking inside me would stop. But instead I wipe up my spilled juice with a napkin, then wad it into a tiny ball and clench my fist around it. So that's why Chelsea checked out my shorts. My mind flashes with images. Mom, meeting with my English teachers the past four years back in Phoenix. After she decided she would no longer take money from Dad, she had to get a job and was forced to enroll me in public school. She felt I was too young to be dumped alone into *the secular world* of middle school, but with house payments to make, bills to pay, and food to buy, she left me at the curb of the *worldly* school and drove off in tears for her new job as an office manager. She'd actually graduated from college with a business degree so that she could get high church jobs, like president of the women's organization. I don't think she ever intended to use her education in the *real world*. I dreaded marching out of English on the days our class discussed "worldly novels" that were on the church's forbidden list. I hated the whole class staring, even though I knew I should be proud to be a witness for Christ. And today no one had stared at me. Today I felt almost normal. Until now.

"Kate?" Chelsea asks again.

I hear my own voice. It's shrill and loud. "I don't think anything is wrong with reading *To Kill a Mockingbird*."

"Oh, so you don't go to their church?" She nods her head again at the table of girls—where, no—they can't be—but yes, they are. They are reading their prayer books in the cafeteria!

"Chelsea!" Douglas scolds.

Everyone has their eyes on me. My heart pounds with the words: *Truth lines the path to Heaven. Falsehoods coat the slippery slope to Hell.* I suck in air before I burst out with words I have never said before: "No, I don't belong to their church."

The table is silent. Do they think I'm lying? Why don't they start discussing calculus again? Why doesn't Chelsea go stalk Richard? Why did this have to come up? I just want to fit in. I just want to be normal.

chapter three

CROSS-COUNTRY PRACTICE has wiped me out. I'm covered with sweat. I slipped on a muddy part of the trail, and now my knee is all bloody and sore from the rock I hit. My calves throb even before I slump onto my bike and start pedaling. The shoulder of this back road is gravel, so I stay at the edge of the pavement, hoping there won't be much traffic. Within the first mile my legs cramp with muscle spasms.

I try to ignore the pain by thinking about our practice. I'm totally out of shape, but still, I think I'm about the second fastest girl, behind Jamie. And it felt so good to run again, to let go of everything.

As I pedal down the road, I notice a tall pine tree ahead of me, silhouetted in silver clouds at the top of the hill. At the end of the road is an old farmhouse with a rickety boat next to it, half buried by wildflowers and weeds. It's so different from Phoenix, which is nothing but brown sand and a cactus here and there. I turn the corner and am greeted by pink and purple lupines. A wide-open field of them, tall and proud, filling every nook and crevice. Dad told me about lupines, one of the few talks we had about his childhood in Maine. He said they grew everywhere, like cacti in the desert.

Dad. A new pain, a searing one that has nothing to do with straining muscles or cramps, rips at my heart. Blinking, I swallow hard as the lupines begin to blur. I focus on the road. Uneven pavement streaks by. Splotches of weeds and wildflowers dissolve at my side. Breathe in and out. Think about today. Now. One thing at a time.

The road slopes upward, so I put more weight on the pedals. I'm working harder and harder to go slower and slower. I adjust the gear to the lowest speed. How stupid to think I could bike so far. I haven't biked in a whole year. And it's not like I was in shape the last time, either. It was the first time I'd been out of the house since Dad died, and I wasn't exactly thinking straight. Pedaling those ten miles under Phoenix's 110-degree sun felt more like a hundred miles. Only one thought kept me from becoming delirious with heatstroke. I had to get to the address on the slip of paper. I had to. I was dehydrated, dizzy, and half-dead by the time I parked my bike, but I had to do it in the heat of the day, while Mom was at work. So I held my head high, walked in, and told the man behind the counter my name. The box was so small. I signed for it, put it in my backpack, and left. So efficient. Like I was picking up Dad's dry cleaning or a package from the post office.

That day the backpack felt light, almost weightless, not like today. I have ten new books stuffed in it. My back is aching and the hill is getting steeper. I have to stand, leaning on the pedals with all my weight. The scene from lunch bursts into my mind. If Mom knew that today I denied being a member of the Church of the Holy Divine, she would probably break into tears and then call every one of our relatives to ask for their prayers and support. Just like she used to do when she and Dad were still together.

When she married Dad, her God told her he would join the church. She spent years fasting and praying, but over time it seemed Dad only became more sure he didn't want religion in his life. And Mom, who used to let me watch Disney movies and play with Barbies, began attending more and more church meetings, praying all the time, and reading the Bible almost nonstop. She bought me a family of dolls from the church bookstore. The mother and daughter dolls wore long skirts like mine. The dad and brother wore white shirts and ties. She also got church cartoon videos and picture books. Together we threw away my Ariel doll and Malibu Barbie because, as Mom explained, they were immodestly dressed. I can still feel my hands letting go of Ariel. I slept with her; I dreamed of swimming in the ocean like her. She fell into our trash can on top of the banana peels and the empty milk carton.

I push harder on the pedals. I gave Mom's faith my whole heart. I played with that church-styled Barbie family. I read the Bible-story picture books. When I was older, I got up at five forty-five a.m. with her and listened while she read the Bible to me for fifteen minutes. When I could read on my own, we sat side by side with our own Bibles, reading in that early morning hour. At six we both went to our bedsides and prayed for fifteen minutes. So many mornings I fell asleep and Mom would have to wake me up again. I really never had fifteen minutes worth of stuff to say to God. I went without breakfast and lunch every Sunday, praying with Mom that Dad would accept God's word and convert. Then our family would be complete—all of us would be part of God's chosen people, the elect of the earth. I even continued fasting every Sunday, alone, after the divorce, when Mom no longer seemed concerned with the eternal welfare of her ex-husband's soul.

I bike on past more farmhouses and think of how finally her High Priest convinced her that divorce was the only solution. Dad probably would have stayed married to Mom forever. Like with most situations in his life, he just let things be, because doing something about it was too much hassle. Besides, if they stayed married, he explained to me, he could spend more time with me. More time.

Now I have no more time. And Mom doesn't even care. She acts like nothing has happened. Nothing at all. But my father died. He's dead. He's gone.

I dig my fingernails into the handlebars. I was so sure God would hear my prayers. So sure that Dad and Mom would fall back in love. So sure of everything. Now I'm not even sure I can get up this hill.

Gasping for breath, I tighten my grip and give the steepest part of the incline everything I have. Push, push, push. Don't give up. Push, push, push. And with one last pump, I'm at the top.

I gulp in air like it's water, relax my legs, and let the bike glide down the road. The ocean dances below. Tiny dots that must be fishing boats shimmer on the water. The woods whiz by. Keeping one hand on a handlebar, I pull the ponytail holder from my hair and let my sweaty strands fly, whipping in the wind. Is this how it feels to fly? Weightless? Effortless?

Too soon I'm at the bottom and the free ride is over. I sigh, brake at the stop sign, and look for traffic before turning onto the highway. Within seconds, from behind I hear a car stereo blaring music Mom would call animalistic. *"If you ever listen to that music, Kate, you'll become like the beasts of the jungle, with no more restraint or brains than dumb animals have."* Before I can move over, the vehicle honks. Startled, I swerve onto the shoulder just as a huge black jeeplike thing zooms past. My bike skids and spins on the small pebbles. I brake and try to regain my balance, pumping forward on the uneven ground. Chelsea Riggs is waving out the window at me. Richard is driving. He turns for just a second and stares straight at me as I fumble to get upright on the road again. What the—? Does he get a kick out of watching me struggle?

Before they disappear, I squint and read the word *Hummer* on the back of the huge SUV. So that's what Jamie hates. Well, Chelsea must be happy—she's finally with Richard. He's on cross-country, too. And he's easily the fastest guy on the team. I watch Chelsea's tan arm get smaller and smaller as they disappear down the road. What would I look like in a real sleeveless top like hers? I've never had anything stylish. Mom would totally freak if she knew I tried on my sports bra for a skimpy top and rolled up one of my old church skirts until it was a mini just to see how it looked in the mirror. Then I twisted up my hair. I tried to imagine my eyes with dark mascara. People say I look like Mom. We both have green eyes marbled with brown tints and light brown, thick, slightly wavy hair. I'm lucky I've never had much acne, and sometimes I think if I'd been born into a normal family, and allowed to wear normal clothes and some makeup, I could be pretty and maybe guys would notice me. But instead, I've been taught my whole life that *Makeup is the paintbrush of the devil* and that *It's the female's responsibility to dress modestly, to keep men's minds pure.* On that score, I should get an A-plus. I look down at my sweaty running clothes and dirty and bloodstained legs and bike on. Even with my immodest Adidas running shorts, I'm certainly not going to be a temptation to any male today.

Two more cars pass. Now one is sputtering and slowing to a chug. Out of the corner of my eye, I notice it's a rusty old truck. Why is it stopping? What does the driver want? My heart beats quicker. *The woods and back roads are dangerous. That's where perverts hide, looking for prey,* I hear Mom's voice echoing in my brain. I push harder on the pedals. The driver whistles. Keep biking, I tell myself. Stay calm. Don't turn. Don't look.

But I do. And my shoulders instantly relax. It's no pervert, just another guy from cross-country. I think his name is Will. He pulls up next to me and calls out through the open passenger window, "Wow, Kate, you really are the athletic type, aren't you? Biking after that workout and with a bloody knee?"

My cheeks, already flushed from biking, now burn. I wipe at my knee and then look up at Will and give him a weak smile. He knows my name. He's a junior and it's his first year on the team. Coach Horne introduced him when he introduced Richard, the two new freshmen, and me to the rest of the team.

He chuckles. "I'd give you a lift but I wouldn't want you to blame me for keeping you from a workout."

Is he teasing me, or is he really offering me a ride? I have a split second to make up my mind. With several more miles still to go, I'd love to throw my bike in the back of a truck and be driven home. And besides, now I'm afraid some crazy guy *will* drive by. But what about Mom? She would never approve.

"Well?" he asks.

"Okay." I gulp, trying to comprehend that I actually accepted his ride, that I actually said "okay" out loud. "If you're offering, I mean. There *is* a lot more traffic this afternoon than there was on the way to school this morning. It's kind of hard going."

Will pulls the truck onto the shoulder in front of me. He jumps out and comes around to help me put the bike in the back. He looks up and down the totally empty road, twice. "Well damn, it really is horrible traffic."

My cheeks warm as I wobble over to the cab. My legs barely make the big step up, but I pull myself onto the seat and manage to shut the door before he puts the truck in gear and we drive down the road, with only his half-eaten double cheeseburger, fries, and Coke between us. The whole cab smells like the Tasty Freeze. My stomach growls.

"Want a fry?"

I shake my head. "No, thank you."

We drive on, as Will munches on fries, with the radio blaring. I swallow, trying to think of something to say. In perfect rhythm with the chugging engine, the words to *The Youth Motto* fill my mind. *I am a youth in God's Army. I represent Him and His purpose.* The words march out as if on autoplay. *I will be faithful and obedient. I will dress appropriately.* I look at Will's long hair, pulled back in a ponytail. *I will resist fads of the day.* I glance at Will's earring. *Modesty will be my motto.* The cab's cracked, vinyl seat rubs against my bare legs, and I pull at my shorts to cover the new tan line I've acquired this afternoon at practice. *I will stay morally clean. I will resist the temptations of the flesh.* I admire Will's bulging biceps, which make him look more like a wrestler than a runner. *As a youth in God's Army I will study His word. I will be a light for Him at all times and in all places.*

I clear my throat. "So, this your first year running?" My voice squeaks. I'm sure I must sound as dumb as I feel.

He grins. "Yep."

Without meaning to, I stare at Will's feet—no socks, only slip-on canvas boat shoes.

"What?" He points to his feet. "You're not telling me these give me away as a new runner, are you?"

"Oh, they're fine," I say. Why can't I make my voice sound more convincing? I wiggle my toes in my expensive, top-of-the-line running shoes. I try again. "Don't your feet get sore though, not wearing socks?"

"Yeah, they did! You mean yours aren't sore from the workout today?"

"No."

"Oh." Will grins. "I confess. I'm a lobsterman at heart. But my mom thought I should, you know, get involved in school. So here I am. And now you tell me my shoes are all wrong. Shit." He fakes a sad frown.

The way he says the word *lobster* sounds like "lob-stah." I like his deep Maine accent. And he'll know if those boats I keep seeing are lobster boats. "How do you fish for lobster?" I ask. "I mean, I see those small boats stopping by the buoys in the bay. Are they lobster boats? Do you use fishing poles or nets?"

Will whistles. "Where are you from?"

"Phoenix."

Will laughs just a bit too long. "Fish for lobster? Maybe in Arizona. But here in Maine, we *trap* our lobster."

"If you knew anything about Phoenix, you would know it doesn't come with an ocean. Most of the year the canals have less than a foot of water and never any lobster."

"Oh, have I made you feel bad?" He smiles again.

I smile back, even though I should be mad at him. Then it hits me—instead of being frightened that I'm alone with a guy who has long hair and wears an earring, I'm having a real live conversation. And we're teasing each other, just like Chelsea did with different guys in classes today.

"Hey," Will says, "I've got a great idea. Would you like to go out with me and my grandfather some morning and see how we *fish* for lobster?"

I don't know what to say. I look down at my knees.

"Oh, so you're not really interested enough in our Maine lobster to come out on my boat?"

"No, I'm interested." I lift my eyes and meet his and notice for the first time how blue they are.

"But . . . ?" Not waiting for my answer, Will continues. "I know what it is—you're a city girl and can't get up at five thirty in the morning."

"I can so."

Will begins to laugh, then stops. "Well, City Girl, what's stopping you?"

My mom. But it's even more. I'd have to think of things to say. I'd be out in the water, where I couldn't run away if something bad happened. What if Will tried to touch me? But didn't he say his grandfather would be there?

The song on the radio blares on, and Will taps out the beat on the steering wheel.

My head hums along. "Sure, I'll go."

He doesn't say anything. Maybe it was a game. Maybe he doesn't want me to tag along. "If it's convenient," I add.

"When could you come?" he asks. "Pick a day, any day."

"You go out even on school days?" I ask.

"Yep. We leave at first light."

"But how do you make it to school?"

"I start late. At eleven. But for you, City Girl, I guess it would be better to come on a weekend."

City Girl again. My heart leaps. "On the weekends, do you stay out all day?"

Will nods.

"Oh."

"Too much for you?"

"Well, I have to help my mom—she runs a bed-and-breakfast. Weekends are the busiest time."

"Oh, right." Will nods.

"But I can get up early on a school morning."

"Okay, let's do this." He points out the window as we pass the dock on Main Street. "Pop and I leave from there every day of the week. Whenever you want to come, just show up and we'll arrange our route so we can drop you off in time for school."

I nod.

"But when you do come, bring a rain slicker okay? You'll get wet if you don't."

"Okay." *Slick-ah*. Like *lobst-ah*.

He drives on, turning up the steep gravel road to the inn, before I can even tell him where I live. My eyes widen.

Will notices and grins at me. "I live in this town, too,"

he says. "One thing you have to get used to, City Girl. Here in Puffin Cove, everyone knows everything about everyone else."

He can't know everything, or he would know I don't want Mom to see us. As soon as the truck stops, I jump out. "I can get the bike."

But Will jumps out and lifts my bike like it's made of air.

"Thanks a lot for the ride." I rush the words together.

"See you." Will smiles as he jumps back into his truck.

I wave and hold my breath. I can't believe I just had a whole conversation with Will. I've never really been alone with a guy near my own age, except for my cousins. At church youth things we were always kept in groups and told never to be alone with a male until we were sixteen, and even then, group dating was highly encouraged. And now my first day at Rocky Point High, I made two friends, Jamie and Will. My heart skips as I wheel my bike down the drive. I turn and wave to Will one last time as he drives away. My eyes dart toward the inn and under my breath I plead, "Please God, if there is a God, please don't let Mom be near a window."

chapter four

I TURN IN BED and look at my digital clock. Four fifty-five a.m. Good—I'll be safely out of the house to meet Jamie before Mom even wakes up for her spiritual time. One tiny ray of light makes its way through my windowpane and reaches out like a yellow finger, glowing, right to Dad's bookcase, one of the few items from his apartment I got Mom to keep. It's packed tight with all his books, most of them classics. I've read only a few, and I've placed them in order on the top shelf. *The Great Gatsby, The Grapes of Wrath, Walden, Poems of Walt Whitman,* and *The Old Man and the Sea.* From my bed I scan through the titles until I find *To Kill a Mockingbird* in the middle of the bottom shelf. I thought Dad had it.

Next week I'm going to start reading *To Kill a Mockingbird.* Mom had called the school. But I simply wrote a note in Mom's handwriting.

Dear Ms. Root, I have changed my mind and decided Kate can stay in class and read the novel with the rest of the class. Sincerely, Ms. Rebekah Anderson

Mom would totally hate the "Ms." stuff. She thinks feminists are turning their back on their true mission in life. And of course she'd totally freak if she knew I wrote the note. But I did.

Books were such a problem for my parents. So much so that my even-tempered, always-logical father almost lost it. It's the only time I remember him shouting. My parents were still living together then, but in separate rooms. "No, I will not get rid of those *horrible* books," he yelled loudly enough for everyone on our block to have heard.

And, of course, when we took care of his things after he died, Mom was totally against saving the books that were full of *worldly teachings*, far from God and far from the *only truth*. So we compromised and they stayed in a box in our garage. Or so Mom thought. But while she was at work, I would sneak out one book at a time. Then, with it tucked inside my cross-stitched Bible cover that read *God's Word*, I read each book with my door locked and would write down quotes I liked in a diary.

When our furniture and boxes arrived and we put most of our belongings into these two basement bedrooms, I unpacked all Dad's books right under Mom's disapproving eyes. She didn't say anything, but she sure stormed out of my room. It's like she thinks just looking at his books will bring the devil into her soul.

But have your father die, stay hidden in your room, refuse to talk or attend church for months, and you discover that even your fanatical mother can soften. I felt I had to read Dad's books after he died, even though he'd offered them so many times and I'd always refused. Now it was my only way of touching what he had touched, knowing what he had known. And trying to understand why Dad used to pat this bookcase whenever I would invite him to come to church. He'd say, "These books are all the religion I need in my life, Kate."

I swallow hard. Right now I'd do almost anything—never run again, attend the Church of the Holy Divine for the rest of my life, *anything*—just to have this sturdy piece of furniture back at his apartment and Dad sitting in his old leather recliner, reading with the shades drawn.

I roll out of bed and flip through *To Kill a Mockingbird*. Midway through I stop and two photos drop out. Two copies of the same shot. I laugh right out loud. Dad! They are two copies of those pictures photographers take of racers as they run across the finish line. About a week later they mail a small proof to you and ask you to buy it for ten times what it's worth. It was my first 5K. Dad ran to the finish line and had just put his arm around my sweaty shoulder. I won for the twelve-and-under division. When the offer came in the mail, he tossed it aside. "Fifteen bucks for one four-by-six photo of us sweating like pigs? A total rip-off."

In the picture my hair is bleached blonde from swimming in Dad's pool, and I'm so tan. I'm wearing my first pair of running shorts. Beside me, Dad looks pale. He always ran in the early morning before sunlight and sat in the shade while I swam at his pool. Sometimes I wonder if I took up running just so I could wear those short running shorts. And I had to convince Mom I needed to wear sport-shorts to run. "As long as you promise to change into modest clothes as soon as you're done." She had the same rules for swimsuits. And like a good girl, I always obeyed. But now, although she frowns her disapproval, she doesn't say anything, and I get away with wearing running shorts even when I'm not running.

I take the photos and place them in my diary, the one I've been writing quotes from Dad's books in, and shake my head at Dad's extravagance. I would so tease him, if he were . . . I bite my lip. I hug the book in my arms, wishing it were him, wishing this book could take me to him, wishing it could whisper to me where he is. Or if he is. "Death is just a big, dark sleep," he used to tell me.

And my mother's cheery report about life after death? "People who don't believe in God, and who never accept Jesus Christ as their Savior, and who never join the Holy Divine Church, will not be allowed into Heaven. Instead, they will endure endless torment for Eternity." Given the small total world membership of the Holy Divine Church, it occurs to me now that Heaven is going to be pretty empty and Hell pretty full. But Mom would just tell me that's even more reason for us to be committed missionaries and save our neighbors and friends from their potential fate. And now there's going to be one less person in Mom's version of Heaven.

Me.

At least when I die, I'll get to see Dad.

I'll be in Hell with him.

Tears burn at the back of my eyes. My lower lip quivers and the familiar dark cloud moves its way inside me. If I don't do something soon, it will be too late. I'll be on my back, on my bed, staring at the ceiling, unable to move. Or think. Or even cry. Hours will pass—days, weeks, and then months. It will be last year. All over again.

I jump up and grab my weights from the floor. Clenching my fists around them, I begin to lift. Up and down. Over and over. Faster. Faster. I lift until my arms pulse, until my shoulders ache. Now I stretch my arms slowly and hold the weights as far above my head as I can and begin to count. One, two, three, four, five. Breathe. Focus. I study the photograph on my wall. My lucky palm tree— the picture Dad took, using his new telephoto lens. He had it blown up and framed. The texture of the trunk reminds me of one of those huge waffle cones. Twenty-five, twenty-six, twenty-seven. I suck in air until my lungs are full.

Fifty-five, fifty-six. My arms begin to shake. Hold. Hold. The entire picture is spinning into a blue, cloudless Phoenix sky.

Seventy-seven, seventy-eight. Every muscle trembles.

Ninety-three, ninety-four. The whole wall is black. I can't see the frame at all. My head begins to spin.

Ninety-nine, o-n-e h-u-n-d-r-e-d! My arms collapse and I let the weights drop to the ground. Exhale. Tiny lights spin around me. I wobble. I lean my arms against the wall. Breathing in and out, I feel the pulse of my heart gradually slow. And as it does, the picture in front of me slowly transforms back to normal.

Before another thought can begin, I sit on the ground, spread my legs and reach my arms out to my toes, stretching until every muscle feels like an elastic band pulled tight. With my head resting against the ground between my legs, I glance up at the clock. Five fifteen. I still have time to make it. And I should be finished before Mom even comes upstairs. She doesn't let even running a bed-and-breakfast interfere with her scripture and prayer time.

Minutes later, pine and salty air fill my nostrils as I run down Main Street. The water is dotted with boats. Is one of them Will's? Does he really want me to come out with him one morning?

I pick up my pace at the *Welcome to Acadia National Park* billboard, and sure enough, there's Jamie waiting for me, and for anyone else on the team who is crazy enough to get up so early and take this extra Sunday run. The wooden sign is half-hidden in pines and birch. The mountains behind it aren't nearly as tall as the Rockies out west, but still they are majestic.

"You came!" She waves at me as I slow to a walk.

I nod.

Jamie looks at her watch. "Well, we'll wait five minutes, but I have a feeling it's only going to be you and me. I don't think any of the other girls seem like the type to get up before daylight on a Sunday."

I shrug.

We wait and Jamie tells me about her plans for college. "I want to go to Princeton and major in environmental studies." And then I notice the words on her blue T-shirt. *If you can't see the forest, don't blame the trees.* We start talking about cross-country and the first meet. "We still need a public-relations person for the team. Would you be interested in the job?"

"Um, I'm not really very good at that sort of stuff." My heart races. "I can't seem to get the courage to tell people about anything," I say. My mind rushes with memories of all my failed challenges. Invite one person to the Youth Activity this week. Did I? No. Share pamphlets with your school friends. Did I? No. Fellowship inactive or nonmembers of your own family. Well, Dad died a solid nonbeliever, so that's another failure.

"Oh, it's not hard. I'll help you." Jamie says it with

such conviction and such ease, like life is a lark, not a big, dark challenge. "Basically it's just writing up little articles for the school paper on our meets, making posters, putting them up, that sort of thing."

I take in a deep breath. Do I really want to start over? Be someone new? Be brave? "Okay." The word slips out. Maybe if I'm around Jamie more, I'll learn how to take life less seriously, too. It's funny because she's so intense about the environment and other things, but then she's like this carefree bird flitting about from one flower to the next.

So we begin our run. I know Jamie is going slower for me, because so far, I've always been following her on the cross-country trail near our school. We stop talking and just run as we turn onto one of the gravel trails in the national park. Green everywhere. Pines and trees that look like the aspen out west. But maybe they're white birch. I'm not sure. I breathe in the scent of a million Christmases. Soon sights, sounds, smells become a distant blur. All I think about is inhaling, exhaling, and keeping stride with Jamie.

I'd guess by my watch and the pace that we've run about five miles.

"Let's cool down and gawk at the summer cottages," Jamie suggests.

I slow to a comfortable jog, sweat pouring off of me, my cramped legs grateful for this slower pace. Back in Arizona, the word *cottage* means a simple one- or two-bedroom bungalow, not the sprawling oceanfront estates with servants' quarters and gazebos that we are passing. "That's Richard's little summer place." Jamie nods toward a big iron gate. *Penrose Cottage, 1870,* announces the brass plaque attached to the stone wall near the gated entrance. It's a three-story Tudor with turrets and a tennis court on the side. I bet there's an outdoor pool around back. The wooded estate goes on for acres and, of course, has a great oceanfront view.

As we jog past, I notice the blinds are still drawn on all the massive wood-framed windows. Is that because the Penrose family and staff are still asleep, or do they keep their shades drawn for the same reason Dad always did—trying to keep their air-conditioning bill down?

At the end of the road, Jamie pauses in front of an old stone church. It's beautiful. The sun hits the northeast corner, leaving one side in the light and the other in the darkness. Decades of moss cover several stones. It's so pretty. Like one of those sappy Thomas Kinkade paintings Mom always wants to buy. Only not. The faded red door could use a fresh coat of paint. The bricks in the walkway are worn down and cracked with age. My kind of perfect.

The church is surrounded by a grove of pines. And behind the old gray granite building with its stained-glass windows, the ocean peeks through. It's so quiet and peaceful. And there's a sprinkler that's running. That's why Jamie stopped. She's grinning at it and then at me.

"Yes!" I say. "Let's."

We giggle and race toward the wet spray, sucking in droplets of icy water. My arms and legs tingle at the coolness. Soon we're drenched. The fountain of water mixes with the rays of the sun and creates a rainbow. I twirl under the umbrella of water, spinning with the ribbons of color. Jamie joins me; we grab hands. Leaning back, we turn and turn, spinning and laughing and letting the water dance on our skin.

"Nice day for an early-morning shower, isn't it?"

I let go of Jamie's hands and jump out of the water. A man who looks too young to be dressed in a black shirt and white collar heads toward us, shattering my dream world where only Jamie and I and the lobster people are awake in Puffin Cove. But, of course, someone had to have turned on the water.

"Yes, it is." Jamie gets out of the water, too, and stands at my side.

"Sorry," I say, and hang my head.

"Sorry?" the thin, sandy-haired minister asks, coming up close. He must be a foot taller than we are. "About dancing in the sprinkler?" As he smiles, a big dimple appears in his left cheek. His green eyes sparkle with fun. "Actually, I'm glad our water can be of service." He puts out his hand. "I don't believe we've met. I'm Pastor Browning."

Suddenly, I'm conscious of my soaking wet white T-shirt clinging to my white sports bra. Jamie's blue T-shirt shows just how much she has, but she doesn't seem to worry about it. While she takes the minister's hand and says, "Jamie Rapp," I slip one arm across my chest, trying to find a dry spot on my clothes to wipe my other hand.

I end up extending my dripping hand. His hand feels huge around mine, and warm. His hold is firm and friendly.

"Kate Anderson," I manage to say. Then I add, "Guess we better get back to our run, Jamie."

"Yes, we should." Jamie grins. She's so at ease, and I'm being a total geek.

"Thanks for the use of the water—it literally saved our lives," Jamie says, like she's just been through some religious experience. Is she making fun of him?

He laughs, like that is the best joke he's heard in days.

"You're welcome to visit here anytime, Kate and Jamie. Inside or outside of our church." He waves as we jog toward the street.

I glance back over my shoulder in time to see him open the massive red door and disappear.

"That was fun," Jamie says between strides. "I heard the town got a new minister last winter. Everyone says he's really liberal."

As we round the corner to Main Street, Jamie turns

to me. "Well, my car is parked here." She slows again and pats a basic-looking red car. After what Chelsea had said about it, I expected to see some weird car with McDonald's French fries printed on the side.

"Thanks for the run," I say.

"Yeah, it was fun. Too bad the rest of the girls missed out. We'll have to play up that sprinkler and make them jealous."

"Right."

Jamie checks her watch as she unlocks her car and gets in. "Perfect, just enough time to go home and take a shower before I go to work."

I wave as she drives away and wonder how she does it all. Good grades, fastest runner, and working part-time at Veggie World.

Then I set the timer on my watch and sprint down the road. Pounding and pounding and pushing and gulping in air, passing estate after estate and trying to forget that a minister just saw me dancing in a see-through top on his church lawn. I whiz past the shops on Main Street. My lungs burn by the time I reach the sign poking out of the pines, announcing *The Whispering Woods Inn.* Ignoring the pain, I gasp for air, lean in on my toes, pushing past the thicket of blue spruce, then the meadow, then more trees, up, up the hill to the turnaround and the parking area. As I pass Aunt Katherine's "Wild Rose Cottage," I stop the timer. Two minutes, thirty-five seconds. I fall against the signpost, gasping for air. Not bad for half a mile.

I pace back and forth on the gravel drive until my heart, pounding nearly out of my chest, calms to a steadier beat. Stumbling onto the back porch, I pull off my wet shoes and socks and collapse on my back. Closing my eyes, I rest my hands on my ribs as my chest heaves, up and down, less and less until finally every muscle is so relaxed, I'm like a corpse, not moving at all. Birds chirp in the trees above, an occasional car hums as it passes by on the highway, a squirrel scampers across the gravel drive. Footsteps on the kitchen floor. Oh no, footsteps! I jump up, every muscle now tense and alert. A closet shutting. I'm too late! I twist the knob a micrometer at a time, inch the door open, and tiptoe into the hall.

"Kate!"

Mom, standing with a broom in one hand and the other firmly on her hip, frowns at me. She's wearing her best Sunday dress, has curled her hair, and has even put on the pearl earrings she won when she was eighteen years old for being the top competitor in a scripture contest. She had memorized about a zillion scriptures. The earrings are called the "Pearls of Great Price," like in the Bible.

"What?" I whisper.

"You're dripping all over the wood floor."

"Sorry." Good, only a scolding about water.

"Do you know what day it is?" She keeps her voice low.

"Um . . ." I pause, like I'm five and don't know the days of the week yet.

"You know better than to run on Sunday."

I stare at my toes, wrinkled from the wet socks. *When Sunday comes, I wear my best. From daily cares I take a rest.* If only I'd come straight inside instead of resting on the porch. If . . .

She continues, "I don't want to discourage you from running. I'm glad you're running again. Glad you're participating at school. It's such a great opportunity to do missionary work."

I cringe.

"Run all you want the other days of the week," Mom continues. Then she purses her lips tight. "But not on Sunday. You know Sunday is a day of rest." Ironically, she says this with the broom still in her hand. "You can't forget what happened to your father."

She can't actually think Dad died because he ran on Sunday? He ran on Sundays for years. Sundays that Mom made me fast, going without food or drink, fasting for his immortal soul. My throat tightens. I blink hard, focusing my eyes on the white marble fireplace in the parlor, beyond her.

"Have you met the girls from church at school yet?" she asks in a kinder tone.

I shrug at the logs I placed there two days ago. She knows I have. I'm not about to tell her they all came up to me Friday at my locker and invited me to the potluck dinner. Besides, she probably already knows and has talked with them about Plan B to get me to church.

"One of the girls lives about fifteen minutes from here," Mom continues. "I met her mother a couple of weeks ago at the women's cultural meeting. She said they can give you a ride to church. They're in Bangor today at their cousin's baptism, but next week they'll be home. I feel horrible I can't go to church myself—"

"Mom, I'm dripping wet," I interrupt. "Can't we talk about this some other time?"

Mom continues as if she hasn't heard me at all. "I guess we had to make some compromises in coming here. I can't leave today, but you know I'd go with you if I could."

Now she's making compromises! I clench my fists. Where was all that willingness to compromise last year, when my father needed a funeral? I stare at her. Does she actually believe God will punish her less for missing church if she still wears her best, blue-flowered dress to sweep the hallway floor? The feeling I had on Monday at the cafeteria pulses through me again. I can feel the door closing, the one in my mind I've been wanting to slam shut for the longest time. I knew at lunch that I didn't want to *ever* go back. A few days haven't changed my mind. I swallow hard. I keep my voice low. "I'm not going to church anymore, Mom."

Her hands clench the broom handle. Her lips purse into a tight frown. Her eyes hold me captive. Glaring at me, her arms begin a back-and-forth swish with the broom, making a wind with her furious strokes. Something clatters in the kitchen. Startled, Mom drops her broom. *Thump.* It falls onto the floor.

Aunt Katherine peeks her head out of the kitchen door. Her short white hair is neatly combed. She's wearing a peach floral dress, with an apron tied around her waist, all ready to help with the Sunday breakfast crowd. "I didn't mean to scare you," she whispers. "I couldn't help over- hearing though. Rebekah," she says, looking up at Mom, "I feel terrible that you have to work this morning. I know it's a big sacrifice for you not to go to church." She sighs. "I wish I was able to manage by myself."

"No, no, it's fine. I'm glad to be here. Glad for the opportunity." Mom's voice is sincere and apologetic. She should be. Aunt Katherine could have asked someone else to run the inn.

Aunt Katherine's blue eyes brighten. Eyes the exact same color as Dad's. "I know. Why don't I take Kate to church?"

My insides groan. Not Aunt Katherine, too!

"I'd love nothing more, but Katherine, you've given up driving. Remember? You don't even have a license," Mom reminds her. "And the church is so far away."

"What's that, dearie?" Aunt Katherine, who is rather hard of hearing, cups her hand around her ear. "Too far? Oh, don't worry." She pauses. "I know it will be a bit of a walk, but Puffin Cove is small. If I can hold on to Kate's arm, I can manage it. I don't believe the church here is more than a half mile away."

Mom's face freezes, and I have to suck in my cheeks and hold my breath to keep from giggling. Aunt Katherine isn't offering to drive me to the Holy Divine Church an hour away in Ellsworth. She just wants to take me to the church here in Puffin Cove, the one with the red door and the liberal, handshaking minister. Mom's trapped. Snared by the most innocent, sweet-looking woman I have ever met. I want to laugh. I want to clap.

Aunt Katherine stands, waiting, appearing pleased with her simple solution.

I've never been to another church before. And even though worshipping anywhere isn't exactly what I'd like to do right now, Aunt Katherine's church has to be better than Mom's. Doesn't it? The silence goes on so long I decide someone should say something. I turn to Aunt Katherine. I put on my biggest, most polite smile. "Okay. Sure, I'll go with you."

"There. See? It's all solved." Aunt Katherine beams. She looks at her watch. "Service starts at ten thirty. We can still help your mother with breakfast before we need to go."

I nod and try to avoid Mom's eyes, which are burning into me like a welding torch. I turn, then skip down the basement stairs to shower.

chapter five

"WOULD YOU LIKE some more orange juice, Mr. Harmony?" Mom asks, using her practiced hostess voice.

"Thanks. I believe I would." The black-haired photographer smiles. "And please, call me Max."

Mom's cheeks flush. Weird.

All four of the dining-room tables are occupied, each set with linen cloths, fresh-cut flowers from Aunt Katherine's garden, and the pale yellow china. Quiet morning conversations, clinking crystal, and the sound of sterling silver sliding across plates fill the room. I serve fresh maple muffins from a basket and the sweetness of them as they hit my nose makes my stomach growl. Across the room, Mom's eyes catch mine. She glares. But with the couple from Texas, the two families up from Boston, and Mr. Harmony all here—busily eating her blueberry pancakes— she can't really scold me about going to an unenlightened church. Not to mention Aunt Katherine, who is serving a tray of fresh fruit to the guests. After all, Aunt Katherine is

Mom's boss. She owns the inn. She just pays Mom to run it. I turn my back so I can't see Mom's disapproving eyes and paste on my own hostess smile as I continue to serve. I refuse to feel guilty.

After breakfast, I sneak out the back door, making sure Mom hasn't seen me, and head toward Aunt Katherine's cottage. My stomach is churning like a blender again, just like on the first day of school, and I regret having stuffed down two maple muffins. Am I dressed okay? I'm wearing my nicest white top with little yellow flowers around the neck that match the yellow flowers in my green, calf-length skirt. Dad and I picked these both out after we shopped for my running clothes last summer. My *first* store-bought outfit, besides jeans and T-shirts. I knew the green was too bright and the yellow flowers were rebellious, too wild for church standards, but it was such a pretty skirt and Dad didn't care what I picked. In the end I never wore the skirt to church, since Dad died the next week. So this is my first time to wear the outfit. It's been a whole year without dresses and meetings and sitting in uncomfortable pews. I kick at the gravel driveway. A whole year free of pulpit-pounding lectures. Mom thought I didn't go to church with her because I was too sad to face everyone after Dad died. But it was more than that. Way more. I kick harder and harder, my foot like a bulldozer digging, until gravel sprays all around me.

"Ready, Kate?"

I drop my foot and look up, then back down at my sandaled toes, which are red and throbbing. My cheeks grow warm. How long has Aunt Katherine been watching?

As we begin our walk down the steep drive, she takes hold of my arm, steadying herself. "Sometimes it's no fun getting old." She sighs. "Before you know it, winter will be here again. With the ice and snow, I may not be able to navigate this hill at all."

As Aunt Katherine leans against me, her touch helps calm my nervous jitters. She smells like soap and flowers and a bit like the rich, dark earth she loves to "putter about" in. When we turn onto Main Street, toward town, Aunt Katherine pauses. She looks at her watch. "Why don't we take a slight detour on our way and walk by your father's old house?"

My heart beats faster. "I've been wondering where he lived."

"You don't know? Oh, Kate, I assumed your mother had pointed it out to you when you moved in. It's just around the corner."

"No. She didn't." I feel tears welling up.

Aunt Katherine peers into my eyes, like so many people have done this past year. My grandmother made several trips all the way from Idaho to Phoenix just to visit me. My cousin Charity who lives with her ten brothers and sisters about an hour outside of Phoenix put me first on her prayer list. My youth leaders at church dropped by with cookies and church books on death and grief. Even the teachers and my counselor at the high school gave me extra attention. But I always squirmed and looked away. This time I let Aunt Katherine look in deep. Aunt Katherine who watches every bird show on the Learning Channel, who reads *The New York Times* and *The Atlantic Monthly* religiously, and who buys organic food and recycles every piece of paper the inn generates. She pats my hand and sighs.

Basic two-story, wood-framed houses fill the block as we turn off Main Street. Not at all grand like the summer estates by the church and the ocean that Jamie and I ran by this morning. Some of these houses are in need of paint and others repairs. Aunt Katherine stops in front of the third house, a blue Victorian with a wraparound porch and a huge tree that covers most of the front yard. I'm happy to see that it has a fresh coat of paint and that all the shutters are hanging straight.

"Oh, they've cut down the rope swing. Your father loved playing in that big old oak." Aunt Katherine's eyes grow misty. "Your great-uncle John and I used to come over on Sunday afternoons for lunch. I probably should have been helping your grandmother afterward with the dishes." She chuckles. "Your grandpa and Uncle John sat on the front porch smoking their pipes and instead of cleaning up, I'd play with Steven. We'd usually end up nestled under the tree reading some of his favorite books. He loved *Where the Wild Things Are.* We read it so much we both had every line memorized."

As Aunt Katherine talks, I try to imagine them younger. I want to go up to the tree, touch it, smell it. It's so nice to hear Dad's name again. Steven. As much as I want to linger, someone, the owner, is looking out at us through the curtains. "We better go," I say, nodding toward the window.

"It makes me sad, thinking of all the years I missed spending time with you and your dad." Aunt Katherine's voice catches a little as we walk back toward Main Street. "But with me afraid to fly and Steven, well, he always seemed to like his books more than people, and he just wasn't much of a traveler, either. . . ."

I know Dad liked Aunt Katherine. His parents died when I was small and I don't remember them at all. But ever since I can remember, Aunt Katherine would phone, send presents and letters, and she came out to visit us on the train about every three years. And he and Mom named me after her. An uncomfortable feeling gnaws at me. Why didn't Dad like to travel? Why was he such a hermit? Why didn't he have close friends? If he had, they could have given him a funeral.

"But you're here now." Aunt Katherine smiles, looking at me. "Steven's daughter." She pats my arm and we walk on down the street, past the buttery smell of the French bakery, the perfumed aroma from the candle shop, and the mystic notes of Celtic music already playing in the New

Age gift shop. I try to imagine Dad walking down this same street—a young Steven living in Puffin Cove, about my age. I try to imagine him alive.

At the stone chapel, an usher stands at the red door, handing out bulletins. I take one and thank him. As we walk inside, Pastor Browning walks by us. Before I can turn away, he heads toward us. Oh, great! Please don't let him recognize me. I hope I look different enough with dry hair and a skirt. If not, he'll probably think his invitation is the reason I'm here. He pauses and looks at us and then grins. Now he's got a long black robe over his black shirt. It goes down to his knees, like a graduation gown. "Why, Kate." He smiles at me like we're old friends, and his dimple seems bigger than ever. "It's awfully nice to see you again. And so soon."

My cheeks grow warm as he grips my hand in another enthusiastic handshake. So much for the dry-hair disguise.

Now he extends his hand to Aunt Katherine. "Hello. I'm Pastor Browning."

"You'll have to speak up, young man, I'm a bit hard of hearing."

"Pastor Browning," he says again slowly and in a louder voice.

"Well, hello, Pastor Browning. I'm Kate's aunt, Katherine Stone."

"Glad to meet you."

Glad to meet you? Jamie said he started here last winter. Isn't this Aunt Katherine's church? Did I misunderstand? But as we leave him and walk down the aisle of pews, people greet my great-aunt like they haven't seen her in years. They act so happy, just like people at our church in Arizona greeted Dad the time he came to hear me sing in the Easter choir. She really must be doing this because she thinks it will please Mom. But there's a twinkle in her eye—it looks like she's having fun, like she's played a big joke on someone.

Aunt Katherine beams, returning everyone's greeting with a friendly wave. When we finally sit in a pew near the front, she leans over and says, "This is where I used to sit with your father."

I feel my eyes grow wide. My father? The same man who said his bookcase was all the religion he ever needed?

"Oh, he never told you that he went to church?"

I shake my head no.

Aunt Katherine continues. "Well, it was years ago. He even brought his own Bible." Her whispering is more like quiet shouting. People on either side of us turn and look.

"Maybe you'd better tell me about it on the way home from church," I whisper, motioning my head toward the pulpit where Pastor Browning is now standing.

Aunt Katherine nods and winks.

On either side of Pastor Browning sit two huge bouquets of flowers. Wow, at the Holy Divine Church, we had flowers only at Christmas and Easter. Pastor Browning is greeting everyone and reading through a list of announcements. As he talks, I rub my hand back and forth on the wooden bench. It's smooth in places, worn down with age and scarred with scrapes and grooves. Did Dad get bored sitting here? Did he fiddle with a tie clip and carve one of these lines in the oak? Did he leave any part of him behind, here in the air? Can I reach out and touch him? If only I could talk to him. If only I knew he was *somewhere*. I look up at the wood rafters above and breathe in their slightly musty odor, and it reminds me of something. I've smelled this scent before. I take a deep breath and my shoulders tingle with some happy memory.

Now the choir sings, and tiny fragments of colored glass in the window across from me shimmer down on the pews and the wood floor of the aisle. The light dances around and around like a kaleidoscope. Mom would love these. She and Aunt Deborah were really into making stained-glass lamps last year. I've only seen pictures of churches with real stained-glass windows; I've never really been in one before. Back in Arizona, the Holy Divine Church met in a square adobe building with ordinary windows and plain white walls. And the High Priest wore a regular suit, no robe or anything.

The choir song is finished and now everyone stands and opens their hymn books to sing. Aunt Katherine and I stand, sharing a hymnal. Her voice sounds loud and happy in my ear.

Amazing Grace! How sweet the sound
That saved a wretch like me!
I once was lost, but now am found;
Was blind but now I see.

It's a song I've never heard. Aunt Katherine, who isn't looking at the hymnal at all, occasionally sings different words from what are written. I can't help smiling. Now the light from the stained-glass windows dances on her creamy white hair. As the organ notes swell, my heart does, too, with warmth and a sense of peace I haven't felt in the longest time.

When the song is over we all sit and Pastor Browning speaks. "That's one of my favorite hymns. It was written by John Newton, who once was a slave trader, and then forced to become a slave himself. Later in life, after escaping his slavery, he found religion and wrote this and many other beautiful songs. He even became a minister. Maybe that's the reason this song touches so many people. Maybe John Newton's words speak to the wretch in all of us." Pastor Browning's voice is friendly and informal, like he's talking to a bunch of friends.

Now it's time for the next song. Everyone stands again. Instead of singing, I crane my neck and spot Chelsea and her family. But no Douglas. And on the other side, across from us, is Richard Penrose.

Richard's hair is different today, all combed and slicked back, and he's wearing nice pants and a button-down, long-sleeved light blue shirt. Something about his face is different, too. He's not wearing the grumpy frown that he had on all week. The frown that says, *I'm here, but no one is going to make me like this place,* broadcasting his message as clearly as he would using the school's loudspeaker system. Not that he's exactly beaming with joy—more like he's on automatic pilot, like his body is here, but his mind is miles away. I know that look. I've used it to survive church, too. He's sharing a hymnal with an older woman. It must be his mom. Her hair is pinned up in a fancy twist that I'm guessing she didn't do herself. She's wearing an expensive-looking pale yellow linen suit and has a perfectly preserved face. She reminds me of those morning anchors Aunt Katherine likes to watch on the news channel. She's not on automatic pilot, though. She's glowing and patting Richard's arm, the one she has hers hooked through, holding on, like if she lets go, he'll escape and she'll never find him again. The man on the other side of him has got to be his father. He's not nearly as tall as Richard, but still he's the kind that you notice in a crowd, a well-built man with broad shoulders and a profile and olive skin very similar to Richard's. The same extra-long forehead and the same unique rounded tip at the end of his nose. He's singing in a booming bass voice. Dad's friend? Did they sit together in church? Go to Sunday school? Shoot spit wads at girls?

After the song, Pastor Browning talks again. "Now, I'd like to share one of my favorite poems." As he reads his voice is gentle, and my eyes begin to droop. I yawn. "'And I—I took the one less traveled by . . .'"

Someone is patting my knee and people are standing. I open my eyes and lift my head off Aunt Katherine's shoulder. I guess I've been sleeping. How long? What have I missed? I stand up in a daze. "Another hymn," Aunt Katherine whispers, and then hands me an open hymnal.

I nod and take hold of the book. After the song, Pastor Browning announces there will be a baptism. A young man and a woman carrying a baby in a beautiful white gown walk toward the front; several other people, who seem to be family members, follow them. Pastor Browning steps down from the pulpit to a brown wooden stand. It's carved, with a wooden bowl in the top. I guess the bowl is full of water. The family circles around the stand, with the mother still holding the baby above the water. Pastor Browning begins asking the family questions like "Do you turn to Christ and accept him as your Savior?" The family answers yes and the questions continue.

I'm finally getting it—this is an infant baptism.

Infant baptisms are a desecration before God. Only when a child has reached the age of accountability and is baptized by full immersion and by those with true authority is this sacred act acceptable before God.

Now Pastor Browning is sprinkling water over the baby and praying. My mind wanders, and I think back to when I was baptized at age eight. Really, did I have the world figured out any more than this infant? I don't even have a clue about life now, and I'm almost sixteen. Does God, if there is a God, even care if you are sprinkled or submerged in water? I mean, how does water and a prayer make you a good person?

I listen as Pastor Browning's voice slows and becomes hushed. "Bless this child with an inquiring mind and a discerning heart."

Obedience is the first law of the Gospel. A questioning heart leads to the path of Satan.

Wow. Is he really asking God to bless this child to question, to discern for herself? Okay. Cool. Now the prayer is over. Pastor Browning takes the baby and walks with her down the aisle of the church. People ooh and ahh. It's like being in a foreign country, but it's a country I think I like.

One more song, then the communion. My eyes about pop out when I see Douglas up front, helping Pastor Browning.

"What's Douglas doing?" I whisper to Aunt Katherine.

"I believe he's an altar boy," she whispers back. Then shakes her head. "No, no, now they have a new name for it, because girls can do it, too—but I've forgotten it. Whatever he's called, he does little things to help Pastor Browning with the service."

So Douglas is religious? Who would have guessed. I watch as people march up to the front to take the communion from Pastor Browning, not like in the Church of the Holy Divine, where young men called deacons pass it around to you in your seat and we called it the sacrament. Of course, no girls could be deacons. Not that I ever wanted to march around passing out bread and water. Here it looks like they have wafers, and is it real wine? Soon the communion is finished and before I know it people are standing and the organ plays. Church is over. How very painless.

After the service, several more people come up to chat with Aunt Katherine. She introduces me to about every family in Puffin Cove. Well, not everyone. I don't see Will or Jamie here. As we make our way toward the door, Aunt Katherine bumps right into Richard's father. "Excuse me," she says.

"Why, hello," Mr. Penrose says as he steps back. "Mrs. Stone, it's so good to see you in church again. How do you like the new renovations?"

"What's that?" she asks, and then cups her hand around her ear.

"Ren-o-vations—how do you like them?" Mr. Penrose's voice booms throughout the church.

Aunt Katherine now scans the chapel with her most serious face, like she's been asked to be the only judge for an architecture contest. Finally, she turns back to him and says, "I must admit I hadn't noticed." She chuckles. "To me it looks as it always has."

"Wonderful!" Mr. Penrose beams, and doesn't seem to realize that Aunt Katherine is poking fun at him. "That was our exact hope. We didn't want to change a thing, just shore it up a bit. Do you know the church is being considered for historic-landmark status?"

"My, my," Aunt Katherine says, and then winks across to where I am standing, half-hidden behind Mr. Penrose.

"Oh, Robert, I want you to meet my niece, Kate Anderson, who's just moved to Puffin Cove." Aunt Katherine puts out her arm and motions for me to step forward. When I do, she puts her arm through mine. "Her mother is running my inn."

Mr. Penrose turns toward me and smiles politely. "Hello." He's wearing some fancy-smelling cologne that attacks my nose. He and Chelsea could fumigate a room together.

I fight it, but I still sneeze. Aunt Katherine hands me a tissue as I try to smile.

"How is Whistling Woods Inn doing these days?" Mr. Penrose asks. "Business good?"

"The *Whispering* Woods Inn is doing just fine," Aunt Katherine answers. Patting my arm, she continues, "Kate is my nephew Steven's daughter." Turning toward me, she says, "I think I told you, Kate, your father and Mr. Penrose played together as children."

Mr. Penrose smiles a puzzled smile like he's trying to remember who Steven is. His eyes dart to the front of the chapel, and whatever he sees makes his eyebrows draw together and his polite smile falls into a concerned frown.

Aunt Katherine continues, not noticing. "Your father and Mr. Penrose were inseparable during the summers. They used to play cops and robbers in the woods behind our home."

"Oh yes, Steven. Of course. Yes, we did," Mr. Penrose answers slowly. Turning back to us, he asks, "So what is old Steven up to these days?"

My heart freezes.

Aunt Katherine sighs. "Steven passed away a little over a year ago."

"Oh. I'm so sorry. I didn't know." Mr. Penrose looks stiff and uncomfortable and his eyes dart away again, like he's looking for an escape, like I did when Chelsea cornered me about belonging to "their church" when she commented on the "skirt girls" at lunch. "Richard," he calls out as he spots his son, waving to him to come join us.

My cheeks flush. How many times did I walk past Richard Penrose at school this week? Now it seems we are actually going to be introduced. What should I say? Thanks for running me and my bike off the road? I realize I'm slouching. I stand up straight, suck in my tummy like Chelsea does, but I can't push my chest forward.

"This is my son, Richard." Mr. Penrose slaps Richard on the shoulder.

"Hello. I'm Katherine Stone. And this is Kate, my niece. But I suppose you two have already met? Aren't you also attending Rocky Point High this year?"

"Yes. Hello." Richard smiles politely at Aunt Katherine and shakes her hand. Then he turns and glances at me for just a second. His eyes dart to the floor like he's totally uncomfortable. He glances back to his dad, then back at us, and opens his mouth like he's going to say something.

Mr. Penrose's eyes seem glued to a group of men who have gathered at the front of the chapel. He barks out, "Excuse me. Nice to meet you . . . uh. . . ."

"Kate," Aunt Katherine says, completing the sentence for him.

But Mr. Penrose is gone and has pulled Richard away with him. Richard follows but turns his head back toward us and nods. They join the semicircle of men who all seem to have knitted brows. I overhear the words "major funding" and "roof repairs."

"Well, now you've met the Penrose family, or at least two of them," Aunt Katherine says. "I don't know Mrs. Penrose. She doesn't talk much to the year-round people. I have a feeling we don't have quite enough silver in our dining room."

"It doesn't look like we had enough to keep Mr. Penrose's interest long, either," I say, realizing Richard's father is exactly what Jamie said—a big snob. Dad wouldn't like him at all now.

"Kate," Chelsea calls, waving from where she's standing with her parents and little sisters, who both have red hair like her, Douglas, and Mr. Riggs. Something's different. Then I realize she isn't wearing makeup, or at least not as much. And instead of one of the low-cut tops she wears to school, she's wearing a sweater buttoned all the way up to her collarbone. Her mom is tall like Chelsea, but her hair is dark, almost black.

"So, you're Kate." Chelsea's mother smiles at me. "You look so much like your mother." She takes in a deep breath and then continues. "I can't believe she's back after all these years. I've got to stop by and see her." She pats the arm of the redheaded man standing next to her. "Did you know Mr. Riggs and I used to double-date with your father and mother the summer she worked for your aunt Katherine?"

"No," I say. How much more don't I know about Mom and Dad's past?

"How is the Whispering Woods doing this season?" Chelsea's mom asks Aunt Katherine.

"Just wonderful under Rebekah's management. She's a wonder."

Aunt Katherine and Mrs. Riggs continue talking about the vacationers and how busy the roads are now. Chelsea introduces me to her twin eight-year-old sisters. Mr. Riggs shuffles back and forth, jingling the change in his pocket. Like Mr. Penrose, he seems more interested in what's going on at the front of the chapel than in talking to us. Finally, he taps his wife and says, "I'll meet you at the car." He joins the group of men. Mrs. Riggs smiles. "That's Douglas Senior for you. He has to be in the thick of any decision. I believe he's convinced the church would fall apart without his input."

I glance at the group. I guess the church men in Puffin Cove are pretty serious about their roof repairs. I look up to the ceiling and expect to see a huge hole. But the wooden rafters seem fine to me. I notice Douglas up at the altar, closing the Bible and centering it on the pulpit. He seems as entranced as if he's in the middle of some calculus problem he's trying to solve.

"Hey, what's up with you being here? I had no idea you were coming," Chelsea says while Aunt Katherine and Mrs. Riggs continue chatting.

I shrug like it's no big deal. "Me, either." But now

maybe she'll believe me about not belonging to "that weird church" and won't bring it up again.

"So what were you talking about with Mr. Penrose and Richard?"

"Nothing much," I say.

"I'm going to bake them a blueberry pie this afternoon and go by to hang out. Richard's dad invited me to stop by anytime. Cool or what?"

Before I can answer, Mrs. Riggs turns to me and asks, "Are you coming to youth group this Tuesday, Kate?"

Youth group? More church?

"We haven't had a youth group in Puffin Cove for years," she continues. "It will be a great way to meet other teens in the area. Pastor Browning is such an excellent minister. Did you know he studied at the Harvard Divinity School?"

I smile but don't say anything.

Aunt Katherine speaks up. "Well, Kate, you can always try it out and if you don't like it, you don't have to go again."

Aunt Katherine pats my back like she wants me to go. Why, if she doesn't normally go to church herself? "I guess," I mumble, and hope that by Tuesday I can think of a reason to be too busy to show up.

chapter six

NO GUESTS ARE chatting and no vacuum is running when I get back to the inn. But from the kitchen, the aroma of Mom's chocolate chip cookies makes its way to me, rich and sweet. Through the doorway I spot her sitting at the kitchen table, thumbing through a stack of papers. Bills, I guess. I don't even know if she's worried about the inn making enough money. But Mom is smart at managing things. Back in Arizona, where she ran a big law office, the top lawyer was always praising her and giving her raises. Aunt Katherine must have made her a good offer or she would never have moved us across the country.

The oven timer buzzes. Mom stands and sees me. "How was *church*?" She spits out the last word like it's cookie dough with way too much baking soda.

"Fine." I decide to go for the friendly approach. "You should have seen the windows, Mom—all stained glass. They were beautiful. You would have loved them."

She removes the pan and slams the oven door. That one

sound, the loudness of it, confirms that we are alone. The hostess with her charming voice and lovely manners is off duty. "I've seen that church. Remember I met your father here almost twenty years ago? The money used on those windows alone could buy thousands of Bibles for children in Africa."

Suddenly, I feel five years old again, trembling and guilty like I've been a very bad girl. Like I did when I tried to hide the half-eaten package of Wint-O-Green Life Savers I'd taken from the grocery store inside my chubby fist. Mom saw the open foil and the white candy in my mouth. Right in the parking lot she grabbed both my arms and shook me. "Don't you know that's stealing? Don't you know you are a thief?"

Pulling me, she marched back into the store. As we crossed the parking lot, she preached, "Satan loves to tempt little children. He always starts with small things, whispering thoughts into your mind, tempting you to take candy that you know isn't yours. If you keep listening, Kate, next time he might tempt you to steal money out of my purse, and then clothes at the store when you become a teenager, and by the time you're an adult, Satan will totally have you in his power and you'll be stealing cars and robbing banks."

I was sobbing by this point and saying, "I'm sorry, Mommy, I'm sorry."

She patted me and said, "Listen carefully, Kate. Sometimes Satan appears in the form of a handsome man wearing a dark suit. You must always be on the lookout."

I nodded and Mom made me apologize to the store owner and she paid him for the pack of Life Savers and then she made me throw them in the garbage can right outside the store door, which was fine with me. The one still in my mouth tasted like poison.

Now in the kitchen, her voice breaks into my thoughts. "I never imagined I would see the day that my own child would attend another church." Her voice chokes. "What would your great-great-grandfather think?" she asks as she wipes tears from her eyes.

I stand soldier-straight and get prepared for a lecture on how I'm going to Hell, but somewhere beneath the layer of guilt a little voice speaks inside me. Maybe he doesn't think at all. Maybe Dad's right. Maybe there is no life after death. But I know what Mom is getting at. My great-great-grandfather immigrated to the United States, leaving Europe and most of his family and friends behind, and became one of the founders of the Church of the Holy Divine. From Mom's point of view, the United States is a chosen land mainly because the Church was started here, not because of George Washington, Thomas Jefferson, or Benjamin Franklin.

"You know we can't do anything if Aunt Katherine goes to a different church." Mom's voice begins to tremble.

"After all, she hasn't been taught any better. She wasn't raised with the saving love of Jesus. But you were." Tears form in her eyes. "How can you turn your back on all you've been given? Does your heritage mean nothing to you?" She brushes at the tears on her cheeks.

What about Dad's heritage? my head demands. But I just stand and examine my sandals. And as I do, I have an uncomfortable memory of Dad doing this, staring at his shoes while she ranted on and on. Goose pimples form on my arms.

"Kate. You were born into the fullness of the Gospel."

I look up. Mom's nose, already thin, seems to pinch tight, her chin juts up, and her eyes stare past me as if her God and Heaven have appeared on the wall behind me. Her voice shakes, like she's making a prophecy, like our High Priest's voice did when he got really riled up calling us to repentance. Every time her voice gets like this, it freaks me out worse than those ghost stories my cousins used to tell at night. Mom continues, "Don't forget, with that blessing comes a great responsibility. Our yeast is pure. We are to share it, so others may rise, so we may be a leaven to the world. God sent us here to Maine to enlighten Aunt Katherine and others."

My fists clench. Mom thinks she's better than Aunt Katherine. Of all the parables I've been raised on, I think the one about all true believers being the yeast to leaven the world's bread is my least favorite. My chest swells. My fingernails dig into my palms. But still I stand, silent.

"You see what's happening in the Middle East. You know what has been prophesied."

I know. I knew. Armageddon. One last Holy War that will begin in Jerusalem and will destroy all the unbelievers before Christ returns to rule and reign over the earth. But I'm not going to be frightened by that stupid prophecy or her shaking voice any longer. Last year I was so sure Armageddon had come. At church the week before Dad died, our High Priest talked about the wars in the Middle East and said the time was near. Then Dad died and somehow I connected the two and thought the end of the world was coming. I huddled in my bedroom, with my eyes puffy from crying, my insides hurting like a million bruises, and guilt pulsing through every vein. At night I stood at my window for hours, looking up into the sky, waiting for the moon to turn to blood like the Bible prophesied. Finally, I fell into a restless sleep. When I woke, I jumped up and ran to the window again, to see if the earth was burning yet, worried constantly that I would burn with the unbelievers, because now I was one.

I was a sinner because I had given up on faith. I had given up on fasting. I didn't fast for Dad the day he died. He had made me so mad that week, I punished him by not fasting. But I didn't mean for him to die. It wasn't because

I didn't fast, was it? It couldn't be. I felt I deserved to die, too. But the sun rose and the sun set and the moon didn't turn to blood. Weeks passed, and then months. The earth didn't explode into flames and Christ didn't appear in the eastern sky. And I quit going to church, so I don't know what the High Priest was saying, probably still predicting that "the end is near," as he probably will for the rest of his life. It's one way to scare people into obeying the rules of the church. It scared me.

"Kate. Kate?" Mom's eyes bore into me.

I close my eyes, squeezing them tight, hoping that if I squeeze hard enough, all of this ugliness will vanish. I'm not going to let her scare me into believing that Satan in the form of a man in a dark suit is lurking around the corner, waiting to pounce on me if I don't follow every stupid rule of the Holy Divine Church. I'm not going to stand still and take what she throws at me. I'm not going to be silent, like . . . Dad.

My shoulders quiver. I feel faint. I need water. I take in a deep breath and raise my eyes to meet Mom's.

And I think back to all those dark days in my room, with the shades drawn, reading Dad's books, reading his old copies of *The Atlantic Monthly* and *The New Yorker*. Slowly, day by day, I began to doubt. I wanted to read more and more. I was so thirsty for information about the outside world I'd always been protected from. I wanted more and more. I learned things. Lots of things. Not everyone believes abortion is the same as murder. Not all people believe being gay is the plague of the modern world. I discovered that people who weren't members of Mom's church actually did great things, like Mother Teresa and Rosa Parks and ordinary suburban families who adopted unwanted pets or handicapped children. How could they all be evil? I don't know when exactly it happened, but one day I just knew they weren't evil. Just like I realized that simply being a member of the Holy Divine Church, this measly little church that most of the world didn't even know about, shouldn't guarantee you a place in Heaven.

So I look at Mom. "Has it ever, even once in your whole life, occurred to you, that maybe God accepts other churches besides yours?" I ask her in a voice that surprises me with its steadiness and calmness. I continue with a speech, one I've carefully prepared in my head for months. "Did you even once wonder if maybe the Holy Divine Church isn't as special as you think? I mean, isn't it arrogant to think that a small group of people who have inbred for generations and make it a practice not to study other religions really have the monopoly on religious truth? I mean, what's so special about *the yeast* they supposedly have? To tell you the truth, I think the yeast needs to be thrown out and a fresh batch started."

Mom's eyes darken; one blue blood vessel along her

temple bulges. Her voice is quiet and so slow and steady it frightens me. "You've. Been. Reading. Your. Father's. Books." As she speaks, she backs away from me, like I'm a monster or an alien from an unknown galaxy. No, it's worse than that. She acts like she's seeing Satan, like I'm the man in the dark suit myself. Tears stream down her face, falling so fast she chokes. Sobbing, she turns away from me. "She's been reading her father's books. She's been reading her father's books," she repeats over and over, pacing back and forth like she's in a trance.

Shocked at her response, I stand, unable to move or to say anything more. Have I ever known who this person is? Did I actually enjoy being homeschooled, leaning so close to her as we pored over algebra that I could smell her gardenia-scented lotion? Did we really cook together? Did she really teach me how to knead bread and make the flakiest pie crust? Could I really have snuggled next to her in bed at night as she read my favorite scripture picture book, *The Good Samaritan*, over and over? Could this woman be the same person who taught me to use a hammer and nails to build a doll house? The house we built after she told Dad that living in two separate bedrooms was a sacrilege to the holiness of marriage and she wanted a divorce?

Outside, footsteps crunch on the gravel drive. Someone laughs. The couple from Texas strolls by the window, hand in hand. Mom stiffens. She stands up straight, smoothes her apron, and wipes the tears from her cheeks. She takes in a deep breath, walks over to her cookies, and begins arranging them in a perfect circle on a silver platter. She lifts the tray and, with a serene calm, glides toward the parlor. She glances at me as she passes. "I'm afraid we'll have to talk about this later," she says in a tone so steady, someone would think we've just been discussing the pros and cons of using margerine in chocolate chip cookies. Somehow she's sucked the shaking limbs and pulpit-pounding, prophetic-sounding voice back inside herself in one deep breath. Out in the hall her voice peals with friendliness. "How was the hike?"

I make my escape down the stairs to my bedroom and through quivering lips whisper, "Seriously, Mom, you should be an actress. We'd be rich!"

chapter seven

SITTING ON MY bed are two envelopes. I guess I forgot to get the mail yesterday. I grab the letters and plop onto my quilt. With my head encased in pillows and my knees bent up, I open the letter from Charity first. She's my favorite cousin. Years ago we promised each other that when we were old enough, we'd be roommates at the church's small college in Virginia. That's not going to happen now.

Dear Kate,
How are you? How is Maine? Have you been to youth group yet?
Big news! The cutest guy just moved here. His name is Jacob and he's in my Bible Study group. He's seventeen and so awesome! He has wavy black hair and these really green, green eyes. He passed off his scripture mastery last year and he's already an Eagle Scout. I overheard Mom tell Dad that he's the kind of boy who will be a disciple for the church one

day, he's that faithful. He smiles at me all the time. Don't tell anyone, but I've been praying about him and I feel like he might be "the one."

And guess what else? Beth called last weekend. She's engaged—going to school for that summer term did it. It's only her second semester at college!! Isn't she lucky? Now she doesn't have to finish. Just think, by this time next year she'll probably have her first baby.

Oh, Kate, I get so sad thinking about you out there all alone in Maine. I hope you're going to church now. I can't imagine Heaven without you. You are my closest cousin. I just want you to remember that I know beyond a shadow of a doubt that the Church of the Holy Divine is the true church of Jesus Christ. I pray for you every day.

Love, Charity.

I hate those words—*I know. I know.* Members of the Holy Divine Church always *know*, they always *know* beyond a shadow of a doubt. Right! How can Charity, who has spent her whole life in a small town in the desert of Arizona, with no cable or Internet access and no newspaper besides the *Weekly Holy Divine*, *know* anything? She's never even read a book about another church or attended any type of service except for the Holy Divine Church's. But she would say, "God told me, Kate. My heart burns with the witness."

I shut my eyes tight. To think I believed just like her that women were put on earth solely to become mothers. Oh, the church leaders made it sound so important, like we would be queens or something. So what do the girls at church do? They pray for it to happen, to find their chosen mate, just like Charity does, before they've had a chance to grow up. It seems horrible now to think that the main reason to attend college is to find *your chosen mate* so you can get married and have all those babies to fulfill your divine purpose of multiplying and replenishing the earth. And if you aren't engaged and actually manage to graduate in four years, you are automatically classified as an undesirable old maid—or worse, a feminist.

I don't know if I have the courage to open Grandma's letter. But I do. Two pamphlets fall out: *Repentance: A Gift for All* and *Renewing Your Faith in Ten Easy Steps.* I wad them up into tiny balls. Grandma's letter is much like Charity's, hoping I'm going to church, telling me how she knows God is watching over me, and finally some report about the apple orchard and the good crop they have this fall in Idaho. I wad up Charity's letter and Grandma's, too. I wipe tears from my eyes. I love them. I miss them. I hate this ache inside me. I twist at the wadded paper. I realize that their letters and pamphlets will make good kindling. So before I end up having a big pity party for myself, I jump off the bed, change into jeans, and stuff the wadded-up papers into my pocket.

As I climb the stairs from the basement, I hear Mom in the kitchen. She's on the phone. Her voice is low. I stand outside the doorway and listen. "No, she isn't going to church yet . . . she's still grieving. . . . She'll come around. . . . God told me so. . . . We have to have faith. . . ."

Right, Mom. God told you I'm going to go back to church? The same God who took my dad when he was only forty-one years old? The same God who told you that you would be the instrument to bring your husband to the truth? What about that one, Mom? Huh? How do you explain your way out of that?

But Mom has buckets and boxes and suitcases full of extra faith. And so does her family. Is it Grandma or Charity's mom, Aunt Deborah, on the phone? I've heard enough. I slink by the kitchen and head upstairs. In the second-floor hallway I rummage through the linen closet and grab a duster, the vacuum, and as much fresh bedding as I can carry. How dare she discuss me with her family behind my back? When I'm halfway down the hall, I pause at the alcove with the window seat and its view of the treetops and the ocean. The faint scent of salt and the gentle rustle of trees from the open window begin to quiet my pounding heart. Every time I've cleaned up here, I have pretended that this is my summer home, and there are no guests. And today, as long as I'm imagining, I'll erase Mom from my life, too. I'm not sad that I spoke up. A part of me feels like I do after I've run a good race, like when I've sprinted past someone right before the finish line.

Besides, the anger or sadness melts away every time I'm up here in this quiet spot, alone. Since I was small, each Sunday while my body sat perfectly still, eyes glued to our High Priest, in my head I created castles in Scotland, châteaux in France, and Victorian mansions in New England. Each estate had turrets, gables, hidden staircases, and velvet furniture. And Aunt Katherine's inn, the place I'm standing in right now, is as fine as any dream place I ever created.

As I put clean sheets on beds, I imagine the original owners, who, in the early 1900s, were rich enough to build this seven-suite mansion for their summer home. Each room has a hardwood floor and thick area carpets and is decorated with period antiques and lace curtains, and there are satin spreads covering the four-poster beds. All the suites have a fireplace and a private deck with views out to the woods or the ocean. After our small stucco house in Phoenix, with its Spanish tile floors and pale green walls, and Dad's drab apartment, the Whispering Woods Inn seems like a fairy-tale home to me. And besides, in Puffin Cove everything is green and alive, instead of brown and hot and dead. And I have Aunt Katherine. I smile, thinking of her telling Mr. Penrose she didn't notice any changes in his fancy church.

So I hurry through my chores and then head over to Aunt Katherine's. "Hello," I call out, knocking on the ancient wooden door of her cottage. I push it open.

"I'm back here, love."

I pass through the front room on my way to the kitchen. Aunt Katherine's home has more windows than walls and more bookshelves than pictures. Trees peek in from every side, and bird feeders hang from several of the nearest branches. Vases of fresh-cut flowers cover the big oak table, ready to place in each guest room. It's something she still insists on doing.

"Can you believe this feeder is empty again?" Aunt Katherine asks as she pours her cooled nectar into her bright red hummingbird feeder. "I tell you, Kate, it exhausts me watching those busy little birds. I must have seen ten of them today. They'll be leaving any day now for their long journey." She sighs. "I'll miss those little critters this winter." Her eyes twinkle and get a faraway look. Then she looks back to me. "Enough about my hummingbirds. I'm glad you stopped by. I was cleaning yesterday and came across an old scrapbook I kept on your father. Would you like to look at it?"

I nod with enthusiasm. Would Aunt Katherine believe that I've never even seen a baby picture of Dad, or that he hardly ever told me about growing up in Maine? Whenever I asked, he'd just say it was so long ago he couldn't remember much.

While Aunt Katherine is in her bedroom finding the scrapbook, I snuggle up in the overstuffed yellow corduroy couch. At Christmas, will I help Aunt Katherine drape pine boughs on the ornate wood mantel? Maybe we'll get a chubby Christmas tree and set it in the corner at the edge of the plush apple-green rug. Will we give each other gifts? Will I sit here and watch real snow fall?

Aunt Katherine sits next to me. She smells all earthy again. I nestle in closer as she opens an old brown leather album filled with pages of thick, yellowed paper. Sometimes Aunt Katherine's breath comes out in a gentle sigh and that tiny sound soothes something so deep in me. My neck tingles and before I even see one picture, I know I want to sit here forever and just feel whatever it is I feel when I'm around her.

"Since your uncle John and I could never have children," she begins, "we were lucky to have your dad in our lives. I inherited this album after your grandparents died. I tried to give it to Steven, but he told me to keep hold of it for him. I guess people would say he wasn't a very sentimental person."

I nod. Mom would agree. She always made such a big deal over holidays, especially religious ones like Christmas and Easter, but Dad didn't celebrate them. He didn't even give me birthday presents.

"'Holiday gift-giving obligates people,' that's what he used to say to me," I tell her.

"That's your dad, all right."

"But he'd buy me things if I needed them or asked, like my running clothes and shoes," I say in his defense. "And one time he came home with a Christmas cactus three days before Christmas. It even had a red bow and foil over the pot. But he made it clear that it wasn't a Christmas present. 'I just thought it was an interesting plant,' he told me."

"I know what you mean. Sometimes I'd find a package from him in the mail for no special event. It would be a book or video he thought I'd like, and once he sent me an ornate bird feeder. No note. No letter. No wrapping paper." Aunt Katherine chuckles. "And yet, somehow it always meant more getting his rare gifts, simply because he didn't follow the traditional customs of holidays."

I nod. "But I still like Christmas and getting gifts for my birthday," I admit.

"Me, too, love." Aunt Katherine giggles like a young girl. She turns the page and tenderly smoothes it. "Here's your father as a baby, with your grandparents."

I lean in close to see a dark-haired baby held up toward the camera by a young-looking woman.

"He was a good baby," Aunt Katherine says. "And curious. He'd sit in his stroller for hours, watching everything around him, taking it all in. I always used to wonder what he was thinking. I do believe babies can think big things." Aunt Katherine winks and pats my hand. "But that, my dear, is a discussion for another day." She turns the page.

We see more baby pictures. Then it's page after page of birthday photos, school report cards, and several news clippings about his high-school track team.

"Aunt Katherine?"

"Yes, love?"

"Did Dad go to church often?"

"Yes, when he was younger. But then when he became a teenager, he seemed to lose interest. Back then, I must admit, I suffered through the preaching part every week, for the social aspects. But your dad, like your grandfather, was never much interested in the social or the religious parts of church." Aunt Katherine smooths her hand over the yellowed page, pressing on the edge of a photo that is coming loose.

My eyes meet hers. Neither of us speaks. But it's as if she knows. Knows that I've stopped going to church, too. That I've started to doubt. I want to ask her if she believes in God. I want to ask her what she thinks happens after you die. But I can't. The darkness starts slipping in around me. The guilt of not fasting and Dad dying that same day. The horrors after that, walking around like a zombie, wishing I were dead. I sit up straight. I blink to fight back tears I feel at the edge of my eyes. To keep busy, I turn the page of the photo album. A wedding announcement and a picture of Mom and Dad with their arms around each other fill the page. They look so happy, so young, and, surprisingly, so in love. The glow in their eyes distracts me from my gloom.

"How did my parents ever get together? I mean, they weren't exactly alike."

"Hmm. Let me see. I needed help for the summer, and I figured the *National Christian Youth Bulletin* I used to see hanging around church would yield some good callbacks, so I placed an ad there and your mom responded. She sounded honest and hardworking, and I hired her right then over the phone."

"And then she met Dad."

"Yes. Steven was home from college for the summer, working at your grandfather's boat-repair shop."

"But . . . how . . . why?"

"You've seen your mother with the guests, Kate. She's very charming. She's talkative and cheerful and a hard worker. She brought life into Steven's eyes."

A cheerful countenance bringeth forth miracles.

"And she was—well—different back then."

"Different?"

"How can I explain? Well, there's really no other way to put it. She didn't seem so religious, or as rigid as she is now."

I nod and remember my early life with Barbie and Disney.

"And your father was such a quiet young man," Aunt Katherine continues. "A real thinker. But . . ." Aunt Katherine pauses.

"But it didn't last," I finish for her.

"No. It didn't last. I'm a bit old-fashioned when it comes to marriage. I think you should be friends first and then lovers. So many young people fall in love first. They like the way they feel when they are with the other person, the sound of the other person's voice. And that is all good. But sometimes if that part comes too fast, it overpowers the friendship side of things. For example, I don't think your parents talked much about their values or beliefs. And if they had, well . . ."

"They would have found out they didn't have very much in common," I add.

"Exactly."

I watch out the window as another hummingbird flits up to one of Aunt Katherine's feeders. Its tiny wings flap so quickly they look like miniature fans.

"I'm sure Steven made it harder, because he wasn't the easiest person to understand," Aunt Katherine continues. "Communication wasn't exactly high on his priority list. He kept most things to himself and puzzled over them in private. I think that must have been very hard on your mother."

My mother? I think as the hummingbird disappears. She probably drove Dad to a life of silence.

chapter eight

MY CLOCK READS five thirty. I shiver, thinking of the dream that woke me. Dad and I were running in Phoenix by the canal, alongside the evenly spread palm trees. He was timing me, like he used to. But instead of a stopwatch, he held a Christmas cactus. It was all in bloom, with bright pink flowers. The pot was wrapped in gold foil and had a bow, just like the one he had given me two years ago. I was trying to make my goal, to run from one tree to the next in ten seconds or less, but I couldn't. My body was dragging. When I finally reached the thirteenth palm, the one Dad said I owned because it was the first palm tree I ever reached in ten seconds, Dad was nowhere. Totally vanished. Instead I found the cactus he gave me lying at the foot of the tree. The blooms were gone and so was the foil and the bow. The plant was brown and brittle. Dead.

I pull my blanket up around my neck. When Dad gave me the cactus, he explained how it would bloom right around Christmas every year because the days were shortest then and the cactus needed at least thirteen hours of darkness to flower. Later when I explained this to Mom, she told me the blooms had nothing to do with daylight and darkness, but were simply one of God's ways of expressing his joy for the birth of His Holy Son. Science or God's joy, one thing is certain: the brown, stiff plant I finally put in the garbage when we were moving out this summer will never bloom again.

It's early. I don't want to think about Mom. Or about our fight. No one would believe she actually got mad at me just for going to church. Suddenly, Will's words, "We leave at first light," enter my thoughts.

Why not? She's already angry with me. How much worse can it get?

I jump out of bed, dress, and grab my rain slicker. "*Slick-ah,*" I hear Will's voice echo in my head, and smile.

With my shoes in hand, I sneak past Mom's bedroom and am grateful no light is showing from under her door. I creep up the stairs to the main floor and outside. The sun's not quite up yet. But the streetlamps along the road guide my way. I jog to town, glad for the warmth the run is pumping through my veins. A few feet from the dock my stomach tightens. Am I crazy? Mom will kill me. And what if Will was just being polite and he didn't really want me to show up one morning? This was a stupid idea. I lean on my heels to turn around.

"Kate?" Will's head pops out of the crowded dock area busy with shadowed bodies moving about, carrying metal cages and buckets.

I wave.

He grins. "Well, hello, City Girl."

"Hi."

"So are you here to go out lobstering?"

"I guess."

"Yep. Sure. We can do that." He looks at me as if he expects me to understand.

I guess my blank expression lets him know I'm clueless.

"If we do our route a little differently today, I think we can drop you back by the dock about eight," he says. "Will that work?"

Eight? The bus comes by my house at eight. I don't have the courage to mention that seven forty-five would be a whole lot better. I'm going to have to ride my bike and I'll be late to school. "I don't want to cause trouble," I say.

"You won't. Pop and I enjoy showing off our lovely yacht." Will extends his arm grandly toward a boat filled with mesh cages and rope. Like the rest of the dock area, it smells strongly of fish. I can make out *Lucky Lady* painted on the back. Is the back of the boat the bow or the stern? I can't ever remember. I hope it won't come up.

"It is a divine yacht," I say, my muscles relaxing. I'll think about getting to school later.

A gray-haired man with a yarn cap and a full beard arrives, carrying two big buckets. One is filled with water, the other with bluish-looking fish or fish parts. Will hoists the water bucket and deposits it inside the boat. Then he hefts himself and the second bucket over the edge of the boat and nods toward me. "Pop, this is my friend Kate. She just moved here from out west. She wants to see what kind of *fishing poles* we use to catch our lobster."

Pop tilts his head at Will, confused. But then he shrugs and nods at me as he climbs into the boat. "Get her a life jacket," he says. His skin is weatherbeaten and leathery. He doesn't really smile, but he's not frowning, either.

"Come on," Will says.

I take Will's hand and step over the side, holding on to the boat with my other hand to steady myself. Pop is already behind the wheel. The engine, chugging, revs as we pull away from the dock.

Will carries the buckets to a spot directly behind the cabin. I follow. "Do you think your grandfather minds my being here?" I say, moving close to be heard over the loud engine.

"Nah, he doesn't mind, he's just not much of a talker."

"What should I call him?" I ask.

"Most people just call him Pop Lane," Will says, and hands me a life jacket.

"Oh. Okay," I say as I put it on, noticing that neither Will nor Pop Lane is wearing one of these puffy bright orange vests.

"Here." Will hands me a pair of oversized rubber boots. "Put these on," he says. I sit on a bench attached to the side of the boat. The spray from the water and the wind hit my face as we leave the harbor and the boat picks up speed. After getting the boots on, I stand and try to keep my feet steady. When Will moves toward the back of the boat, I tag along, grabbing on to whatever I can. He begins sorting through a pile of metal cages.

"Are those cages for the lobster?" I shout.

He smiles and hollers, "Yep, guess you could call them that. We call them traps," he says as he pulls one up and ties a long piece of black rope around the top.

"Oh. Can I help?" I call out.

Will nods, cupping his hands around his mouth, and says, "When we stop at our buoys, you can help rebait the traps, after Pop and I empty them."

We hit a rough spot and I reach out, grasping the boat's railing, and barely stop myself from falling onto Will. I feel my cheeks grow hot as my shoulder rubs his.

In the early-morning light, buoys of every color greet us every few yards, like flocks of striped seagulls resting on the water. "Are all those yours? How do you know where to stop? How do you remember where you have them all?" I shout over the engine.

Will laughs as he ties rope onto another trap. "Whoa, slow down," he calls back. He finishes his knot. Then he tugs at a blue tarp, exposing several yellow-white-and-black-striped buoys sitting on the floor of the boat. "These are Pop's. Everyone has their own special color design," Will explains as he picks up a buoy and hands it to me.

I hold it and turn it over and examine it.

Will laughs again.

"What's so funny?"

"You." He's standing so close to me, we don't have to yell. So close I could touch him or he could touch me. But we don't. "I mean, I never thought about it, but I guess it's like you said—in Phoenix there isn't exactly an ocean around. You've never seen all this?" he says, tilting his head toward the lobster equipment.

I shake my head. "Just like you've never run six miles when it's one hundred ten degrees and the only other livings thing outdoors besides you are lizards. And instead of pine trees on every corner, you're surrounded by cacti and desert hills."

"Okay, okay. You get pretty defensive about your desert now, don't you?"

I feel my lower lip beginning to stick out the way it used to when Dad would tease me about not knowing something he thought everyone in the world should know. It's like most of the time he totally forgot and acted shocked when I reminded him that Mom didn't have cable television or subscribe to a single magazine or newspaper besides the weekly church bulletin.

Will chuckles and then explains all about traps and buoys. He goes on to show me different equipment and various parts of the boat. We have to stand close to hear each other. My body tingles every time his arm brushes mine. Is this how it feels to want someone to touch you?

The boat slows. Pop pulls up near a buoy painted like the ones under the tarp. Using a machine-powered pulley, Will brings a trap up to the surface of the water and lifts it over the side of the boat. Pop takes it and Will goes back to the pulley and soon a second trap appears.

"We normally have two traps to each buoy," he explains as he opens the second trap and pulls out one of the two lobsters. The antennas on it move. Its claws go into attack mode. Without meaning to, I jump back. Will glances up and grins. "Shit," he says, and just before the pincers close in on his hand, he tosses the shelled animal back into the water.

Pop clears his throat and mumbles, "Watch your language around the young lady."

My cheeks color.

"Ah, Pop."

Pop gives Will a serious look.

"Um, why did you throw that lobster back in?" I ask, trying to ease the uncomfortable silence.

"Too small," Will explains.

"How do you know?"

He pulls out a measuring gauge from his pocket. "By law they have to be at least three and a quarter inches and no bigger than five inches from the eye to the beginning of the tail. But the actual size changes a bit from year to year." Then using a small tool, he puts rubber bands over the nipping claws of the second lobster. He tosses it into a bucket, half-filled with seawater, where Pop has already dropped two. "A keeper," he says, and it sounds like "keep-ah."

"Do you ever get pinched?"

"Plenty," he says as he lifts his hands and points to several scars.

"Why don't you wear gloves?"

"Gloves? Gloves are for sissies, right, Pop?"

Pop grunts.

We continue to stop at all the yellow-white-and-black buoys. Will operates the winch that pulls up the traps and Pop rubber-bands the lobsters. I fill the bait bags with slimy dead fish, which they attach to the empty cages before they send them back down into the ocean. At first I'm afraid to hold the slippery, cold bait and Will offers me a pair of rubber gloves, but I don't want to be thought of as a wimp. After a few minutes I actually get used to seeing the dead eyes of fish stare back at me every time I fill a bag. We work without talking; only the loud hum of the boat engine fills the air.

After a while I ask, "How do you know where to put your traps? I mean, are there rules?"

"Yup. Well, that's sort of complicated. Most people who *trap* lobster have been doing it for years. Father to son. So we all grew up knowing where we could put our buoys, where our family's territory is. Every once in a while someone gets a little greedy and puts their traps too close to ours."

"What happens then?"

"Oh, we Down-Easters have our ways."

"What do you mean?"

"We'll move the traps back out of our area, and if that doesn't work, then we gather up their buoys, cutting them loose from their traps, and tie them together with rope. We call it a bouquet. We leave them in the water as a warning."

I gasp. "But don't you get in trouble? I mean, shouldn't you call the police or the coast guard or something?"

"Nah. Why involve the government? We just try to stay clear of them. Government and politics just mess things up."

I nod my head. I've heard this before. Dad used to tell me that the secret to life was "Mind your own business,

pay your taxes, and avoid the rest of the whole political
and religious mess if you can." But Jamie, Aunt Katherine,
and especially Mom seem to want to change the world.
Jamie, who doesn't eat meat, drinks only out of her reus-
able water bottle. She thinks all the discarded water bottles
will make this country a mountain range of plastic. Aunt
Katherine is on a committee for recycling and insists that
Mom buy organic food and paper products, which cost so
much more that Mom's lips become thin every time the
topic comes up. And Mom? Her solution is simple—everyone becomes a member of the Holy Divine Church and
we'll have Heaven here on Earth.

A sudden gust of wind blows the loose strands of
hair across my face. I brush them away and my thoughts
as well. Taking in a deep breath, I realize how different
the view is out here on the water. There are several little
islands I've never noticed from the shore. What fun Dad
could have had with his camera. I can almost feel him
peering around the tip of Puffin Cove to other parts of
the mainland. Along the rocky ledges, peeking between
trees from high perches, the windows of several huge
houses blink as the rising sun hits their panes. My watch
reads seven a.m. Mom's cooking breakfast by now. Will
she notice I'm gone?

Splash! The water near the boat explodes. Something
big and black shoots toward us. A shark? I freeze. But

neither Will nor Pop even stops his work to look. After a few seconds, I inch toward the edge of the boat, just as the black thing explodes again, spraying water upward like a huge geyser. I jump back. "A dolphin!" I cry.

Will looks up from the bait bucket and chuckles. "Hot damn! Let me guess—never seen those in Arizona, either?"

I shake my head and turn back to watch as it swims by. It glides so easily above the water, making a fountain of spray. Then down, making another splash. Gone. Then up again. It seems to be following us, going our same direction. Up. Twirling in the air. Down. Up. Twirling around and around. Down. It's like the dolphin is dancing. I clap. I laugh. I love it. It's so free and happy. I want to dance, too. I want to stay on this boat with Will and his grandfather and watch this dolphin forever. Freeze this moment. I think of dancing with Jamie in the sprinkler at the church. Is this what it means in the Bible when it says to become as a child? Is this what it is to have childlike faith? Could it mean joy? Just simple joy?

Now the dolphin is swimming away from us. Two more dolphins rise into the air above the waves. They jump. They touch and dive back into the water. I wait and watch. A minute passes. Two. They're gone. It was so magical. Did it really happen?

Sighing, I return to helping with the bait. A couple

of traps later, Will shouts to Pop, "Let's stop by the old osprey's nest before we head back to shore."

Pop just grunts and continues steering the boat.

Despite my curiosity, wondering what, exactly, an osprey is, I'm worried about getting back home. "We don't have to see the nest if your grandfather doesn't want to."

Will laughs. "Don't take Pop seriously. He'll want you to see it. He's proud of that old nest. You just watch."

The engine slows as the boat approaches a tiny island. Pop pulls out a pair of binoculars from a cupboard. "Here," he directs, but it sounds like "he-ah," as he hands me the glasses. Pop's accent is even stronger than Will's. "Take these and look straight up there, at the top of that big rock."

At first all I see are trees. Then I focus on a huge brown nest, four or five feet tall, made up of thousands of little twigs and branches. Just above the top, something moves. I angle the binoculars up and make out the head of the bird that must be the osprey. "Wow. It's huge. It looks like an eagle."

"A sea eagle," Pop clarifies.

"That nest is one hundred and fifty years old, isn't it, Pop?" Will asks.

"Ayuh." Pop revs up the idling engine again.

I watch the nest shrink as we head back toward Puffin Cove. Did Dad ever come on a lobster boat? Did he see this nest? Did his father? Did his grandfather?

When the nest is a tiny dot, I help Will clean up. I wash out the empty bait bucket. I sponge down the area we worked at. "So, do you eat lobster a lot?" I ask as the engine slows.

Pop hears me and grunts.

Will chuckles. "Yeah, Pop and I have both had our share of lobster. Lobster soup, lobster sandwiches, which I used to trade for peanut butter and jelly sandwiches in grade school, lobster pot pie, lobster salad. Hell, we've even had lobster for Thanksgiving."

Pop grunts again, but I think I see the corners of his lips turn up a little.

"He's not used to being around people much, especially women," Will whispers.

"But don't you both live with your mom?" I ask when the engine is too loud for Pop to overhear.

"Oh, well, that's different—she's his daughter."

"But your name's Lane, too," I say without thinking.

"Right. My mom didn't marry my dad, whoever he was. So she, Pop, and I all have the same name."

"Oh, I'm sorry." My cheeks grow warm.

Only the sin of murder is greater than the sin of fornication or adultery.

"Why are you sorry? You don't like the name Lane?" Will's eyes are full of teasing.

I shove away the ugly, haunting words and smile. "I

like it," I say, and to myself add, I also like your boat and my hair whipping in the wind. I lick my lips and taste salt. My skin tingles.

When we get to the dock, I thank Pop and he says to Will, "Why don't you go in with the girl? You can take that makeup test your mom keeps scolding you about. I'll be fine."

"Ah, Pop."

Pop tries to look stern. "You don't want to be on your mom's bad side, do you?" There's a certain rhythm to his speech. So Maine. It almost seems like he's reciting poetry.

Will shrugs. "Okay."

"Here." Pop hands me a Styrofoam bucket with three lobsters in it, making sure the lid is secure.

"But . . ." I start to protest but look into Mr. Lane's eyes. I can't refuse. It wouldn't be nice. "Thank you, Mr. Lane."

Will drives me back to the inn to change clothes and he's even going to pick me up in fifteen minutes. I won't be late! A big yawn slips out.

"Early morning, City Girl?"

I nod. "I don't see how you have enough energy to run cross-country after school every day. Aren't you tired?"

"Well, maybe that's why I'm not as fast as you."

"Maybe it's because you don't wear running shoes," I say before I think. It's dangerous to feel this free around someone. Maybe he can't afford any new shoes.

He doesn't seem to mind, though. He chuckles. "Shit. So you think I need running shoes?"

I shrug my shoulders. I'm not about to say more.

"Okay. Maybe I do. Will you help me pick some out?"

My heart jumps. Is he asking me to go shopping with him? Isn't that almost like a date? A real date? Does that mean he liked me coming out this morning? Me, walking side by side with Will at the mall, just like regular people. But shoe stores aren't exactly open at six a.m., when Mom is still safely in her room studying the Bible. "Maybe," I say, trying to stay calm even though my insides are exploding.

"Maybe? You mean, after your fine educational experience this morning, you aren't sure you're willing to help out your great lobster instructor?"

"Well, since you put it that way . . ." I pause and pretend to be really thinking. "Okay." I grin and Will smiles back. My heart leaps. Not that Mom will ever let me go to the mall, which is, of course, evil all by itself, without adding Will to the picture. But lately, I've been doing tons of stuff she wouldn't normally allow, so I let myself hope. I glance out at the road. We're almost to Aunt Katherine's drive. "Just drop me off at the bottom of the hill," I suggest. "It'll save you time." I jump out as soon as Will slows the truck.

"Don't forget your lobsters."

"Oh, yes. Thanks."

I jog up the hill and make a slight detour to Aunt
Katherine's. The door is unlocked, but she's not inside.
She's probably already over helping Mom. I swing open her
fridge and stash the bucket inside. I grab a scrap of paper
and scrawl out a note and tape it to the bucket.

> *Aunt Katherine. Some lobsters. I'll explain later.*
> *Love, Kate.*

Now, if I can just slip into the kitchen to get some food
without Mom noticing that it's past time for the bus.

I make it. She's busy talking to the guests in the dining
room. I grab the lunch she packed and the blueberry muffins she left on the kitchen table for me. I ignore the glass
of apple juice she placed on the counter and dash out the
back door.

chapter nine

GRAVEL SCATTERS ACROSS the road behind me as the bus, full of chatter and laughter, pulls away from the bottom of the drive. Aunt Katherine looks up from her hose and waves. "Hello," I call to her as I trudge up the steep hill to the inn.

I'm heading over to the flower bed and Aunt Katherine, planning to explain about the lobsters in her fridge, when Mom calls from the inn. "Kate, Kate?" She waves at me from the back porch. "Can you come here?" Her voice is singsong happy, like we're best friends. Like the last conversation we had was about how much she admired my maturity in making my own decisions about church. Like she wants every guest at the Whispering Woods Inn to know what a great relationship she has with her daughter. If that's all true, why are my legs suddenly wobbling?

"Let's go downstairs," Mom says when I reach her.

My stomach muscles tighten at the idea. But what can

I do? Ignore her? Say no thanks? Mr. Harmony, the photographer guy, is on his knees in one of the flower gardens, taking close-ups of Aunt Katherine's prized begonias. I don't exactly feel comfortable walking away from her like I haven't heard a word she said, or replying, "No way," in front of him. So I wave good-bye to Aunt Katherine. As I pass Mr. Harmony, he looks up and asks me, "Isn't the color of this flower amazing?"

I pause and take a good look at the velvetlike red petals and nod. They are spectacular, like they're made of fabric from fancy theater curtains, soft and elegant and vibrant. No wonder he's taking a close-up.

"Kate," Mom calls again.

"Coming," I grumble under my breath. And as I tromp off, I swear Mr. Harmony chuckles.

Once downstairs, she opens her bedroom door, waits for me to follow her inside, shuts the door tight, and then sits on her bed. She pats her star-patterned bedspread, the one she and I quilted by hand the last year I was home-schooled. Before the divorce. "How was school today?" she asks as she motions for me to sit beside her.

"Fine," I answer, and stay standing.

"Lots of homework?"

I shrug.

"So, do you feel like you're beginning to fit in at this new school?"

I nod. "Sure."

"Good." She sighs, then frowns. "Kate, I might as well be honest." The hostess voice is totally gone. "I went to dump some garbage this morning and saw you in that boy's truck."

No. Not Will. Please, no. I hold my breath and examine the ruffled white skirt covering the base of Mom's bed.

"First, you try to sneak off in the dark to ride your bike to school." Her voice becomes high and shrill. "Then, you go running on Sunday. On a Sunday, Kate!" Mom shakes her head. "And then if that isn't bad enough, you purposely misled Aunt Katherine into thinking her church is absolutely fine to attend, turning your back on all you've ever been taught." Mom rises from her bed and stands, pacing in front of the large print of Jesus kneeling against a stone in prayer. "And then when I think my heart is totally broken"—her voice begins to quiver—"you stab at it even harder. Now I find you're sneaking off with some long-haired, wild-music-listening boy."

My eyes dart to Mom's locket, sitting on her night-stand. The locket she and all her fellow church sisters have with the same three engraved words. The locket I stupidly used to look forward to receiving when I turned twenty-one and joined the women's organization. *Charity Never Faileth.* Yeah, right. And charity is supposed to be the pure love of Christ. Is that what you have in your heart toward me right now, Mother dear? Is it really Christlike love? Was it that same Christlike love that kept you from helping me give Dad a funeral?

"I expect you to look at me when I speak to you. Have you forsaken everything we've believed in? Even the fifth commandment?"

"Honor thy father and thy mother: that thy days may be long upon the land which the Lord thy God giveth thee."

I want to remind her that the fifth commandment includes honoring my father, as well as her. But I say nothing and study my running shoes and my sweat-stained, dirty socks.

"Who *was* that person, Kate? And for Heaven's sake, what were you doing riding with him? I was worried that he was taking you away to who knows where." Now the tears begin to well in her eyes. Her lips quiver.

I can't help it—I roll my eyes. My mom the drama queen.

"Don't you care about how worried I've been? If I hadn't phoned the school . . . if you hadn't been there . . . what would I have done? Called the police to chase down my daughter?"

"He's just a guy on the cross-country team," I answer.

"Whoever he is, he's certainly not the kind of young man I approve of you being alone with." More tears. "He looks like the type who has pierced some part of his body or is into drugs." She sniffs, reaches for a tissue from her nightstand, and blows her nose.

I bite my lip hard to keep from laughing. She certainly has lots of opinions on a person she could barely see through the trees. What does she do, carry binoculars in her apron? She moves closer to me, so close I can smell the gardenia-scented lotion she always wears. She glares down at me, her dark eyebrows arched.

My chest feels tight. Darkness crowds in. The old familiar urge to hide away in my room, to stare at the walls until I can't feel anything rushes over me. My insides quiver under her scrutiny. I wish I was as tall as her. Why couldn't I have inherited her height genes and her thick, dark lashes, the two good things she actually has in her DNA? Then at least I would be able to look straight across at her and be on equal ground. And then maybe I wouldn't have spent so much of my early teen years trying not to be tempted by the lure of mascara. I used to think God gave dark-lashed women an unfair advantage if he was going to make wearing mascara a sin. Now I think, if there is a God, that God is probably much more concerned about love and kindness than a little color on your eyelashes.

Why does she make it all seem so ugly? I want to reach back and remember how I felt this morning—the dolphins, the lobsters, the sun coming up over the ocean, Will's smile, Pop and his osprey nest—all the magic, all the good feelings. Why does she make it sound bad and dirty, like I'm some cheap prostitute?

"He just offered to give me a ride, Mom."

"But it was a planned ride."

"Yes. A planned ride, with a guy from my cross-country team. A nice, hardworking guy who helps his grandfather every morning on a lobster boat before he goes to school."

Mom's eyes widen. "A lobster boat? And is that why . . . ?"

I bite down on my lip.

"Is that why your raincoat is soaking wet and stuffed in the bottom of your closet? Please don't tell me . . ." Mom pauses. "Exactly where were you this morning, Kate?"

Great! Me and my big mouth. And why has she been going through my closet? Just how far did she go searching? My heart beats faster. Did she find it? She couldn't have, could she? No. Please no. But she's only talking about Will. Maybe she just found the raincoat when she was in my closet. I sigh. "Yes, I went on his lobster boat this morning. That's why he gave me a ride."

"How could you? You know the rules." Her voice is stronger now, firm. "No dating until you're sixteen."

Dating is the first step of courtship. At the age of sixteen, it is appropriate for young men and young women to begin dating, preferably in small group outings.

"A date?" I chuckle.

Her frown lines crease deeper into her skin.

"Will's grandfather was with us. I wouldn't exactly call that a date."

It's no use to try and tell her how harmless it all was. How fun. How interesting. I can see that from her eyes. They're like steel doors. They have all the answers. No matter what I say, I can't win. I'm looking at the only person in the state of Maine who would actually call helping out a guy and his grandfather on a lobster boat at five thirty in the morning a date.

"Kate, you know better than to be alone with a boy before you're sixteen. I didn't see any grandfather in that truck this morning."

I stare at her in disbelief. Does she really think something magical will happen on my sixteenth birthday? That miraculously on that day I will instantly become all-wise and all-knowing around the opposite sex? Is that the day God comes down and gives me a chastity belt and protects me from all evil advances? Fine. Before I know it, as if I'm possessed, the words tumble out. "I bet if I'd taken a ride to school with someone from *your* church you'd be planning my homecoming date—because, of course, no one from *your* church would ever do drugs or have one tiny impure thought—because, of course, they belong to the *true* church—what a bunch of garbage."

"Kate! How dare you speak to me like that? *My* church? It's *our* church."

I say nothing but my wrists are pulsing like they do

when I sprint at the end of a race, running faster and faster until everything blurs and I use all my reserve to cross the finish line.

Mom stares at me and paces back and forth, breathing in and out like she, too, has just finished a race. Her face is bright red, but slowly the color drains and her breathing becomes more regular. Finally, she speaks. "Kate." Now her voice is calm and sweet. "It didn't work out with your father and me. Do you know why?"

I've heard this line a hundred thousand times and I hate it. "Because you married someone who didn't belong to *your* church. You thought Dad was a good man, and that he would come around. But he didn't," I answer in a singsong voice, rushing the words together as if I were quoting one of the hundreds of memorized scriptures she used to quiz me on each morning at the beginning of our homeschool day.

Mom doesn't seem to hear the sarcasm in my voice. She beams, likes she's so pleased I've remembered, that I've said the right words. "Yes." She puts out her hand and touches my shoulder. Every muscle stiffens at her touch. "Kate," she says, stroking me, "you marry who you date. I want you to have dates. I want you to go out. But I want you to pick boys who share our standards. I want you to learn from my mistakes."

"So I won't get divorced? So I can homeschool my kids

and be a stay-at-home mom? So I can let my husband support me while I have baby after baby? Then I can fill up a whole church pew with my offspring, instead of having to slink into church every Sunday with only one puny little kid."

"Kate!"

"You think Dad has gone to Hell. Just admit it, Mom. Hell. Hell. Hell. There, I've said the bad word. Damn. Damn. Damn." Tears stream down my face. I think of her heartless phone call and how she told the person that she wouldn't be collecting her ex-husband's remains. I grab her locket off her dresser and throw it against the wall. I shove open her door and race for the hall. In a voice loud enough for any guest in the house to hear, I shout, "I have news for you. It is *your* church, not *our* church. And I don't think Dad is in Hell. I don't think it's bad to be alone with Will Lane, either. I don't think like you at all."

chapter ten

I RUN UP the stairs and out of the inn. Tears burn my eyes and I lunge forward onto the gravel driveway. I trip and my knee scrapes against the pebbles. Staggering to my feet, I brush the tiny rocks off and blood oozes out. As I try to ignore the throbbing from the cut, the open curtains and lamplight from Aunt Katherine's cottage beckon. But if I go to her, it will put her in a bad place, between Mom and me. So I run. Down the hill, down the highway, down Main Street, down to the dock, down, down, stumbling and running until I hit the rocky shore.

Then I stop. The water in the bay is calm. The tide is low and as I stand still, panting, I hear how loud my sobbing is. In the half light of dusk I pick up a stone and hurl it out into the water. My chest heaving, I watch the circles my little rock makes. The circles I always heard about in church, where one little action can have such a big influence on others, making bigger and bigger spheres. The circles grow, making ripples as my crying stops. I wipe my face and watch as the bay gobbles the last of the round lines in the water. I can't see them at all now. In just seconds they've totally vanished. I stand, staring for a long time. It hits me how the water looks exactly the same as it did before I threw the rock. Neither the rock nor the momentary ripples changed anything at all. I wish I could show Mom. Show her how stupid all those church analogies are. "They're all lies, Mom, can't you see that?" I shout. "All lies!"

I watch as the water gently ebbs and flows, covering a large boulder on the shore, then moving back around, leaving the jagged edges exposed, then covering it again. I breathe in the smell of shells and lobster and fish. I wish it was this morning and I could be out on Will's boat again. But this time I'd come home to a mom who'd say, "Let's cook up that lobster tonight." And as we stood by the stove together, she'd ask, "Now, when do I get to meet your new friend, Will?"

I climb up and cross a long ledge of rocks until I'm perched on the last one, water surrounding me. I stand, watching as the sun drops and the islands, houses, and even my body become shadows. My face is dry, but inside something still quivers, shaking from what I said. Still, I don't feel sorry. I hate what she did. Doesn't everyone deserve a funeral?

Of course *she* knew best. Standing on the wet rock, I

think of how Dad would offer to take me shopping or out to eat on Sunday and I would say no because I knew the Sabbath was supposed to be a day of rest. And of how he'd want me to read some of his books. But then I believed Mom. I didn't want the books to be an evil influence in my life. I didn't want the devil, dressed as a man in a dark suit, to appear to me.

"I've been reading your books, Dad. Can you hear me?"

Fresh tears drip over my lips, leaving their salty taste behind. I feel them drop, mixing with the salty water below.

The beach is quiet tonight. No one can see or hear me talking. No one alive. Maybe no one at all. It's dark enough now that all the boats are in. The weekenders are back in their cities. But in the remaining dim light of the setting sun, some dark form breaks the stillness of the shadows. I scramble back over the rocks to the sandy shore. It's a man heading this way. My heart beats faster. Could it be Mom's devil after all? A shiver runs through me. Just as I'm about to jog up to the road and head home, I hear a cheery voice call out. "Hello, Kate." I turn. It's only Pastor Browning.

"Hi." I hope it's too dark for him to see my tearstained face or scraped knee. Did he hear me sobbing to my dead father? Or shouting?

"Lovely evening for a walk, isn't it?" he asks.

"It is." My voice sounds scratchy and hoarse.

"And peaceful. I love it when the beach is this quiet. Do you?"

"Yes." He can't even begin to imagine.

"Are you heading home?"

"Yes."

"Good idea, since it's getting dark. I happen to be heading your way. Do you mind if I walk with you for a while?"

"No." And I really don't. For some reason Pastor Browning feels like one of the harmless shadows around me, like a dream in this half light. Add this to your list of my sins, Mom. Now I'm walking in the setting sun with a minister, someone so deluded, so far from the light, that he's chosen to devote his life to preaching false truths.

Our feet crunch in rhythm as we cross over the rocks. The sound grows more noticeable with every step we take. After a minute or two, Pastor Browning turns to me and says, "I'm glad I ran into you, Kate. I normally like to visit new families in our congregation."

"Uh, that's okay," I stammer.

"However, today when I ran into your aunt Katherine at the post office and suggested a visit, she explained that your mother might be uncomfortable."

So Aunt Katherine does have things figured out. Despite

the state of my mind, my lips curve up into a half smile.

"Do you mind, Kate, if I ask what your religious background is?"

"No, I don't mind." And as I begin to tell Pastor Browning about the Holy Divine Church, my words spill out easily, like I'm talking to a friend. I'm not stiff and tongue-tied like I always was with the High Priest in our church back in Arizona. Each year I had to go into that dark office of his for my annual birthday interview. Couldn't he just have given us a card or a cupcake?

He'd sit on one side of his monster-sized desk and I'd sit on a chair on the other side. He'd lean his elbows on the desk, look straight into my eyes, and then ask those same awful questions. *Do you smoke? Do you drink? Are you morally clean? Do you know what being morally clean means?* I died when he asked me that the first time. And it only got worse. *Do you masturbate?* I had no clue, since at age twelve I didn't even know what the word *masturbate* meant but figured I hadn't if I didn't know what it meant, so I said no. *Have you ever been with someone of the opposite sex?* And the last confusing question. *Have you ever been with someone of the same sex?* Of course I'd been with people of the opposite and same sex. What did he think, that I lived in total isolation? He'd seen me with my mom all the time. I just shrugged my shoulders in answer to that question, and I guess he figured out his question was above my head because he moved on. It wasn't until I confessed my confusion to Charity after the interview that she explained what "been with someone of the same sex" or "the opposite sex" and "masturbate" meant. She's smarter about these things because she has older brothers and sisters. She was sleeping over at my house, and I felt so stupid and humiliated that I hid my face under my pillow.

But as I walk along the shore, the whole religious mess just pours out. Mom and Dad, their opposite views, how when I was ten we moved from Idaho to Arizona, away from a place with so many church members and Mom's family—a fresh start so my parents could try and save their marriage. But then a year later they divorced. I even tell him how Dad, who had perfect health, had a heart attack and died after one of his morning runs. But I don't tell him about not fasting that very same day.

Pastor Browning pauses, and a light from a nearby house illuminates his face. "I am sorry for your loss, Kate. It's extremely brave of you to tell me. I imagine it's hard to talk about him."

I nod. We walk on in silence. The water laps. A breeze blows though my hair. Finally, I ask, "Pastor Browning, do you think it's a sin to be cremated?"

"No. Was your father cremated?"

"Yes."

"And I take it your mother's church is against that sort of thing?"

"Yes."

"I see. So what did you do about a funeral?" he asks.

I look at the stones as we walk over them. This is the hard part. I swallow the lump in my throat and then blink to keep the new tears I feel forming from seeping out. "He didn't have one."

"Oh. I'm sorry." Pastor Browning pauses, and I can feel his eyes on me even though I can't see them. Are they full of pity, confusion, sorrow?

"So your church isn't against cremation?" I ask.

"No, people choose that option all the time. It's what I have chosen for myself, after medical science has salvaged the parts of my body that could be useful."

The body is a sacred temple. It should not be cremated or cut apart. Keep it pure and whole so you may rise with the Just on the Blessed Day of Resurrection.

I'd been taught this doctrine since I was very small. And each time I heard it preached, my mind filled with a vision of resurrected bodies. Glowing, dressed in white gowns, hundreds and thousands of them rising from their graves. But a few with holes where their eyes should have been and empty red spots where their hearts once pumped keep sinking back down into their caskets. Members of the Holy Divine Church don't believe in organ donations.

A gust of wind off the water makes me shiver. In all the times I've imagined Resurrection Day, I never even imagined people who were cremated. They don't exist. They are just ashes. My fists clench. How unfair. Some people die in fires. They didn't choose to be cremated. The sun has set so low now that the trees and houses are just gray outlines against the black sky. I look up into the darkness and wonder for the millionth time if Heaven exists. I bite my lip. I clear my throat. Ask him, my head commands.

"Um, Pastor Browning?"

"Yes?"

"Um, well, that is, what do you believe happens after you die?" I ask.

"Do you mean, what do I believe, or what does the church I preach for believe?"

That surprises me. I look at him as the floodlights from a nearby house shine in his face.

"You see, sadly, I must admit, they aren't always one and the same."

"Oh."

"Let me explain. Our church believes in Heaven and Hell. Good people go to Heaven, sinners to Hell. I think our church has a more liberal definition of what a sin is, though, than your mother's faith. Stealing, beating your spouse or children, murder, rape—those kinds of things are considered sins. And then only those who don't regret what they have done actually end up in Hell. That's what the church teaches. But me, Kate? Well. I honestly don't know."

I look at him again, confused.

"I'm the minister, right? And I'll tell you, I've prayed and read and walked so long I've worn out several pairs of shoes. But Kate, in the end, I can't say that I know whether or not there is a God who created us or a place called Heaven. Sadly, no angel has visited me and shared all the answers."

I nod and almost trip over a rock in front of me.

Pastor Browning grabs at my elbow and steadies me. "Are you okay?"

"Yes. It's the same for me. I don't know what I believe."

"Can I share something with you? Something personal?"

"Sure."

"People talk about spiritual experiences, moments of wisdom that change their lives, epiphanies. One day I had an epiphany of my own. I was pondering over a Bible verse that had haunted me for years. 'Now we see through a glass darkly.' Are you familiar with it?"

Am I familiar with it? My cheeks flush, remembering how I had it all memorized. How I fasted. How I got up in front of the audience at the speech festival. How my mind went totally blank. The humiliation of it all pulses through every vein. But I answer. "Yes. First Corinthians, chapter 13, verse 12. 'For now we see through a glass, darkly; but then face to face: now I know in part; but then shall I know even as also I am known.'" The words march automatically out of my mouth so simple, like they've always been there, from birth, just waiting to be spoken.

"Very good." Pastor Browning chuckles.

My heart swells with his compliment, and I must admit I feel rather proud of myself.

"Like you, I was quite familiar with this verse. But this time, the words hit me in a new way. Maybe our lives are actually meant to be experienced in the half dark. Not knowing all the answers. Being open. Questioning. Always searching, but never being finished. And maybe not knowing the answers to all the cosmic questions can actually make us kinder, more accepting, and more loving." Pastor Browning pauses. "Does that make any sense?"

My feet slow as his words begin to sink in. "Yes."

Is that why Dad liked this scripture passage, too—one of the few, he said, that actually made sense? Fresh tears run down my cheeks. Does Pastor Browning see them? Does he know how his words soothe the ache inside of me? The ache that's been with me this whole long year?

chapter eleven

I CREEP IN the back door. Low voices hum from the glassed-in sunporch at the front of the inn. I tiptoe across the parlor carpet and, using one finger, slip the lace curtains open a crack. Mom's sitting on the wicker sofa, right next to that photographer, Mr. Harmony. They're both sipping tea. And out of Aunt Katherine's best set of china. The tea has to be herbal, because Chelsea was right about how members of the Holy Divine Church aren't allowed to drink caffeine. Mom's lit the new scented candles, the ones that smell like vanilla. She laughs at something and her dimple shows, like she has no cares or worries. Like it doesn't matter that less than an hour ago, her only child stormed out of the house in tears. No, instead, Mom has combed her hair up in some sort of twist, and she's wearing a blouse and skirt she usually saves for Sundays! Her hand brushes across Mr. Harmony's. My stomach feels queasy. I stomp away. And she has the nerve to tell me to stay away from nonmembers like Will!

I guess I wanted to come home and find her crumpled

on her bed, sobbing. Hearing me come in, she would run to find me and say, "Oh Kate, I'm so glad you're back. Are you okay? I love you, Kate. I'm sorry. I was so wrong. Date whomever you want. Go to church wherever you want. I trust you. Are you hungry? You poor thing, you haven't even had any dinner." But no, she's laughing, sipping tea, and touching this strange man. Does she realize it's dark out and she doesn't know where I am? Pastor Browning, a *deluded* minister, was more worried about my safety than Mom is.

In the kitchen, though, just like normal, a plate with mashed potatoes, a breast of chicken, and cooked peas sits out for me, along with a big glass of milk and a note:

Kate, I love you and am praying every day for you to find peace about your father.

Find peace? Does she actually believe that? I rummage through the fridge, tipping a pitcher of apple juice. I don't wipe up the spill. Let the perfect hostess wipe it up! She's the one who keeps buying the stupid apple juice anyway. Doesn't she notice I always dump it out? No cookies left. The guests must have eaten them all. I open the cupboard where Mom keeps the supply of candy to refill the candy dish in the parlor. Spotting a bag of Jelly Bellys, I lean in, open my mouth, and grab it with my teeth, then take my dinner over to Aunt Katherine's.

I put my milk in the crook of my arm, knock on her door, and let myself in. Aunt Katherine turns down the volume on her television and smiles at me.

I drop the Jelly Bellys on the coffee table. "Can I eat my dinner here?"

"Certainly." She pats the couch and motions for me to sit beside her. "So, how are you and your mother getting along?"

I tilt my head. That's a strange question for her to ask.

"Your mother was here a while ago, love, looking for you," Aunt Katherine says.

Fresh anger stirs inside of me. I kept away from Aunt Katherine so I wouldn't make her feel sorry for me or make her feel like she was taking sides. And what does Mom do? Comes and blabs everything. I should have known! What kind of a horrible daughter did she make me sound like? I stare down at the bag of candy in my lap.

"Maybe this Mr. Harmony will keep your mother occupied and she'll have a little less time to fuss over everything you do." She strokes her fingers through my hair. "I don't like to interfere, but to tell you the truth, I didn't see anything wrong with going out on the lobster boat this morning. Granted, the lobster folk aren't exactly known for having clean vocabulary, but everyone should go on a lobster boat at least once." Aunt Katherine chuckles. "Now

I know where the lobsters in my fridge came from."

I smile and my neck tingles with the stroke of her fingers on my hair.

"Did you know I used to date Charlie Lane's big brother? Will's grandfather's brother, that is. A couple of times Charlie had to tag along on our dates."

"Really?" I feel my eyes grow wide.

"My, yes. And was Charlie ever a handful to watch, climbing out windows, jumping off the top of fences." She chuckles and looks through me like a movie is playing on the wall behind me, a movie of her and Will's grandfather and his big brother, when they were all young.

As I rip open the bag of Jelly Bellys, I try to imagine Will's grandfather without a beard, as a small boy, and Aunt Katherine without white hair, without her wrinkles, young like me. And as I do, I see how her smile is just like Dad's. I've never noticed before. Digging through the rainbow of candy, I pick out two of my favorite yellow-and-white-speckled pieces. I pop them in, and within seconds, my mouth tastes like buttered popcorn. I offer Aunt Katherine some.

"No thanks, love. I'm afraid candy gets stuck in the few good teeth I have left."

"Aunt Katherine," I ask, sliding the candies to one side of my mouth, "do you think Mom and Mr. Harmony like each other?"

"It appears that way, doesn't it. I know he is reading lit-
erature and meeting with missionaries from your mother's
church."

"Where? I haven't seen missionaries lurking around the
inn."

"Do missionaries lurk? Interesting."

Despite this upsetting news, I can't help but grin.

Aunt Katherine chuckles, then says, "But to your question, I don't know. I assume he meets them at their church
in Ellsworth. He seems to be very excited to talk about it
all with her."

But they've known each other such a short time. True,
he was our first guest, and he's been here for over two
weeks. But am I really surprised about the church part?
Duh. Mom has brought tons of *unenlightened* people *to the*
truth through her missionary efforts. I have been so blind.
I think back and realize Mom's been showering him with
her extra-special treatment for days. She's handed me the
best linen for his bed, the thickest towels for his bathroom,
even the prettiest bouquet of flowers to set by his nightstand. How much longer will Mr. Harmony's big photo
project on the national park take? Where does he live?
And why would any adult seriously be interested in the
Holy Divine Church? At least my father had the sense to
see through it. So Mr. Big-Shot Photographer likes Mom's
church, does he? Or is he just playing along? I don't like

this. Mom had a couple of dates with single men back in Arizona, but they were really old widowers, and already members of *her* church.

Aunt Katherine's words play in my head. "You've seen your mother with the guests, Kate. She's very charming."

Mom's also been putting those stupid church brochures in every guest's nightstand. And it looks like she is scoring big-time with Mr. Harmony. That should assure her of that huge mansion in Heaven she's always dreamed about. Whenever she became discouraged by our small house with its leaky kitchen faucet, linoleum floors, and Formica countertops, she'd say, "It doesn't matter, Kate. We have a humble house now, but if we continue as true ambassadors for Christ, He has promised us a mansion on high."

Aunt Katherine pats my hand. "It may turn out all right. Mr. Harmony seems like a nice man, and your mother certainly deserves some happiness."

Why? Why does she deserve some happiness? I don't like the idea of Aunt Katherine having any pity for Mom. I don't want her to wish Mom well. But of course, Aunt Katherine doesn't know everything. I've never talked to her about what happened after Dad died. And Mom has had every reason not to tell her. Aunt Katherine probably just thinks we had a funeral for Dad and sprinkled his ashes around his favorite palm tree or something fitting like that. She doesn't know what really happened.

chapter twelve

"ARE YOU REALLY going to Douglas and Chelsea's youth group tonight?" Jamie asks before she puts her head into the locker-room sink and guzzles water straight from the tap.

"Um . . . um, well, maybe." At lunch today, Chelsea pestered me about going, and after talking to Pastor Browning, I sort of want to, but what will Jamie think of me? I've heard Douglas call her the Environmental Atheist.

"Great!" Jamie says, splashing water on her face. "Because I'm going and I don't want to be stuck sitting by Chelsea. She'd drive me totally nuts. She's always telling me how I should show off my figure with something besides T-shirts. Like I need style advice from her! Anyway, I'm writing this research paper on different Christian denominations for my comparative religions class and I've only been to, like, two churches in my whole life. I'm basically pretty much agnostic. But that's probably because I'm totally ignorant about religions. I signed up for the class because I think I should know what churches believe before I give up on the whole God thing."

As I put on a jacket over my sweaty running clothes, I can't help but think how lucky she is to know so little about church. I read Jamie's clean T-shirt as she slips it on. *I worship trees.* "Anyway," she says, "I think that thing tonight will be a good place to pick up some information, and besides that pastor guy seems pretty cool."

"Yeah," I say, and think again of last night. His words, about how maybe not knowing all the answers actually makes us more loving and kind, play again in my head like a song.

"Do you think we'll have a lesson?" she asks as she splashes water on her short hair, then shakes her head back and forth, spraying water across the mirror.

"I guess," I say, realizing I have no clue at all and I still have to tell Mom I'm going.

"Cool. Hey, do you want a ride home? I don't have that much time before this thing tonight, so I figure I'll just head toward Puffin Cove and go to Veggie World and mooch some dinner off of my boss." She grins.

"Sure. Thanks."

As we walk outside, I notice Richard Penrose's dad talking to the coach. More like barking orders, I'd say. "I expect him to be in tip-top shape for basketball."

"We try to keep all our athletes in good shape," Coach

Horne replies, flipping through his clipboard as he and Mr. Penrose walk and talk.

Jamie rolls her eyes and the two fade out of our hearing range. "If he's so worried about Richard, why doesn't he hire a personal trainer, or stick around this town more and help him himself? I mean, Richard is totally alone with the housekeeper and gardener all week, then his parents fly up from Boston for the weekend. This must be some special occasion that his dad is here midweek."

Just at that moment, Richard comes around the corner toward us. He had to see his dad with the coach. Did he hear Jamie as well? All I know is that his face is as red as a cardinal, the school mascot. He barely nods at us as he zooms by.

"Isn't he a trip?" Jamie asks. "I could almost feel sorry for him, but then I look at that monster Hummer of his. Oh, what my dad would say to Richard if he saw him driving it."

When we get to Jamie's rather beat-up red VW Jetta, I ask, "So, does your car really run on used French-fry oil?"

"Yup. I get fifty miles to the gallon in my modified engine. Some of the local restaurants, including Veggie World, save their used oil for me. So I drive for free."

"Sounds good, but wasn't it hard to alter your car?"

"Nope. Dad and I got all the things we needed at an

auto-parts store in Boston. That's where he lives. I usually spend the summers with him. He couldn't afford to buy me one of those new hybrid cars, but we're both mad about the whole dependence on Middle East oil thing, so we did this. Now he's bought a Chevy Suburban and has it running on straight grease as well."

I nod, trying to act like I understand at least half of what Jamie is talking about. But I got lost after hearing that Jamie's dad lives in Boston. "Are your parents divorced?" I ask.

"When I was ten years old."

"Mine divorced when I was ten, too," I say.

"So is your dad still back in Arizona?"

I shake my head no. But can't bring myself to form the words *My dad is dead.* So instead, I clear my throat and say, "Remember the other day at lunch when Chelsea thought I belonged to the same church as those girls with the long skirts in the cafeteria?"

"Ah. Sort of. But you don't, right?"

"Well, I did. I mean, I guess technically I still do. I was baptized and I'm still on the official records, but . . ."

"But you don't believe?" Jamie glances over at me.

I shake my head no. "And I haven't been going for the past year."

"That's cool," Jamie says as she brakes at the stop sign.

"I feel kind of guilty that I lied at lunch."

"Hey. Religion's personal." She shakes her head and blows out a deep puff of air that flutters through her bangs. With her eyes on the road, she says, "Chelsea had no right to bug you. She's too nosy for her own good. And besides, if you don't belong in your heart, you don't belong. Right?"

"Right." I smile.

"But maybe you could tell me about your old church sometime, I mean for my paper?"

I laugh. Jamie is so into her school stuff I believe she wouldn't care if I were a monk with blue hair. She'd still hang around me, and she'd like me more if she could use my strange life in her research paper.

"Are you hungry?"

"Of course." I laugh. "I'm always starved after practice, aren't you?"

"Totally. Want to taste the best fries in the world?"

"Um, sure." I don't tell Jamie how I usually avoid oily stuff that may slow down my running times.

"My boss will load us up with them for free."

So the next thing I know, I'm in Veggie World with Jamie, dunking fries in this really good sauce and realizing I had forgotten how wonderful fried food really is. As we munch away, I tell her about how I was homeschooled most of my life, and she tells me about how her mom is always on a diet, so the only good food she can get is here. We giggle and eat, and my stomach is so full by the time I wave good-bye to Jamie. She's going to do her homework at the restaurant until it's time for youth group, and I'm going to use the five blocks walking home to think of some way to announce to Mom that I'm going to youth group tonight, only not at the Church of the Holy Divine.

Echos of laughter and the sweet aroma of pastry greet me as I open the back porch door.

"Kate, is that you?" Mom pops her head through the doorway, all cheery. "Come in, we've got company."

I walk in and see Chelsea's mom. "Michelle, this is my daughter, Kate. Kate, this is Mrs. Riggs."

"Hi, Kate." Mrs. Riggs smiles at me. "Kate and I actually met on Sunday at church."

For the slightest second, a frown slips across Mom's lips, but it is quickly replaced with her familiar Christ's-ambassador-to-the-world smile. "Look what Mrs. Riggs and I just baked." She proudly lifts a pie off the counter. "Michelle just taught me how to make a blueberry pie, from scratch. She shared her old family recipe with me. Doesn't it look delicious?"

"It does, but Mom—"

Before I can go on, Mom interrupts with, "Do you want a piece?"

I can't believe it. Does Mom expect me to fall for this? Michelle is beaming. She's obviously been taken in. So I give the polite smile Mom's eyes are begging me to respond with and don't mention the tiny fact that my mother has a whole scrapbook full of blue ribbons she's won for pie baking—some of them blueberry—at county fairs in both Arizona and Idaho.

Look for situations where you can bring up people's talents. Make them feel important. Make them feel loved. After you have prepared the soil with friendship and trust, then introduce the seeds of the True and Everlasting Gospel of Jesus Christ.

"Maybe I'll have a piece after I shower," I say, and head downstairs, nodding to Mrs. Riggs as I go. Mom may be comfortable with ranting at me one moment and being polite the next, but I am not.

Halfway down the steps I overhear her saying, "Why don't you come with me? My church in Ellsworth is having a class next week for women, on keeping romance alive."

They both giggle, and the sick pit I had in my stomach last night at seeing Mom with Mr. Harmony returns. It isn't just her new romance, though. I know what Mom is up to. It's like I'm watching a movie, one that's played over and over my whole life. But now for the very first time, I'm seeing beyond the surface of Mom's intense friendliness with people to what is really happening. She wasn't known only for her pies back in Arizona. Our High Priest was always praising her for her missionary efforts. She helped convert two people from her work, then Sally the UPS lady, and even the clerk from our 7-Eleven store, and that was just last year. *And ye who are the true light of Christ shall be the leaven of the earth. Share the gospel of Christ with those around you and the whole earth will rise at His coming.*

Sitting on the bathroom counter is a new bottle of my favorite shampoo. I guess Mom noticed mine was almost empty. She's good about those kinds of things. I never run out of deodorant, soap, sunscreen, or anything. But as I undress and turn on the water for my shower, the discussion from English class replays in my mind. Ms. Root read a sentence from *To Kill a Mockingbird*:

Sometimes the Bible in the hand of one man is worse than a whiskey bottle in the hand of [another].

I shiver and turn the faucet farther toward hot. Mom is so worried about bringing Chelsea's Mom to *the truth* that she would lie and pretend she doesn't know anything about making pies. I think the Bible is dangerous in her hands. Is it dangerous to base your whole life on the Bible and reject any other book? Like Dad's books? Like not wanting me to read books for English class? Because if you read, you begin to think. And if you begin to think, you begin to see how crazy stupid the Holy Divine Church really is.

I let the hot water pour down on my back, washing

away the sweat and the dirt, and then I turn so the spray hits full strength on my chest. Maybe if I stand here long enough, the water will wash away this anger inside of me, this feeling of being tricked my whole life. Maybe it will be sucked down into the drain and out into the ocean.

High-pitched giggles are still coming from the kitchen. I stand at the bottom of the stairs, dressed in the same skirt and top I wore to church Sunday. I pace back and forth. Should I go up now? Maybe it's better to face the youth group thing with Chelsea's mom here. She and Chelsea are the ones who brought it up in the first place.

As I climb the steps, I try to clear my expression of all emotion and walk in like I always change into a skirt and nice top after cross-country practice. "Mom." I pause. "Um, Chelsea, Mrs. Riggs's daughter, invited me to her youth group meeting tonight."

"Oh yes," Michelle interrupts, twisting her wrist so she can see her watch. "Goodness. The time. Where has it gone? I've got to get home and get those kids a quick bite to eat." She grabs her purse off the counter and picks up a second blueberry pie. "We may end up having only pie for dinner tonight." She chuckles. "Now, Kate, why don't I have Mr. Riggs pick you up, say"—she glances at her watch again—"in half an hour?"

I nod. "Thanks." To myself I add, Please Mrs. Riggs,

invite me to go with you now. If you leave me alone with the Queen of Pie Making, you may never see me alive and well again.

Mom stands with her mouth half-open. Her eyes are frozen and icy. She seems to have lost her ability to talk. And so I speak, hardly believing I'm daring to say what I say. "You really should have Mom show you how to make bread. She has her own special yeast—it sort of leavens the world. It makes her bread very unique."

Mom's face turns bright red, and I swear she is using every ounce of reserve to keep from exploding at me. She knows I'm making fun of her.

Michelle smiles, grateful, interested. "Oh, I will. I'm always up for learning more about yeast breads." She doesn't know. She's totally taken in, like a mouse who smells cheese but doesn't see that little wood trap with the wire snap until it's too late.

"Thank you, Rebekah." Michelle leans over and gives Mom a one-arm hug. "I've had a great afternoon. It feels like we're still two college girls working for the summer in this little town. It hasn't really been twenty years, has it? And I will go to your women's class. It couldn't hurt." She laughs.

Mom seems to perk up at this last bit of information, and her scarlet cheeks fade to just a high pink. "I'll phone you with the details."

144 * Beckie Weinheimer

Mom walks Michelle out to the back porch. I pace back and forth in front of the kitchen window. She's going to throw a huge fit! I can't sneak down the hill. She's standing in the middle of the drive watching Michelle back out. But guess who is pulling in? Mr. Harmony. And guess who's walking toward his car to greet him? Thank you, Mr. Photojournalist! I'm not impressed with your wavy black hair or your big, fancy camera and I think you're totally stupid if you are seriously considering joining the Holy Divine Church, but maybe Aunt Katherine's right. If you stay around, Mom might not have so much time to fuss over me.

I hide in the dining room as Mr. Harmony and Mom walk into the house. Once they've passed through the back hallway, I sneak into the kitchen and out the back door and go over to visit Aunt Katherine for a half hour before I walk down the hill to wait for Chelsea and her dad. Simple as pie!

chapter thirteen

MY STOMACH RUMBLES despite the fries, and I wish I had grabbed something to eat. As Mr. Riggs's white patrol car pulls up, my stomach stirs with more than just hunger pains. Jamie told me Douglas's father was a cop. The car stops and I open the back door. Chelsea pats the empty seat next to her. "Hey."

Douglas is sitting in the front seat next to his father, who is still in his black uniform and yes, is wearing a gun belt. He could kill someone. I don't think I've ever been this close to a gun before. I mean, I've seen my uncle's rifle he uses to go hunting with. But it's on the wall in a locked cabinet. I can't keep my eyes off his gun.

"Good evening, Kate," Mr. Riggs says.

"Hey, Kate." Douglas turns and lifts his hand in a half wave.

I swallow my fears and clear my throat. "Hello. Thanks for picking me up." I manage to get out the words as I scan my surroundings. There is a steel screen between the front seat and the backseat and no door handles on the back doors. I guess Mr. Riggs or Douglas will have to open the doors for us. It smells antiseptically clean. The plastic seats are hard and very uncomfortable. We drive down Main Street. No one talks. Douglas's profile is as stiff as that bust of Beethoven that Aunt Katherine has sitting on the piano in the inn's parlor. Chelsea reminds me more of a store mannequin, almost lifelike but definitely not moving. I've never been with her when she wasn't jabbering away. Today she about drove me nuts whispering to the girl next to her throughout our entire English class.

As we pass store after store and the only sound is the hum of the car engine, I suddenly feel like Douglas, Chelsea, and I have been arrested. What am I doing going to this youth group? More church?

The silence is freaking me out, so when we pass by the dock, I nudge Chelsea. Pointing to stack of traps, I ask in a low voice, "Have you ever been out on a lobster boat?"

"Yeah," she whispers. Then frowns. "You haven't missed anything. It totally sucks, let me tell you. And you can't wash the smell off. Have you ever been in the same zip code as Will or any of his friends?" She scrunches up her nose.

I'm relieved to hear Chelsea talk. But I didn't think the lobster boat totally sucked. And yes, I have been up close to Will and I happen to like the way he smells. But what do I know about normal life and what's cool? What I do know is that Will pulled at my ponytail again today at practice before he went off to run with the guys. I touch my hair where his hand was and bite my lip to keep the smile inside from showing.

Finally we pull up in front of the church. "I'll be checking with Pastor Browning later, so don't either of you get any ideas about ditching," Mr. Riggs says.

"We'll go, don't worry, Daddy," Chelsea says in a little-girl voice. Douglas doesn't say anything as he opens the back door for us. But I'm beginning to seriously doubt he is choosing to come to youth group all on his own, and I wonder if it's his dad's idea for him to help Pastor Browning at church, too.

In the chapel, Chelsea tugs at me and says, "Stop with me at the bathroom, okay?"

We climb the stairs at the back of the chapel. I follow her to the end of a dark-paneled hallway and then inside the women's restroom. Once the door closes behind us, Chelsea whips lipstick and mascara out of her purse. I lean against the wall, not sure what I should be doing, and watch Chelsea as she transforms her pale lashes, brightens her lips, sprays perfume behind each ear, on her wrists, and behind her knees, and finally unzips and removes her sweatshirt, revealing a spaghetti-strap top. Leaning forward, she tucks her breasts up in her skimpy top to show as much as possible, then shakes her bouncy red hair and fluffs it out.

"There," she says, smiling at her reflection in the mirror. "Now I'm ready."

Robot Chelsea is gone. Real Chelsea has returned, very alive and unharmed. Why was she acting so weird around her dad? Is she really scared of him? We leave the bathroom and I follow her. She seems to know her way around this church like it was her house. She stops in front of a tall wooden door that's open to a paneled room.

A huge round table fills most of it. Several familiar faces from school stare at us as we enter. At the far end, Jamie and Douglas are talking. The dark table reminds me of one in an illustration in a picture book Dad and I once checked out of the library, where King Arthur and Sir Lancelot and the rest of the knights sat. At age eight, I had loved Merlin and pretended to be like him, dressing up in my long nightgown and a handmade cone-shaped paper hat and carrying a stick for a wand. "No one but God has special powers," Mom informed me. It was about the same time she had decided Barbies were evil and made me throw mine away. She grabbed the stick from my hand, threw the hat away, and took the book back to the library the next day. It's like every day she became more scared that any outside thing would pollute my soul and fill me with the devil.

Chelsea pulls out a chair. I start to take the seat next to

her, but she puts her purse down on it. "For Richard. He wants me to save him a place."

My cheeks flush. Fortunately there's an empty seat next to Jamie.

As I sit, Pastor Browning walks in the door. "Well, well." He glances around the room, counting heads. "Good evening. It looks like we have nine brave teens tonight."

"Don't forget Richard Penrose." Chelsea pats the empty seat next to her. "I'm sure he'll be here soon."

Douglas rolls his eyes.

Pastor Browning nods. "Well, let's get started, shall we? As most of you know, I'm fairly new to Puffin Cove and the ministry here. When I took this position last January, there was no organized youth program. I've been looking forward to getting started ever since. I'm hopeful that together we can learn a few things and have some fun, too."

The door opens and Richard walks in. Chelsea waves and taps the seat next to her and beams at all of us, as if to say, See, I told you.

"Welcome, Richard." Pastor Browning smiles.

Richard slumps into the seat Chelsea has saved for him. He doesn't say anything or look at anyone.

Pastor Browning pulls out a vacant chair, sits down in it. "I suggest we introduce ourselves and share what we expect to gain from this group."

Chelsea volunteers to go first. "I've always dreamed of being a part of a real church youth group," she says, using her sweetest, most innocent voice.

Jamie rolls her eyes and Douglas coughs.

Jamie goes next. "I don't really belong to any church, but when I heard this group was starting, I decided to check it out, mostly because I'm taking a comparative religion class at school and I need to do research."

Pastor Browning chuckles at Jamie's honest answer. "And it looks like you are into trees."

Jamie glances down at her T-shirt. "Yep."

Two juniors speak, then three freshmen, all saying things like "It sounds fun" or "It will be a way to socialize with people who have similar beliefs." Finally, it's just Douglas, Richard, and me. None of us volunteers.

"Kate?"

My stomach flutters. Everyone, including Richard, seems to be staring at me. "Um." I pause, feeling dumb. "I'm not sure."

"A perfectly legitimate answer. I'm not always sure why I'm here, either." Pastor Browning chuckles. He turns to Douglas.

Douglas sighs. "Well, to be honest, I'm basically here because it makes life at home more pleasant."

Chelsea gasps. And her eyes look really frightened.

"Hmm, I see," Pastor Browning says.

Richard, who has been rolling a pencil back and forth on the mahogany table, looks up as Pastor Browning asks, "And Mr. Penrose, what exactly do you expect to gain from your association with our group?"

"Wheels," he says, his eyes concentrating on his pencil again.

"Wheels?" Pastor Browning tilts his head as if he's confused.

"No church, no car. Get it?"

Before Pastor Browning can reply, Jamie coughs really loud. Everyone looks at her. "Sorry. I just think calling that tank a car is a slight understatement."

Richard says nothing but clamps his fingers tight around the pencil.

"Okay. My turn." Pastor Browning rests his back against his chair and scans every one of our faces. "For me, this group is important because I can still remember all the crossroads I faced as a teenager. I hope together we can create a safe environment where we will be free to explore all our thoughts. I can't promise you answers, or even direction, but I will promise to be someone you can bounce your ideas off of." He pauses and smiles.

Pastor Browning's words roll over in my mind like a gentle tide washing up to shore. "Explore all our thoughts . . ." What a novel idea.

Pastor Browning clears his throat and leans forward

on his elbows, like he's about to tell us all a secret. "I also—and this is the tricky part—have this horrible dislike of being with people who really would rather be somewhere else. We have Douglas, who is coming to keep his parents from being upset, and we have Richard, who wants to drive his"—he clears his throat—"vehicle. What should we do?"

Silence. Does he really want us to decide? All eyes are on Pastor Browning now. Even Richard's.

When no one speaks, Pastor Browning says, "Gentlemen, the computer room downstairs is vacant tonight. Douglas, you and I have already had several conversations about our mutual interest in Latin. Perhaps you could pass the time tonight perusing that Latin Bible of mine and using one of the computers if you need to look up anything online?"

Douglas's serious face breaks into a smile. He nods like someone just offered him candy. And if I didn't see him with that Latin book constantly open at lunch, I'd think he was being polite. But I know he's genuinely excited.

Chelsea lets out a tiny gasp. When people turn toward her, she blushes and starts digging through her purse.

"I believe my Latin Bible is stuffed somewhere on the bookshelf in my office. It will only take me a minute to get it," Pastor Browning says, and stands. As he opens the door to leave, he turns to Richard. "Mr. Penrose, would you like to join Douglas?"

"No thanks."

"We do have two computers in the computer room." Pastor Browning winks.

Richard looks up, tilts his head to one side like he's considering it.

"Internet access . . ." Pastor Browning offers.

"Nah."

"While I'm locating the Bible then, perhaps you could come up with something else."

Richard shrugs.

After Pastor Browning leaves, Jamie laughs. "Not exactly the kind of minister I expected. What do you think, Douglas?" she asks, turning to him.

"Great." He glares across the table at Chelsea. "That is, if she doesn't blow things."

Chelsea frowns. "I don't know." Her lips tremble and her voice sounds different, not like her school "hey, look at me, world" voice, more like she sounded with her dad, like a timid little girl.

"What's the big deal?" Richard asks, and drops the pencil. It falls onto the table and rolls onto the floor.

"What, Richard?" Chelsea turns all her concentration to her favorite person.

"Nothing." Richard leans over and picks up the pencil.

"Well, if you think it's such a great idea to skip out of youth group, maybe you should go use the computer," she says. I'm surprised at Chelsea's sharp answer since I've seen her *skip out* of biology more than once.

"No offense to that pastor dude, but I've seen those computers. My dad donated them, like, five years ago. With those Model Ts it would take the whole night to go from one screen to another," Richard mutters.

The door opens and Pastor Browning hands Douglas the Bible. After Douglas leaves, Pastor Browning turns to Richard. "Now, Mr. Penrose, what should we do for you?"

Richard shrugs again.

"I've heard a few moments spent in solitude does wonders for the soul." Pastor Browning's voice sounds almost playful. He's smiling. "You could go down to the chapel and meditate. Sort of count your blessings."

Richard scowls at the idea at first and then slowly his frowning lips turn up. "Yeah, I think I will," he says. It's the first time I've ever seen Richard smile. "Thanks." He stands up and leaves the room. Chelsea watches with her mouth open.

The meeting continues. Chelsea, who pouts for a few minutes, finally gets involved and volunteers to find a scripture or uplifting passage to start each meeting with. And I find myself feeling comfortable enough to volunteer to bring the refreshments next time.

Then we have the lesson. Pastor Browning talks about Gandhi and Martin Luther King Jr. He doesn't even read from the Bible or have prayers or sing hymns. He reminds me more of an English teacher than a minister.

Through the lesson, Chelsea keeps glancing at her watch, staring at the door, and thumbing through all the photos in her wallet. But Jamie is so interested, she's taking notes. Maybe that's just for her report, though.

After the lesson, we make our way to Pastor Browning's office for refreshments. "Kate?" Pastor Browning turns to me. "Would you mind going downstairs and telling Douglas and Richard we're done?" he asks.

"I'll do it," Chelsea says.

"Oh, why don't we let Kate. I was hoping to show you a couple of books I thought might help you select some messages to start youth group with. The computer room is just at the foot of the stairs," he adds.

Chelsea frowns but follows Pastor Browning to a bookshelf. I stand frozen. Why me? Chelsea actually wants to go. I look for someone to rescue me. But Jamie is busy talking to the two juniors I don't really know.

I head downstairs and knock on the first door I see and open it a crack. "Douglas?"

Click. He spins around in the chair. He has two Bibles open at the side of the computer. His cheeks are flushed.

No wonder. I caught one glimpse before the computer

screen turned black. Those two naked guys on the video clip couldn't have been reciting Latin translations.

I blink, hoping my eyes were playing tricks on me. "We're done," I say, suddenly remembering why I am here.

"Oh. Good. Thanks. Be right there." Douglas stands and hurriedly gathers the Bibles and notebook paper he has written on.

I want to gag as I hurry out of the room and head toward the chapel. Mom is totally upset just because I came here tonight. She would die if she knew this church had access to pornography. I guess that's what I saw. Mom's so paranoid about me seeing stuff like that, every year she makes sure my school has blocked all access to any sex-related Internet sites. And, of course, we don't have a computer in our home, where its evil influence could tarnish the light of Christ. Like I'm going to surf sites with stuff like Douglas had on that computer screen! Right, Mom. I'd rather vomit! Does he know I saw? I've never seen him even look at a girl . . . or guy.

I shudder as I make my way down the darkened stairway.

Pornography is an evil that will steal all the purity from your soul. Avoid it like the plague.

Real pornography before now has always seemed as far away and unreal as starving children in Africa. I didn't think ordinary people like Douglas really looked at such things. Do other guys look at things like this? Do girls?

Does Chelsea? Jamie? Will? Did Dad? I mean, the High Priest made it sound as bad as robbing a bank or raping someone. I try to push the horrible image out of my mind, but my heart is pounding faster and faster like it's heading downhill on that roller coaster in Idaho Dad used to take me to.

Inside the chapel, the moon shines through the tall stained-glass windows, providing an eerie light. I scan the empty pews. Richard must have gone straight home. He did show up, which is all he really had to do. I wouldn't stick around either if I felt like him. I'm glad. Glad to be alone in this quiet place. I pause at the stained-glass window in front of me. The bright pieces of red, blue, and yellow glass form a picture of the Virgin Mary and infant Christ child. A bronze plate below it reads, "In memory of James Penrose 1798–1845." That must be an ancestor of Richard's.

"How beautiful," I whisper. Even my whisper seems to echo in this quiet, musty place. As I stand in the moonlight in the stillness, slowly the horror of what I found Douglas doing fades. How would it be to create a beautiful window in your loved one's memory? What a nice tradition. What have I done for Dad? What's been made for him?

I breathe in the ancient wood smell of the chapel and my neck tingles. And like on Sunday, the smell tugs at my memory. And suddenly it clicks. The scent. I breathe in and remember it all. My grandparents' cabin smelled like this.

When we lived in Idaho before the divorce, Mom, Dad, and I would often take the hour drive up to the mountain cabin and stay there alone. At night I used to snuggle under about ten handmade quilts piled on top of me in the cabin's loft. From that musty spot, I'd watch the shadows of swaying pines, their branches rustling, and listen to the gentle hum of my parents' voices in the bedroom below. They mingled into a sweet lullaby. I never wanted to leave. I never wanted to fall asleep.

Some low, small sound from the back of the chapel startles me. I turn but don't see anyone or anything. I tiptoe down the aisle. When I reach the last pew, I notice a dark form lying across the bench. I freeze. It's Richard Penrose. He is here. His eyes are shut and his breathing is heavy.

I back up. I'm certainly not going to wake him up. I'll get Chelsea to do it. It will make her night. As I climb the stairs to find her, I realize something. Richard doesn't look so angry when he's asleep.

chapter fourteen

THE SCENT OF lemon oil greets me as I open my bedroom door. I sniff and my eyes zoom in on Dad's bookcase.

"No!"

I fall to my knees at the side of the freshly polished shelves. Two of my own books are still here, both on running. And next to them, five new books. They manage to fill only a tiny bit of the space on the now almost empty shelves. *The Holy Bible, The Gift of Forgiveness, Christ and the New Millennium, Miraculous Stories from the Youth in God's Army,* and *Twenty-Five Missionary Tips for Today's Teens.* But Dad's books, which only two hours ago crammed this bookcase, are gone.

Every. Single. One.

My fists clench. I hit at the carpeted floor, smacking and punching, losing track of time, losing track of everything, until my knuckles are red and raw. In exhaustion, I collapse on my back, draw up my legs, and wrap my arms around them. I rock back and forth, my eyes shut tight.

Stretching out flat, I stare at the empty white ceiling, then roll over and run my hand across the wood shelves. I rub at the traces of lemon oil on my fingertips. Trust her to have even cleaned the wood! As if she could actually wipe away every speck of his dangerous, worldly books. I jump up, grab her precious Bible, cross the room, open my window, and hurl the red leather book out into the thick woods at the edge of the yard. It's raining, a gentle drizzle. Back at the bookshelf, I pile the other four books in my arms. Then one at a time, using all my strength, I throw each toward the Bible and watch as they land with a quiet thud on years and years of pine needles.

"They're all lies. All lies," I cry to the woods. To the sky. To any god who will listen.

I lean out, looking upward, breathe in the fresh air the rain has brought, and the droplets dribble down onto my T-shirt. The T-shirt with the tiny flowers that I wore to church youth group. The youth group that caused Mom to steal all my father's books. The same youth group that Douglas's and Richard's parents won't allow them to miss. I smile as Mom's books receive a baptism from Heaven. Not the Church of the Holy Divine immersion kind, sadly, only a sprinkling. Too bad. But maybe if I'm lucky it will rain and rain and rain and they'll be covered in a puddle and then every tiny part of them will be covered and they can get a baptism that is acceptable to Mom. After all, I know how important it is to be baptized with total immersion. I learned that lesson on my eighth birthday.

We lived in Idaho then. Grandma, Grandpa, my aunts, uncles, and cousins filled most of the chairs that surrounded the church baptismal font, which to me looked like an oversized sunken bathtub. I didn't know how to swim and was frightened of the whole thing. Maybe if I'd spent more time at a swimming pool, I would have known what to do. The first time the High Priest drew me and my long white dress under the water, strands of my long hair stuck out. On the second attempt, my big toe popped out just before the High Priest said "Amen." When I came up, I heard snickers from my cousins, and one glance at Mom's red face told me how embarrassed she was.

Who knows, I think now as I watch the pattering rain, maybe even back then, my subconscious knew it didn't want to be baptized a member of the Church of the Holy Divine.

Finally, on the third try, while the High Priest prayed, I stayed far below the top of the font. His arm cradled my head firmly down in the crook of his elbow, assuring me that this would be my last time. Every fiber of me was covered up with the holy baptismal water.

"I thought I was going to drown," I later told my father, who hadn't come. When the High Priest finally let go of me, I came shooting up, coughing, spitting, and gasping for air.

Dad shook his head. "Maybe your mother should get one of her church friends to teach you how to swim and not just focus on you memorizing the whole Bible." Mom overheard him and the next summer actually did take me to the home of a church member with a swimming pool and taught me to swim herself.

The rain is doing its job on Mom's books. They'll be drowned soon. Why couldn't Dad have taught me to swim? Why did he let me get baptized? Why was it so hard for him to fight her like I am? I wrap my arms around myself.

Wasn't I worth it?

In the morning, my stomach growls as I walk into the kitchen and inhale the sweet aroma of baking muffins. Mom seems busy stirring oatmeal, and she doesn't look up or say a word, even though she sees me opening the fridge. Maybe she's waiting for me to apologize for going to Pastor Browning's youth group. Or is she hoping I will weep and cry and beg for Dad's books? She may have stolen all of his books, but has she forgotten we live in the United States of America, where long ago Benjamin Franklin started the idea of a free lending library? And besides, *To Kill a Mockingbird* and my diary with quotes from all Dad's books I've read are safely tucked in my backpack. In fact, I make a new goal on the spot. Mom made me memorize a scripture a day when she homeschooled me. I knew hundreds of scriptures. Now I'm going to start memorizing again. One quote a day from Dad's books. It will do my head good. It will keep me from wanting to scream at Mom.

I grab my lunch sack that is sitting in its normal place on the counter. I peek inside. Another apple juice box.

With her lips pursed tight, she takes fresh orange cranberry muffins, my favorite, out of the pans. Without a glance my way, or offering me any, she begins arranging them in one of her perfect circles. If she wants to sulk, that is fine with me. I don't need her muffins or her rules or her silent ways of trying to make me feel guilty. I can be silent just as long as she can.

After lunch, Will stops at my locker.

"Hey, when are we going to get me those running shoes? We have a meet on Saturday, remember?" A dimple in his left cheek appears that I never noticed before.

"With that workout we had yesterday, how can I forget?" I try to act casual, but he's standing so close I worry that he'll hear how fast my heart is beating. It's like a kettle of hot popcorn kernels. Does he have a reason for being in the sophomore locker area or did he come here just to ask me about shopping?

"Well, if I'm going to look like a real runner, I think we better go soon." He tugs my ponytail. "How about Thursday after practice?"

Thursday? Is he asking me out? Is this like a real date? I've already promised Jamie and Aunt Katherine that I'd go to the Rocky Point County environmental meeting with them. I so want to go with Will, but Mom's never going to let me. What story can I make up?

"I can't on Thursday, but how about Friday?" I try to sound like I'm talking about cross-country practice or any other unimportant thing.

"Great. Meet you after practice then, City Girl." He tugs my ponytail again and disappears down the hall. My head is singing Handel's *Hallelujah Chorus*, just like it's Christmas.

In the locker room the next day I tell Jamie about Will inviting me to the mall.

"So, you two kind of like each other?" She elbows me as I comb my hair in the mirror.

"I guess." My cheeks burn. "But it's never going to work. My mom won't let me go and I didn't dare tell Will."

"Why won't your mom let you go?"

It's getting so easy to tell her stuff. Things I normally don't tell anyone. But she seems to find me fascinating because I've lived such a different life, and she never makes fun of me. So I answer, "One. Malls are evil. Two. She's already seen Will drop me off and told me he was the kind of guy who she was sure was into drugs, and she hinted he would take advantage of me. In other words, he wasn't a member of her church."

"Whoa. You're kidding!" she says as she slips her *Trees bleed too* T-shirt over her head.

I frown.

"I guess not. Sorry. Seriously, your church—I mean your mom's church—is so, um, well, unusual."

"Right. That's one word for it. Want to try it out for a year or two?"

"Okay, it's not that interesting!" Jamie leans forward and tosses her wet hair back and forth. She doesn't even use a comb or look at herself in the mirror. "Hey." Jamie slaps her forehead. "I've got an idea. Douglas and I are going to the mall on Friday to stop by the bookstore and read up on different universities. Why don't you tell your mom a bunch of us from cross-country are going to the mall to get running supplies? You, Will, and I—that makes a bunch, and you and I can each buy a pair of running socks, so you won't even be lying." Jamie's eyes are dancing with mischief.

"Hmm. Maybe. If I catch her while she's busy and distracted, maybe she won't ask too many questions. Thanks, Jamie. It's worth a try." We walk toward the lockers together and gather our backpacks. "So." I pause, a bit afraid to go on. I swallow, then say, "Do you and Douglas kind of like each other?"

Jamie hoots. She actually slaps her knees. "Douglas? No. We're just friends. I don't think Douglas is ready to announce it to the world yet, but I'm pretty sure, like ninety-nine-point-nine percent, that he bats for the other team."

"Oh."

The other team? Does she mean gay? *Homosexuality is an abomination and plague practiced by followers of Satan.* I think back to that porn site I saw Douglas looking at on the church computer. It did have two guys making out on it. I've never known anyone who is gay. Is she sure? He seems so normal. Well, totally nerdy, but not evil, not a follower of Satan. I want to ask Mom if followers of Satan get good grades, bring their Latin textbooks to the lunch room, hang around geeks, and go to Harvard.

At home I try to tiptoe through the hallway. But before I can escape downstairs, Mom calls out from the kitchen. "Kate? Come in the kitchen, dear."

Dear? I walk in and see Mr. Harmony. He waves at me and I nod.

Mom looks a little flustered as she clears her throat. "I'm not sure you two have ever been properly introduced. Max, this is Kate. Kate, this is Mr. Harmony."

Is she crazy? He's only been staying here for two weeks now. I've served him breakfast at least twice, changed his bedding both weekends, bumped into him outside two or three times, and seen them making goo-goo eyes at each other more than I want to mention.

"Hi, Kate." Mr. Harmony is tall. He has dark hair and seems fit and trim. He dresses in khaki pants and sports shirts. He has one hand in his pocket and the other on his belt, twisting it back and forth. He has bushy black eyebrows that grow together, like one big black line. He finally quits fidgeting with his belt and extends his hand.

Does he want me to shake it like we're at church or something?

I give him my hand and he barely grasps it, like he's afraid he'll break it or something. It feels all slick, like he oils it. Up close his cologne is really strong. I much prefer the smell of lobster and ocean.

"So, your mom says you run cross-country?"

I nod.

"What would you think about me coming to your next meet and taking a few pictures?"

I shrug and hope it's one of those polite comments adults make but don't follow up on.

"It's this Saturday at ten at the high school in Ellsworth, right?"

I sigh. "Yes."

Mr. Harmony doesn't seem to notice my frown. Or maybe he thinks that all I do is frown since I'm usually mad at Mom for something. But Dad always took pictures of me at races. Of course, he didn't sell his work to big-shot magazines and have ten cameras and about a million lens attachments. Still, he took great pictures. And no, I do not want Mr. Oily-Hands-Strong-Cologne-Wannabe-Member-of-the-Church-of-the-Holy-Divine-So-He-Can-Score-with-My-Mom to take a single picture of me. But what can I say? I mean, he knows the date and place and everything!

He glances at his watch. "Nice to chat with you, Kate. I'm going to have to leave now or I'll be late. I'm meeting a magazine editor for dinner."

Great, fine. Go. Never come back. I give him my big fake Church of the Holy Divine smile. It's scary how automatic it is.

From the kitchen window Mom watches as he pulls out of the driveway. "He's won several photography awards and had pictures in *National Geographic* and tour-guide books," she says as she waves to him.

I scrounge through the fridge for something to snack on before dinner as Mom brags on. "He just got an assignment today to photograph the national park through autumn and part of winter. And the best part is, he's going to church with me this Sunday, Kate. Aunt Katherine said she could take care of the breakfast shift without me. I would love for you to come to church with us."

I squeeze my eyes closed tight. Will she ever stop? Without turning, still rummaging inside the fridge, I mumble, "I think I better stay and help Aunt Katherine."

Mom's hand reaches out and strokes my shoulder and I stiffen.

"Now I know for sure this is where God wants us to be and why Max was given this particular photographic assignment."

Where God wants us to be? I crush a container so hard as I pull it out that the cover pops off. As I set the pasta on the counter, I look up to meet her eyes, but she's seeing beyond me to that glorious, Heavenly place she believes in. Her eyes shine now, like I'm sure Charity's did when she wrote me her letter telling me she knew that God lived and loved me. Her eyes are full of Max and her God and that stupid Holy Divine Church.

I'm about to escape to my room and eat cold pasta rather than have to microwave it and hear any more about God's miracles in our lives. But then it hits me—Mom is in an exceptionally good mood.

"Mom," I say as I put the pasta on a plate and set it in the microwave for one minute. "A bunch of us from the cross-country team are going to the mall after practice on Friday to get running supplies. I really do need some new socks before our meet on Saturday."

"The mall?" Her face turns serious, like one trip there will make me a drug-taking video-game addict.

"Yes. That's where the sports store is."

"You know what I think of the mall, Kate. It's just a place for kids to waste time and get into trouble."

"But we aren't going to goof around. We have a purpose."

She holds in her breath and looks up at the kitchen ceiling like she's praying. She probably is. I hope her God tells her the mall isn't such a bad place.

The microwave beeps. I tiptoe over to it and take out my plate.

"Okay. But you have to promise not to go into the video store or any stores that sell horrible animalistic music."

I should hide a tape recorder in my pocket and record all this for Jamie. She wouldn't believe it! But right now nothing else matters. "I promise, Mom."

She reaches out and runs her fingers through my hair. Instead of backing away, I let her. "Kate, I know we've had our differences about things lately. I've held on to too much tension. I've been talking to Max—uh, Mr. Harmony. He's teaching me how to relax and let things be. I just want you to know, I trust you and love you. I think you're old enough to start making some of your own choices."

I stare at her. Am I really hearing this? My own choices? "So does that mean you're going to give me back Dad's books?" I take a fork out of the silverware drawer and then slam it so hard the counter rattles.

"Well." Mom pauses, sucks in her breath, and, I swear, mentally counts to ten. "Yes."

I smile and my grip on the fork relaxes.

"When you're eighteen, if you still want them, you can have them then. And I'll be praying for you, as always, hoping God will be with you and guide you to make the right choices."

"Any fool can make a rule, and any fool will mind it." —*Henry David Thoreau.* My head chants one of the new lines I've memorized. "When I'm eighteen? Eighteen!" I stomp out of the room, leaving my pasta uneaten.

chapter fifteen

AFTER A FEW minutes of listening to Will's blaring radio, I reach over in the cab of his truck and turn it down. "Want to play the car punch game?" I ask.

"Never heard of it."

"You've never heard of the punch buggy?"

"Whoa there, City Girl. I'm not the one who thought you used a fishing pole to catch lobster."

I roll my eyes. "First you pick a car color and then every time you spot a car of that color, you punch the other person on the upper arm until they say something like 'Red pickup two cars behind us.'" I smile, thinking of all the times I used to play this game with Dad.

We drive along and play. "I'm winning six to two," I say, hitting Will's shoulder an extra time when we're a few miles away from the mall.

"Damn." He rubs his shoulder like I've really hurt him. "Well, it would be easier to punch you if you weren't so far way. I do have to keep my eyes on the road," he says as he pats his truck's steering wheel.

"Excuses, excuses." I grin and tilt my head.

"Hey, seriously, I don't bite, you know. You could sit a little closer."

I look at Will, so tan, with his long blond hair in a ponytail as usual. His blue eyes dance with mischief. I clutch the edge of the seat. "But what about the seat belt?" Will's truck has only two; the middle one is broken.

"Like we're going to crash on this busy road? Come on." He pats the vinyl seat.

So I take off the seat belt. Now I can imagine both Dad's and Mom's disapproval. Dad was very particular about seat belts, bike helmets, and filtered drinking water. And Mom—well, that's easy. Too close to a nonbelieving male who listens to animalistic music. I scoot way over until my bare legs are touching Will's jeans. He lets go of the steering wheel with the hand closest to me and puts his arm around my shoulder. My muscles stiffen, just like when Mom touches me. I guess it's because I'm not sure what to do, what to say. I have a feeling, though, that playing punch buggy is over. I'm quiet. Will doesn't seem to notice. He hums along as we drive. I feel a caressing squeeze on my right arm pulling me even closer to him. Then he leans over and kisses me on the cheek. I keep my head looking straight out the window. If I turn and look at him I know the next kiss will be on my lips.

Once we're out of the car in the mall parking lot, my muscles go back into normal mode. I feel safer now with other people around. And suddenly I realize I'm at the mall. With a guy. I try to be more carefree. "So, do you think you'll wear your new running shoes on the boat in the mornings? I mean, maybe you can get done faster with those speedy things on your feet."

"I've got a better idea. Why don't you come? You're not so bad with those bait bags."

I shudder at the thought of those slimy sardines, but just smile and start walking faster until soon we are running and I say, "I'll beat you to the door."

"No fair," Will hollers. "You've got good running shoes on."

"I know." I giggle and then race to the door and open it for Will.

"Why, thank you, madam," he says, and bows to me.

Inside, the mall is so alive and bright with lights and music and people. The cigar shop smells the way the woods do after one of our guests smokes on the back porch. The bath-and-body store has the aroma of rose and lavender. Winter coats, sweaters, boots, and woolen hats are on display in the clothing stores. Will has his arm around my shoulders. I feel like I'm in some fairyland, and I want to stay and stay and buy pretty clothes and fancy shoes and jewelry and even makeup. I guess Mom's right—the mall does tempt you. I glance at Will. What would he think if I was dressed up in the latest style? He seems to like me even in my running shorts and plain old T-shirts. He makes me feel pretty. I touch my cheek where his lips were only minutes ago.

At the sports store Will turns to me and says, "Okay, City Girl. Where do I begin?"

I'm about to answer when I notice Chelsea and Richard on the other side of the store. Chelsea waves and hooks her arms through Richard's and drags him over toward us. Turning back to Will, I say, "Um, well, first off, why don't we sit down and take a look at the bottom of your foot to see if you have a high arch, a normal arch, or are more flat-footed. That really helps determine the best type of shoe for you."

Will sits down and kicks off his boat shoes. As usual, he has no socks. I take his foot and turn it over in my lap.

"Kate, what are you doing holding Will's foot?" Chelsea says with her nose scrunched up as the light above her shimmers on her glittery purple eyeshadow. She backs away like Will has the worst case of athlete's foot in the world—which, thankfully, he doesn't.

"She's checking my feet to see what kind of shoes I need."

"Flat," I say, and try to ignore Chelsea.

"Bad?" he asks.

"No, it just means you probably overpronate. You need

a shoe that will keep your foot from rolling in too far, a motion-control shoe. I'm flat-footed, too. So," I say, standing and heading toward the line of men's running shoes on the wall at the side of us, "we need to look for shoes that have a straight shape and a firm midsole and a firm heel counter."

"Wow, Kate, you sound like a shoe salesman," Will says.

Chelsea snuggles closer to Richard, who I notice is still frowning and staring at Will's feet like he's really interested in the fact that they are flat.

"Saleswoman," I say.

"Whatever. But did you work for a shoe store in Arizona or something?"

"No," I answer as I take a shoe off the display shelf. "My dad liked to run, too. He and I did a lot of reading about different shoes before we bought ours. The best time to shop for running shoes is in the late afternoon because that's when your feet are their largest, and feet tend to expand when you are running. So our timing is perfect!"

"Kate's father died last year," Chelsea pipes in.

I wince. Chelsea's words hit my stomach like a punch that comes when you have your head turned. "This one seems to have good heel support," I start, but I swallow hard and can't finish.

"Yeah, I think it does." Richard surprises me and takes

the shoe from my hand and examines it. He hands it back to me and our eyes meet for just a second. Is that kindness I see flicker in his green eyes? Whatever it is, he's stopped Chelsea from going on about Dad.

Will takes the shoe. "Looks good to me," he says. He motions to the clerk to come over.

"Come on, Chelsea," Richard says. "I need running shorts, not shoes."

I sigh with relief that they are gone and focus on lacing one of the three pairs of shoes Will's going to try on. I watch out of one eye as Richard and Chelsea walk to the shorts area. Chelsea stops him before they reach the shorts, though, and takes a skimpy bright pink sports bra off the rack and puts it in front of herself. "What do you think, Richard?" she says loud enough to make the whole store look.

Will looks up and whistles. "Maybe you should get one of those, Kate."

My cheeks burn as I focus on the shoe, lacing it up carefully as if I didn't hear his remark.

After I finish, I pull a packet of running socks off the wall near where Will is sitting. "You'll need good socks, too. No running with just shoes."

"Ah, you are spoiling all my fun." Will grins.

Out of the three pairs Will tries on, he picks a neon yellow pair. "No one else has these."

"I wonder why."

"Hey, if you haven't noticed, I don't like blending in with the crowd."

"I've noticed."

With his new yellow shoes and a pair of the socks on, Will pays and stuffs his old shoes into the store bag with the rest of his new socks. "I might as well get used to them now," he says, "while my running expert is still around to give me advice." He pulls at my ponytail as I pay for my socks, and my heart leaps like it's jumping hurdles.

Just as we're about to leave, Jamie and Douglas join us. "Gotta buy my running socks," Jamie says, and winks at me. "Then Douglas and I are heading to get some food. Want to join us?"

"Food sounds excellent," Will says, and does a little tap dance to show off his yellow shoes.

"Whoa, awesome treads, dude." Jamie high-fives Will.

"See, I told you they were great." Will puts his arm around me.

Jamie stares at Will's arm and moves her eyebrows up and down like she's saying *ooo-la-la*.

At the food court, Jamie and I head for the smoothie place while Douglas and Will go for the burgers. We meet back at the table, and Will is carrying this monster-sized plate of chili fries. As luck would have it, Richard and Chelsea and some of the cool kids are at the next table.

"Are you seriously going to eat all that?" Chelsea looks over at Will and frowns at the pile of greasy carbohydrates.

"Hey, running revs up a mean appetite."

Then Will kicks me with his shoe under the table. "Wait until you see me run tomorrow! I feel like I could fly in these, City Girl."

I laugh.

Soon the four of us are talking, and Douglas starts his jiggling-leg thing, then says, "Kate?"

"Um, yeah?"

"Well, I just wanted to thank you."

"Me? Why?"

"Well, the other night at youth group, when Pastor Browning asked us why we were there, the last thing I thought of telling him was the truth. But then you said you didn't know why you were there, and well, it gave me the courage to be honest myself." Douglas's face gets so red I can't see his freckles.

"Aw, that's so sweet, Douglas." Jamie pats him on the cheek.

I'm too blown away to say anything. Douglas takes a big bite of his burger and gulps it down and stares at his tray. I guess that conversation is over.

Later, on our way out, I spot a big candy shop. "Can we stop here?" I ask.

They have a great selection of Jelly Bellys. Jamie,

Douglas, and Will wait for me at the entrance. Jamie and Douglas are flipping through their new college guides like they've just purchased the latest best-selling novel. I notice Douglas also has a book titled *College Degrees in Latin or Carpe Diem*. Will looks bored. I'm sure he is, since he told me he's going to take over his grandpa's boat and doesn't need a college degree. When I put a whole pound of popcorn-flavored Jelly Bellys in the bag and pay for it at the counter, Chelsea and Richard walk by. I'm beginning to think they're following us. Snoopy Chelsea has to come in to see what I've bought. Richard ends up talking to Will, Jamie, and Douglas. As we walk toward them, she says, "You're not really going to eat that whole bag of candy all by yourself, are you, Kate? Think of the calories."

"Hey, running revs up a mean appetite," I say as we approach the rest of the group.

Am I seeing things, or does even Richard's frown turn into a tiny smile?

chapter sixteen

I JOG IN PLACE at the starting line. Dad's voice fills my mind. "Remember, Kate, relax. You've trained hard, now just let your body take over."

The gun sounds. My muscles tense. I grind my shoes forward into the dirt. Don't sprint ahead, I warn myself as Jamie shoots to the front of the pack. I lock my eyes on the back of her short-cropped hair, though, and set my stride. Her philosophy is run ahead, stay ahead. But my strength is endurance, not speed.

After the first mile I start to pass runners who have made the mistake of starting out too fast and are already beginning to fade. I squint. I can still make out Jamie's form. Time to rachet up the rhythm of my stride. I pass several more runners. I draw close to a girl from Blue Lake High, with her blue tank top and bobbing brown ponytail. I can almost feel the hairs on her arm as I try to pass her. But she pushes ahead. I run harder until I'm at her heel. Now at her arm. I nose past her! After a few seconds I can't hear her behind me. I glance over my shoulder for a brief millisecond. She's there. She's gaining on me. I push harder into the gravel trail. She passes me. I hear Dad's voice.

"Kate. Never turn. Never look, never."

Now she's several feet ahead. I push on. Don't think about the Blue Lake girl. Don't think about the Blue Lake girl. Focus on Jamie. My strategy works. I keep my eyes on the tiny form way out in front. I pass runner after runner. At mile two I pass the Blue Lake girl again. Only one runner in front of me—Jamie.

Push, push, push, my head instructs. Then out of nowhere, like a surprise quiz on a Friday afternoon, in my head I hear the sound of Mom's silly giggle and the annoying way she laughs when Mr. Harmony is around. I'm surprised she isn't here today. I mean, she hasn't come to any of my meets, but he's here. I heard him call out, "Go, Kate," as the gun fired. Her perfect darling man. "Good luck, sweetie," she'd said, and kissed my head as I left this morning. "Wish I could come, but you know."

I know—the guests. And she never went in Phoenix because running was something I did with Dad. But she did advise me about my races. My hands, already balled into fists, tighten as I remember her advice on the first race I ever ran with Dad. "Go fasting and praying, Kate. Then you know God will be with you and you will do your best." Fasting for members of the Holy Divine Church means not only going without food for an entire day, but liquids as well. I finished that race all right. But the last mile my head was spinning, I was so dehydrated. As I crossed the finish line I collapsed and passed out for a few seconds. On the way home Dad asked if I'd had enough to drink in the past twenty-four hours. "Probably not," I'd admitted. A slight understatement. Now, I drink nonstop on the day before a race.

I look ahead on the trail. In my mind's wanderings I've lost sight of Jamie! I look behind me. Where is the Blue Lake girl? The other runners? Frantic, I spot a red flag in a tree several yards back. Right where the trail forked. Stupid! I strike out at the air with my fists. I pivot, sprint back, and regain the right path. How could I miss the red flag that marks the trail? Now I've used up precious energy, energy I had hoped to save for the last few yards. Through the trees I spot Jamie's petite form and her red Rocky Point High tank top just as she crosses the finish line. The Blue Lake girl is about twenty yards ahead of me. I push and push, exerting every ounce of drive I can muster. I sprint so close to her the dirt she kicks up hits my legs. She must hear me because she pulls out faster. Every muscle quivers in spasms as I try to follow. My lungs are on fire. With feet still to go, I become aware of the bleachers breaking into cheers as she crosses the finish line. I stumble and stagger over the chalk-drawn line behind her into Jamie's arms. Everything spins around me. The announcer's words seem to come from miles away. "Third-place runner, Kate Anderson from Rocky Point High, with the time of twenty minutes fifty-six seconds."

Twenty fifty-six. Twenty fifty-six! My best time ever! Even with the lost time running on the wrong trail. I sway and the ground seems to tilt in the opposite direction. Jamie swings my arm around her shoulder. "Walk, Kate, walk. And breathe, too. You're chalk white." As we walk, Jamie talks to me. "You did great. I did great."

I nod. Then between breaths I say, "'*Tomorrow we will run faster, stretch out our arms further.*'"

"Hey, Kate, that sounds, like, profound. I've heard it before. Where is it from?"

"F. Scott Fitzgerald—*The Great Gatsby*," I gasp.

"One of your dad's books?"

I nod. I told Jamie all about Mom taking away Dad's books. It seems I tell her everything now.

As soon as Jamie assures me I have color back in my cheeks and lips, I hurry to my backpack and get out my notebook. It's my job as PR person to keep track of the times for our school newspaper. I gulp down water and write down the times as the rest of our team finishes. We get second place. Maybe we could have been first if only I hadn't let my thoughts go to Mom. If only I hadn't lost the trail. And speaking of Mom, here comes Mr. Harmony.

"Great race, Kate."

"Thanks," I mumble.

"Can I take your picture now?"

No. You. Can. Not. *Dad* takes my picture. *Dad*. Do you hear me? I shrug.

So he gets down on his knees a few feet away from me and clicks away.

Jamie notices. "Hey, that's great. Can you take some pictures of our whole team, for the school paper? I was going to bring my camera but I forgot."

"Sure." Max reaches out his hand to Jamie. "I'm Max Harmony, a friend of Kate's. I'm staying at the Whispering Woods Inn for several weeks."

My friend. My *friend*! Jamie notices my frown and tilts her head, puzzled, with a look in her eye that says, *You're going to have to tell me about this guy later.*

Jamie and Max begin to talk, and she soon discovers what a big-shot photographer she has asked to take pictures for our school paper. While they are deep in conversation, I wander over to the finish line, where the first guy runners should be coming in within the next minute. The big clock above me reads sixteen minutes twenty-seven seconds when Richard Penrose breaks through the red tape. I do the math as I write down his score. He ran under five and a half minute miles! So fast! Right beyond the finish line, Chelsea and Richard's mom and dad are cheering. Chelsea shouts out, "Yes, Richard! You won!" He shrugs like it's no big deal and jogs right past her toward the table of water bottles. He grabs a bottle, opens it, and as he guzzles it down, seems totally unaware of the cheering bleachers or the announcer saying, "First-place runner, setting a new Rocky Point High record for the three mile, Richard Penrose." A record! And he doesn't even care. But Max does. He comes over and shakes Richard's hand and then meets his parents and takes several photos of him. Poor Chelsea—she isn't invited to be photographed. Jamie comes up to my side. "You really should do a feature article on Richard. I mean, he just broke a school record."

"Me? But . . ."

"All you have to do is ask him questions like how long he's been running, what his hobbies are. I mean, besides driving that tank of his. You can do it, Kate."

I look at Richard and then at my notepad. I can do it. *Just kidding.* I can't even say hello to him. My mouth freezes up every time I pass him in the halls at school. We walk past each other like we're strangers. And to think our dads were friends growing up.

It's a whole minute before the next runner comes in. When the clock reads twenty-one minutes and thirty-five seconds, I spot Will yards from the finish line. On impulse, I shout, "Go, Will, keep it up." And then wish I could swallow back my words. I hate it when people call out to me, as if I'm not trying my hardest already. But Will turns and gives me a thumbs-up as he sprints across the finish line. He places sixth for our team. Now he'll have one of the coveted varsity slots for the next meet. I put stars and smiley faces around his time. Maybe I should do a feature on Will instead. He's just become the most improved runner on our team, thanks to his friend's insistence that he get real running shoes. Besides, I already know his hobbies, or at least what he does with his spare time. Lobstering.

"It's the shoes," he calls out to me as he jumps in the air, kicking his feet together.

I chuckle. Where's Max now? This is the picture I want, of Will clicking his heels together in midair. Too bad, he missed it. I turn back—he's still talking to the Penroses.

After the last runner is in, we gather around Coach Horne. Max, as Jamie is already calling him, takes a group photo, and then Coach gives us one of his pep talks before he dismisses us to load on the bus. I'm one of the first people on, eager to get away from Max before he can offer me a ride home. As people pile in, I spot Will. He's scanning the seats, and smiles when he sees me. "That seat next to you taken?"

"No," I say, and try not to let my happiness burst into an ear-to-ear grin. But inside I feel as happy as if I had set a running record for Rocky Point High. I'm so pumped about my running time, and about our new friendship, I don't even feel nervous or stiff sitting close to him this time. As the bus drives back toward our high school, we talk about the race and then he asks about running in

Arizona. I tell him how Dad and I used to run along the canal from palm tree to palm tree. He nods, his eyes start to droop, and then without saying a word, he's asleep. I hope he's snoring because he got up so early, not because my story is that boring. We hit a bump in the road and the next thing I know, his head is resting on my shoulder. My back stiffens. But Will is really out. I relax against the seat. His sandy lashes are longer than mine. And he has a sprinkle of tiny pin-dot freckles.

I glance up and for the first time notice who is sitting across from us. Richard Penrose. But no Chelsea. Did she take the ride home with his parents? Why didn't he? We don't have to ride the bus. His eyes meet mine for a second. How long has he been watching me? But before I have the chance to say "nice race," he twists his head away, back toward his window. I cringe. Why do I always feel so uncomfortable around him? Will lets out an extra loud breath, and his chest heaves in and out like the bellows we use to start the fires at home. His new yellow shoes are caked with dust. His white socks are now mostly brown. We both smell like a sweaty locker room, but I couldn't be happier if we were dressed in silk and fine linen and bathed in those expensive oils we have in the guest bathrooms.

chapter seventeen

WHEN THE BUS lets me off after cross-country practice, I jog up the hill to Aunt Katherine's. She's promised to help me make banana bread for our youth group to have for refreshments tonight. I wanted to take something semihealthy.

Mom's been too distracted and frenzied with the guests all weekend to harass me about attending a misguided church or any of my many other sins. I've helped when I've been home. At least she can't complain that I'm lazy on top of everything else. And every time I'm cleaning, I search cupboards and closets and the storage rooms, even the garage, for Dad's books. I'm beginning to think she burned them. I can't find them anywhere. But she said she'd give them to me when I'm eighteen, so they must be somewhere.

I knock, then open the door and walk into Aunt Katherine's cottage.

"Back here, love," Aunt Katherine calls from the kitchen.

Even though it's almost dusk, the kitchen is bright and cheery, with its yellow-painted walls. But maybe some of the cheeriness is because the room is rich with the aroma of fresh chicken soup.

"I hope you're hungry," Aunt Katherine says from the stove, where she's stirring a big pot.

"Starved."

Soon I'm spooning down the delicious broth thick with chicken, carrots, celery, and homemade noodles. Meanwhile, Aunt Katherine shuffles through an old tin box of her recipes at the counter. She always makes such a big fuss about Mom's cooking, but I've discovered she's quite a cook herself.

Waving a small card in the air, she narrows her eyes like a scheming underworld spy. "I've got a special recipe. Mable Simpson won a blue ribbon at the church bazaar for this banana bread ten years in a row. We found out later that her secret was to mash the bananas in fresh lemon juice. It makes the bread a light golden color and adds just a hint of tang. She was furious when Michelle Riggs figured it out and showed up at the church potluck dinner with white, tart banana bread. Mable never would share her recipe, but Michelle shared her copycat verison with all of us."

I grin and feel like I used to with Charity, when she and I shared a secret or a private joke. "I think you could win a blue ribbon with this chicken soup."

"Why, thank you. That's so nice of you to say. I have always thought my chicken soup was pretty good, myself."

"So, your church has bake-offs?"

"Oh, Kate, I don't even know if they do anymore. Between you and me, before you came, I hadn't set foot inside that church in over ten years."

I nod and busy myself with my soup as my heart fills with a mixture of guilt and gratitude. I know she's going now only because of me. And why? Is it because even if she thinks her church isn't that good, it has to be better than the one that ruined her only nephew's marriage?

Soon I'm measuring out flour and sugar, and before I know it, two tins of banana-bread batter are baking in the oven. I race home to shower and come back just in time to help take them out of the oven to cool. Aunt Katherine and I have slices of one of the loaves, with tall glasses of milk from an organic farm, where the cows graze outside and don't stay all day in steel stalls. I call it happy-cow milk. We sit on the couch, watching the news on CNN. More fighting in the Middle East. High oil prices. Starvation in Africa. Protests against gay marriages in several states. "Oh, Kate, why do I watch it?" Aunt Katherine sighs. "Will it ever be good news?"

"Maybe if everyone buys happy-cow milk, joins their town's environmental club, and drives cars fueled by used French-fry oil." Jamie and Aunt Katherine already knew each other slightly from going to Puffin Cove's environmental group, but last Thursday we all sat together and I asked Jamie to tell Aunt Katherine about her car. Right now, with my stomach full of chicken soup, banana bread, and happy-cow milk, sitting next to Aunt Katherine, I really do believe that good things can happen in the world.

"Yes, yes." Aunt Katherine reaches over and takes my hand in hers and pats it. "You and your running friend, Jamie, with her interesting car, are our future, Kate. You really are. I will take hope in that." She pats my leg. We sit in silence for a moment and I feel so much love and understanding in the air, I wish I could bottle it.

I'm sitting at the huge table at the Puffin Cove church, keeping my eyes on the door, hoping Jamie will walk through. What will I do if she doesn't show up? Douglas is already in the computer room. I saw him as I passed it, and this time he was mumbling in Latin and seriously studying what I assume was Pastor Browning's Latin Bible. Slowly, everyone from last week, plus two new freshmen I've noticed at school, show up. And finally Jamie. She slumps down in the chair next to me. "I'm so beat from that workout today, aren't you?"

I nod as Pastor Browning walks through the doorway, his arms loaded down with a box and books. He drops the box on the table and scans the room. "Good evening, everyone. Well, well, I haven't scared too many of you away."

He turns to the freshman girls. "Welcome, ladies, glad you could make it."

The girls smile and blush.

Pastor Browning clears his throat and points to the box. "One of the twelve-year-old boys in our congregation is a Boy Scout," Pastor Browning says. "He's selling these candy bars so he can go to a winter wilderness camp. He asked if I'd help him out and I said I thought I knew a few people who liked candy." He chuckles. "So if any of you are inclined, they're a dollar fifty a bar."

"I'll buy two," Chelsea offers, sounding as noble as if she had just volunteered to adopt two starving orphans from Africa. "Scouting is such a wonderful program," she adds as she rifles through lipstick and other makeup in her purse. Grinning, she waves three wrinkled dollar bills.

The new freshman girls each buy two. The two juniors that are friends each buy one. Richard buys five. I didn't bring any money and feel my cheeks burning as Pastor Browning exchanges candy bars for money.

"Hey, I don't mean to be the spoilsport here," Jamie pipes up. "But you are aware, Pastor Browning, of the current exclusionary stand the Boy Scouts of America have on who can join the Scouts or be an adult leader?" Today's T-shirt reads *Shoot the breeze. not Bambi.* She would so get killed if she wore that out west, where every guy over twelve is a hunter.

Pastor Browning, who is leaning over the box and counting out five candy bars for Richard, hands them to him and then stands up straight and faces Jamie. "Yes, I am aware."

"Knowing this, do you think you should really be promoting their group?"

Pastor Browning, his hands in his pockets now, paces back and forth. Everyone is quiet. Chelsea rolls her eyes. I have no idea what exclusionary stand Jamie is talking about. I understand her reasoning in not using gasoline to fuel her car, and wanting to use recycled paper and eat organic food, but to my knowledge, the Scouts have always been squeaky clean. My uncle in Idaho is a Scoutmaster, and all of my cousins who are old enough have become Eagle Scouts. Scouting is a major part of Mom's church. I mean, it's actually one of the programs that makes sense. What is so harmful about hiking and fishing and learning to build fires? Who are the Scouts excluding? Girls? But girls can join the Girl Scouts.

Pastor Browning finally speaks. "Jamie has brought up an excellent point. I won't go into the specifics of the Scout case, but maybe we can talk for a minute about what to do when you are faced with a moral dilemma like Jamie's." He tugs at his white collar.

"Boycott," Jamie answers.

Chelsea sits up straight. "Oh my God, Jamie. It's only chocolate. Do you have to spoil everything? It's not like we're buying illegal drugs or supporting the Ku Klux Klan."

I'm surprised Chelsea even knows what the Ku Klux Klan is. I guess she's been paying more attention in history class than I thought.

"No, it's more like the Hitler Youth Group. A group that promoted national pride, exercised, sang songs together, but didn't let anyone who had an ounce of Jewish blood join. The Scouts have picked their own group to exclude."

Pastor Browning's face is serious.

Chelsea yawns loudly. "This isn't history class. It's just candy for a campout or something."

Pastor Browning picks up the box and puts it on a side table. Then he faces us. "It's a hard thing to know what to do when something isn't all bad, or all good. I guess I'm just hoping that the Scout program, which has been around for a long time and only recently added an exclusionary clause, will come to see the error of its position. I guess I'm hoping reason will prevail."

Jamie shakes her head. "I think I will just boycott, thank you."

Pastor Browning tilts his head and watches Jamie. And I can tell he likes the way she stands up for things. But Jamie is too busy frowning to notice. Most of the rest of the group looks almost as bored as Chelsea. Richard, however, is not rolling a pencil tonight or staring at the table. He has his eyes up and is listening to it all.

And when the lesson starts, Richard stays, even though Pastor Browning invites him to return to the chapel if he'd feel more comfortable. Chelsea beams like she actually thinks Richard is staying just to be near her and hear her spiritual thought, which she proudly stands and recites. Maybe before she gets too cocky, she should notice how he's watching Pastor Browning and paying attention through the whole lesson.

After class we go into Pastor Browning's office and everyone has a piece of my banana bread and Pastor Browning offers sodas, juices, and water bottles. Everyone tells me how good it is, and I try not to smile too much. As the rest of us chat and munch on the bread, Jamie sits in the far corner with her eyebrows knit in thought, oblivious to the rest of us giggling and talking.

Afterward, as we walk out of the church, Jamie trails behind. I slow down, and when I'm sure no one else can hear, I ask, "Jamie, who do the Scouts exclude?"

"Homosexuals," she answers as she studies each cement square of the sidewalk. This word, rarely said but often hinted at in my religious past, seems to linger in the chilly night air.

"Oh." I shiver and don't know what to say. That topic again. Guys who bat for the other team. Douglas. I remember all the protests the Holy Divine Church participated in back in Arizona a couple of years ago, trying to stop gay rights. Mom's church, of course, thinks sex is a sin unless it is between a married man and his wife. If someone has sex and isn't married, or has an abortion, she might as well be like Hester Prynne in *The Scarlet Letter*—which we've started reading in history—and sew a scarlet *A* on her clothes. I remember one girl who came back from the church college and people whispered she'd had an abortion. She wasn't allowed to take communion for a really long time or sing in the choir, and she had been a soloist in our Christmas program. And it was even worse if you were gay. People whispered about this one guy in our congregation liking another boy at his high school. After a while he stopped showing up with his family at church. Charity told me the High Priest sent him to this place where they do extreme therapy on you to help you like girls instead of guys. They did things like show him pictures of naked guys and then gave him medicine that made him throw up. A few months later, I overheard Mom on the phone telling someone from church that he ran away from that place and his family had no idea where he was.

I wonder if she's upset because of Douglas? The Holy Divine Church thinks people are tempted by Satan to become gay. But why? I mean, who would want to have people call them ugly names? Who would want churches to label them *the perpetrators of an evil plague*? I mean, if I really liked guys, which I do—at least I like Will—could any devil really *tempt* me to want to kiss or touch a girl instead?

I've been watching Douglas. I didn't like what I saw him watching on the church computer, but he's not bad or mean. He's a bit weird, I'll admit. Yesterday, he was reading to himself from his Latin textbook. Out loud. At the lunch table. But that's eccentric, not evil. *"Be curious, not judgmental."*—*Walt Whitman.* Some people can't see— does that mean all blind people are sinful because their bodies don't work the way most people's do? Or people who are crippled or deaf are evil? Couldn't people who are homosexual just be wired differently?

I glance at Jamie. I'd like to ask her. I'm sure she'd have something to say. But she's still so quiet; she's staring at a streetlight ahead of us now, like it's a crystal ball that might help her solve the world's injustices. Her shoulders, usually straight and strong, are slumping, and she's trudging down the street without her normal pixielike bounce.

"Um, Jamie? I don't like anything that excludes people, either. I won't buy the Scout candy bars."

She looks up at me for the first time all night. "I'm glad, Kate."

chapter eighteen

OKAY, I'M TURNING into a total geek. I'm so into *To Kill a Mockingbird* that I'm rereading the section we discussed in English as I walk down the hallway. I can't believe how Boo Radley's father kept him locked in the house for all those years. And I thought my mom was strict. *Bump.* I trip and stumble, crashing right into Richard Penrose. My left foot is right on top of his. I jump back. "Sorry," I say, quickly closing my book.

"Me, too," Richard mumbles. His eyes flicker intently into mine, like he's trying to figure something out. What? What are you looking at? Haven't you ever seen someone reading a book while walking before? But before I get all defensive, I realize this is the perfect opportunity.

"Um, Richard, actually I was hoping to bump into you." My cheeks burn. "I mean, not literally. I mean . . ."

Richard looks at me like I'm from Mars. And why not? I certainly sound like it.

"What I mean is, I was hoping I could interview you

for the school paper—you know, about the school record you set last week in the track meet."

"Oh." Richard nods. "Sure. Don't you have lunch now? You could interview me at the cafeteria."

He knows I have the same lunch as him? "Um, sure."

As we walk toward the cafeteria together, Richard bends over, glancing at the book in my hand. "So, you like *To Kill a Mockingbird*?"

"Oh, I have to read it for English."

"In the hallway?" He smiles. Richard actually smiles. I'm so confused.

"Well, no." I bite my lip and wonder what to say next.

But fortunately we are entering the lunchroom, and before you know it, I'm sitting across from Richard with my notebook, asking him the list of questions I had carefully prewritten at home. "Have you always liked to run?"

"No, I actually hate running, but it's good to get me in shape for basketball."

"Really? But you're so fast."

Richard shrugs.

"So, you love basketball. I mean, that's your real sport."

"No. My dad loves basketball." He frowns. That prisoner look again. Sometime Richard and I should have a chat about his dad and my mom.

"Oh, not basketball. So, what sports do you like?"

"Um, I like sailing okay. And hiking."

"Hiking?"

"Yeah, you know, the whole backpack-and-sleeping-bag-thing, climbing uphill, escaping people, and listening to the birds chirp in the trees."

Is he messing with me? I have no idea, but I write it all down.

"Any hobbies?"

"Planes."

"Planes?"

"I play a lot of fighter-jet computer games online with my buddies out in California." He actually chuckles. "And, eventually, I want to join the coast guard as a pilot."

"Oh." I know even less about computer games than I do basketball, but I write it down.

"So," I ask him, "do you have a favorite game?"

"Absolutely. *Heroes of the Pacific*. It's the greatest. You can have eight people playing at once and the graphics are great."

He's actually smiling and animated. He's serious about his fighter-jet games.

I look down at my list of prepared questions.

Do you have any goals to run a marathon? (*My answer: Yes*)

Who is your favorite runner? (*My answer: Prefontaine*)

How does it feel to break a school record? (*My answer: I have no idea but I bet it feels like Heaven.*)

Somehow none of these questions seems right now.

"Rich-ard." Chelsea sneaks up behind Richard and kisses him on the cheek.

He turns to her and the smile drops to a frown. His eyes darken and it seriously looks like he's about to punch Chelsea. Or vomit. I'm not sure which. But I thought he liked her. He's always with her. Correction, she's always with him.

"Well, I think that's about it," I say. "Thanks."

"No problem." He lifts his hand in a half wave and smiles at me as I leave the table.

It's Friday morning. No school! I skip as I make my way to the travel bus. We get to miss the whole day of school for the Super Sports Weekend. We're going to Bangor, where six different high schools compete in cross-country, golf, lacrosse, and volleyball. The school with the most points wins this huge trophy. Rocky Point High won it four years ago, and Jamie says we have a good chance of winning it this year.

Jamie and I are sharing a room in the hotel. When I climb on the bus, I'm hoping to sit with Will, but he's already sitting with some girl from the volleyball team. She has way long blonde hair, big brown eyes, and a low-cut tank top on. They are giggling and Will doesn't even see me when I pass by. My heart feels like it has just fallen to the bus floor. I trudge on and find Jamie and the seat by her is empty. "Kate." She waves. I sit down without even saying hi back. Jamie, who has her calculus book open, doing homework, smiles at me and doesn't notice my silence or frown. Her head is already back in her book. Through the whole bus ride I stare out at the farms and churches and villages we pass and try to ignore the sound of Will's chuckling, four rows up. I thought we were like boyfriend and girlfriend. Boy, did I get that wrong!

Once we arrive, our cross-country team hangs out together to watch the girls' volleyball match. I feel a tug at my ponytail. "Hey, City Girl."

"Hey," I say. Obviously, the pretty blonde girl can't be with him now since she's down on the court, thumping balls over the net time after time. I guess I'm second choice. Great. Will cheers and claps with the rest of the team. But he seems a bit more excited about the volleyball team winning than I wish he would be.

And when the afternoon comes and we're watching golf, he's off to the blonde girl again. Chelsea is rushing around giving out water and towels to the team. She stops by once and I ask her, "Who's that girl with Will?"

"Oh her? Candy. Why?"

"No reason."

By dinnertime, our girls' volleyball team has taken first and the girls' golf team takes third. The guys' golf team takes first and Chelsea is beaming with pride. Jamie whispers to me as she passes, "Couldn't have done it without Chelsea. We'll owe it all to her if we win that trophy, and she'll never let us forget it!"

At dinner, at the all-you-can-eat buffet near the campus, Will eats with some of his buddies. But afterward he comes up to me and asks if I want to go see a movie with him and a bunch of other people. Before I can even ask if Candy is one of the other people, Jamie shakes her head no. "We all three need to go straight to our hotel rooms. Coach Horne wants us to be good and rested."

"Fine." Will sticks out his lower lip like he's pouting. But he tugs at my ear and says, "See you first thing, City Girl."

I totally don't get him. But I like the way I feel when he looks in my eyes, tugs at my ear, and calls me City Girl. Maybe he and Candy are just friends. I mean, he can have friends. After all, he's lived here all his life. I'm sort of friends with Douglas. They were just talking. It's not like they were making out.

In the room I share with Jamie, we each have a double bed. I feel just like I used to when Charity would sleep over, like I've known Jamie forever. Well, I still change in the bathroom, but I mean I'm not worried about what to talk about with her. And we don't go to sleep. We are in our beds, sitting up with the lights on, and we start talking.

"So where does your dad live?" Jamie asks. "I mean, do you ever see him?"

My chest stiffens. Here it comes. I've got to tell her. I twist the top of the sheet and, looking down, I say, "No, he died last year."

"He died?"

"He was a runner, but he had a heart attack. I found him." My head floods with memories. The chair. The books in his lap. The last sound of his laughter, mocking me about fasting. I shake my head and bite my lip to keep the thoughts from taking over.

"Oh, Kate." Jamie comes over from her bed and puts her arms around me. She pats my back just like she's Aunt Katherine. It feels good. Tears roll down my cheeks. Jamie says nothing but keeps her arms tight around me while I cry.

Finally, I brush away the tears from my face. I try to smile. I try to move on because I know what happens when the darkness takes over. "Do you see your dad much?" I ask.

"Yeah. Most holidays, and I spent last summer with him and we built our car together. We get along really well. Sometimes I've thought about moving down there and living with him. But this has always been home, and I'd miss my friends."

"So, do you get along with your mom?" I ask.

"Ha. About like you do with your mom. Only for different reasons. She worries about me because in her opinion I don't pay enough attention to guys. She actually asked me if I was a lesbian."

I swallow hard because I've sort of wondered that myself.

"Don't tell anyone but I actually have a sort of boy-friend. He's a year older than me and goes to NYU. We had some classes together last year. We chat online and call sometimes. He's coming home for Christmas."

"What's his name?"

"Anthony Salcedo. His dad is from Ecuador and he has the sweetest eyes, and the darkest, sexiest hair." Jamie grins.

I giggle. It feels good to know a secret about Jamie and to know she likes guys, too.

Finally, we fall asleep, or Jamie does. As I listen to her heavy breathing in the dark, I feel all cozy and warm and not even scared about tomorrow's run.

In the morning, we're dressed and ready to go a half hour before we need to meet downstairs. Jamie pulls out a notebook from her backpack and says, "So tell me about your mom's weird church, will you?"

I tell her the church is led by a prophet and assisted by his twelve disciples, all male, of course.

"Like in the Bible? Like Jesus had?"

"Yeah."

"Interesting." The whole time we talk, she scrawls down notes to use in her term paper. "And so, basically, the men call all the shots and tell the women to have a ton of babies and homeschool their kids?"

"Basically."

"Well, that should keep most women too busy and demeaned to think for themselves."

I nod. I've been thinking that a lot lately myself. Even Mom. Is that why she is the way she is?

Today I'm running, though, not sitting at home learning how to cross-stitch. Today is our race. And we really have a chance to take home that big trophy with the wins Rocky Point High had yesterday. But we pretty much have to take first in both girls' and guys' cross-country to win, since we don't have very good lacrosse teams. I try to ignore the nervous knot in my stomach. The calmness of last night is gone, and the familiar churning I always get the day of a race has come.

When it's time, we head downstairs. As we walk across the marble floor to the group gathered in front of the huge floral arrangement in the center of the lobby, angry voices make their way to us. Coach Horne and the golf coach are answering questions.

"What's going on?" Jamie asks, tapping the shoulder of a senior girl on the volleyball team.

"You haven't heard?"

We shake our heads.

"Richard Penrose, Chelsea Riggs, and two other cross-country guys snuck out last night after curfew and got caught. Now they can't compete."

"You're kidding! How could anyone be that stupid?" Jamie puts her hands on her hips.

No wonder people are angry. Now what are our chances? Richard's first-place run would have brought in a lot of our needed points. And the other two would have seriously helped. My fists clench. Chelsea! My article about Richard will be in the school paper on Monday, like he's a champion or something. And now he's totally ruined our chances of winning. Just because he doesn't care about running, does he have to ruin it for everyone else?

I feel someone grabbing me from behind at my waist. I turn around and come face-to-face with Will.

"Aha. Got ya, Running Machine."

"H-h-hi," I stutter, and worry Will might be one of the other two runners, but at the same time, I am so happy he touched me again!

As if he read my mind, he says, "Man, I was out like a light at nine p.m. That's what lobstering will do for you. Shit, it sounds like I missed out on all the fun." He nods his head toward the coaches. He grins at me, like a friendly, harmless pup who doesn't care about trophies or winning. My hands loosen, and that silly sparkle in his eyes melts the anger inside of me and I find myself smiling back.

"Look's like we're going to have to run extra fast today, City Girl, if we're going to take home the trophy."

And we do run fast. I stay with Jamie almost the whole way and am just a few seconds behind her at the finish line. When my lungs and ribs felt like they would rip in two, I just kept thinking, Run for the trophy, the trophy. Jamie,

Will, and I each post our best times of the season, but it isn't enough. We don't get the trophy.

And who sits by me on the bus on the way home? Will! We play punch buggy again. I can almost forget yesterday on the bus ever happened. But then I notice Candy isn't on the bus. She must have been driven home by her parents, or, better yet, her boyfriend.

But I slip away from Will in a hurry when the bus pulls into the school parking lot. "See ya," I say as I dash off. All I need is for Mom to see him walking me to the car. Instead Jamie walks with me to the other end of the parking lot, where her car is parked and where Mom is waiting for me.

"Hey, introduce me to your mom. I want to meet this woman I've heard so much about."

I glance at Jamie's sweatshirt. *Straight but not narrow.* When she put it on after our run, she said she was tired of people thinking she was a lesbian. I swallow. It is dark. But the parking lot is well lit. Oh, who cares.

So I walk up to the car and open Mom's door. "Mom, this is my friend Jamie. She's captain of our cross-country team."

"Nice to meet you, Ms. Anderson."

Mom nods and then her eyes zoom in on Jamie's sweatshirt. She glances at her watch and frowns. Where is the wonderful hostess tonight? Doesn't she want to help Jamie find the truth?

"So, I'll see you Monday at school?" Jamie says, and when Mom's not looking, she grins at me, like she's saying, *Yeah, she's a trip, all right.*

After Jamie leaves, I get in the passenger side of the car, and before I even have my seat belt on, Mom says, "So, I hear there was a bit of trouble at your event." I know she means Richard and Chelsea. She must have already talked to Mrs. Riggs. It really is a small town!

"Chelsea just needs friends who can influence her in a good way," Mom says, patting my leg when we come to a stoplight. "Not people like that Jamie girl, who is a walking sign for accepting homosexuality. Really, I can't believe people have such horrid things printed on their clothes." I think of my yellow *Keep the Faith* T-shirt with the small words *Be happy, be Christian* and wonder what Jewish people or Muslims think of it.

"But Mom, Chelsea got drunk! She broke curfew. If I did that I'd be grounded for the rest of my life."

"But Chelsea hasn't been born with the saving love of Christ. We can't judge her in the same way," Mom says, keeping her eyes on the traffic.

But she can judge Jamie? And Will? I hit the armrest on the passenger-side door over and over with my fist.

"I think you two should do more together." She glances at me, then back to the road.

"Oh, so now you want me to drink, wear low-cut

shirts, flirt with every guy at school, and spend hours on the Internet?"

Mom slows for a red light. "No. Just invite Chelsea to do more wholesome things."

"I'm sure she'd love to help me clean the guest rooms." Hasn't Mom noticed? I go to school, I run, I do homework, I clean the inn, and I sleep. Very exciting options for Chelsea.

"Kate. I'm serious. You can be a witness for Christ."

You have to *believe* to be a witness for Christ, I think.

But as Mom glances my way, I see it in her eyes. The glow. She's thinking of her mansion in Heaven again. She's seeing Max and me and now the Riggs family all in it, sipping herbal tea and reading the Bible. I mean, what else will we do in Heaven, since there will be no one to convert? All those who didn't accept the true gospel will already be in Hell. Seriously, Heaven is beginning to sound really boring. I mean, I've read Exodus. And Leviticus. All the begats and other boring lists the Bible seems to think are so important. Total sleeping pills. But Mom gets up as early as Will every morning so she can read them and kneel on the cold floor forever, praying to her God. Then she wears ugly clothes all day every day and no makeup and never sees real movies or reads real books, all so she can have that stupid gold mansion in Heaven. And what if she dies and there's nothing? What if Dad's right? Maybe eat, drink, and be merry isn't all wrong. I mean, I like my life here, now. I like Aunt Katherine's house. I wouldn't trade it for a gold mansion, with its views of the ocean and scent of pine trees. Maybe Heaven is here. Maybe Heaven is now. My arms tingle at that thought, and a warm feeling floods over my shoulders like someone just put a wool cape around me. Heaven is here. Heaven is now. I like it.

"So what do you think, Kate? Can you try to be friends with Chelsea?

I shrug.

"I don't think those Penroses are a good influence on her. Michelle says they threw their money and power around to hire Pastor Browning, which Douglas Senior was totally against. She said she's forbidding Chelsea to hang around that Penrose boy."

Interesting. "But, Mom, Pastor Browning is writing Douglas a letter of recommendation for Harvard."

"Yes, but some of his values." She shakes her head. "I told Michelle that's what happens when you let the congregation decide who is to lead your church instead of letting God make the decision."

I bite my lip to keep from screaming out, You really think your church leaders don't do the choosing? You think God really tells them what to do? I've got news for you, Mom. I've spent hours on my knees, too, thank you very much, and I didn't hear a lot of things coming from Heaven. It was pretty quiet, to tell you the truth. And I was as sincere as I could be.

Mom takes her right hand off the steering wheel and pats my leg again. "I'm counting on you, Kate. You could be an influence for good to Chelsea."

"Mom. How can I—?"

Before I can finish, Mom interrupts. "Now, we need to stop by the store, we're out of orange juice." She glances down at her watch. "And I've got to hurry before the grocery store closes." She hits a bit harder on the gas pedal. "I just hope Douglas Riggs isn't parked behind some tree, waiting to catch me and accuse me of driving one mile over the speed limit!"

That's Mom. She's moved on. One minute she's some judgmental priss, glaring at Jamie's shirt, the next a missionary extraordinare for the Church of the Holy Divine, planning Chelsea's conversion to the only true church on earth. And only seconds later, she's the stunning-speed-limit-breaking hostess of the Whispering Woods Inn. Does she ask about the run that was my fastest time ever? No. Does she ask about sleeping in the hotel room with Jamie? No. Does she even care who Jamie is? No, because she isn't trying to convert Jamie's mom. Mom is like one of those gauzy designer dresses—everything shows if you look too closely.

chapter nineteen

I'M HEADING DOWN the stairs from the guest rooms with a huge bag of trash Sunday afternoon, when I hear someone knocking at the back door. Mom doesn't seem to be around, so I set the trash bag on the hallway floor, wipe my hands on my jeans, and open the door.

I freeze. Two young men in dark suits, starched white shirts, and very familiar name tags pinned to their lapels stand in our doorway. The tags are, and have been, ever since I can remember, black plastic rectangles. Across the top in white lettering is the word *Missionary*, and then the person's last name. And at the bottom in bolder white letters, *A Representative of the Church of the Holy Divine*.

Right there at the door a flash of memories rushes over me. How we used to have the church missionaries over to our house for dinner once a week. How Mom started baking in the morning for the young adult volunteers, who spent eighteen months away from their families and good home cooking. How our house filled with the aroma of yeasty breads, sweet fruit pies, and cheesy casseroles. Mom would fill up their stomachs and in return hoped they would influence Dad to join the church. I hoped so, too. I believed in them because they "were in the world but not of the world." At Mom's church they were looked up to, like the marines—the few, the proud, the brave. Only, instead of being commissioned by the United States government, they were, of course, commissioned by her God. They had been set apart by church leaders with a special prayer for their divine mission.

But the main reason I looked forward to their visits was that they livened up our normally quiet house. They spent most of their days going door to door, from neighborhood to neighborhood, trying to interest people in their message. They told us stories of dogs chasing them, of women answering doors with skimpy nightgowns on, and of ministers from other religions who'd invite them in and debate the Bible for hours. And then, of course, they'd have the occasional *perfect contact*, the person who had been waiting for their message and accepted it with a full heart. Mom would always lean over the table and pat their hands when they told those conversion stories. Her eyes would fill with tears of gratitude as she realized another soul had found God's truth.

After dinner we'd play Uno or the church's version of Monopoly, called Holy Divinopoly, where the properties were named after historically important places connected with the Holy Divine Church. I had to admit when I became a teenager, I had crushes on a few missionaries who served in our area, even as my perfect childlike faith began to fade and I had less hope that they were the miracle answers for converting Dad to the *truth*. So what if they didn't convince him to change his ways? They were cute and fun to be around.

Seeing missionaries here in Maine, though, standing at Aunt Katherine's house poised, straight, and tall, so confident in their knowledge that they were God's true representatives on earth, I want to rush past them out the door, running as fast and as far as I can. I'd left that world behind in Arizona and I didn't appreciate the sight of them bringing it all back to me. "Hello," one of them says while I stand there struck dumb.

"Kate?" Mom comes up behind me. "Oh, hello. Do come in."

I move aside like a zombie and watch as Mom shakes their hands and then introduces them to me. "Kate, this is Missionary Packer and Missionary Dunn. They've come to talk to Max, um, Mr. Harmony, and Mrs. Riggs about the church."

As they put out their hands for me to shake, I walk toward them like a programmed robot who has done this a thousand times before and accept each of their handshakes.

"Please feel free to join us for our lesson, Kate," Missionary Packer says, with his hand still holding mine. "We've got a message that will bring you the answers to all your spiritual questions."

"What?" His voice jars me back from my trance. "Oh. No. Thank you." I pull my hand from his strong grip. "I have homework I had better get to. Um, nice to meet you."

"I cannot be awake, for nothing looks to me as it did before. Or else I am awake for the first time, and all before has been a mean sleep."—Walt Whitman

Yup. A mean sleep was what I was in for the first fifteen years of my life.

Mom frowns as I disappear down the steps.

Mom is worse than frowning the next morning. The mood inside the inn is terrible, and the view outside isn't much better. Bare brown trees frown in at me from the frost-covered window of the kitchen this morning. Overnight the weather changed. All the cheery signs of autumn blew away with the wintry wind. The air looks bitingly cold. I assume from the chill in the air inside the kitchen that Max didn't decide to be baptized right away. And last night I overheard him telling Mom that he's leaving today for California on some big magazine assignment. Maybe those missionaries gave him the same desire to run away that they gave me.

I hear him coming down the stairs as I toast my bagel for breakfast. He drops his luggage in the hallway. Mom, who is stirring muffin batter for our two guests, leaves her bowl and meets him in the hallway. They hug. She holds on tight, and I can hear her sobs. The Holy Divine Church teaches youth not to kiss until they meet their chosen mate and even then the first kiss should be over the wedding altar. But with her arms around Max, I sense something in her tight grasp on him. A wanting I have sometimes when I'm around Will. Ever since he kissed me on the cheek, I've had a longing to be near him, to be touched. Go ahead. Kiss him, my head orders. You know you want to. Instead of telling her, though, I creep downstairs to my room, leaving them alone, and wonder if abstinence really is a virtue. I remember reading somewhere in the Bible that if a person lusted after another person, it was the same sin as doing the physical act. So since Mom clearly wants to kiss Max, shouldn't she at least get the satisfaction of doing it, if it counts against her anyway?

When I come back up, coat on, book bag over my shoulders, ready to head for the bus, Max's bags are gone. He's gone. I hear Mom in the kitchen, crying.

"Oh, Kate"—she turns to me as I enter the kitchen—"do you think Max will come back?"

Her eyes are wide and her voice sounds so much like

a timid five-year-old's, that it spooks me and brings out a pity for her I haven't felt in a long time.

I nod. "He's hooked, Mom. I don't think he can go two weeks without your blueberry muffins." And suddenly I hope I am right, because her pathetic sobbing for Max freaks me out just as much as her high-pitched, nose-pinching preaching does. Max did say he might come back in December to take pictures of the national park with snow. I hope he does.

chapter twenty

WILL HASN'T BEEN at school all week. I've checked in the junior locker area and at the library computers, where he sometimes goes during lunch. On Saturday I even walked to the dock, hoping to run into him. At lunch, Jamie, Douglas, and all the seniors at our table are so busy talking about college applications that they barely notice I'm around. And someone else has been missing from the cafeteria—Richard. I did see him in the computer-lab part of the library, though. He and Chelsea haven't been together at all since the curfew fiasco. Chelsea's dropped by to chat with me a couple of times. She doesn't even notice I'm mad at her. Or that Jamie is shooting angry bullets at her from her eyes for ruining our chances for the big sports competition. Today as I munch on my bagel, she's sipping her Diet Coke and talking nonstop about this guy named Andy.

"He graduated last year. He's studying marine biology! He's going to work for one of those big lobster companies in Portland when he graduates. He was home last weekend and took me out to a movie. College guys are so much more mature. I wouldn't be caught dead with a high-school boy. They are such babies!"

My eyes roll. What a different song she was singing a week ago—"Rich-ard" was chirping from her lips 24/7. But Mom must be right—Chelsea's forbidden to be around him.

Cross-country is officially over, so today I'm going to take a run after school and see if I can find Will. Minutes after the bus drops me off at the inn, I'm in sweats and running down Main Street. The air stings my cheeks and feels damp, like it might rain or even snow. No summer people. No weekenders. No kids playing on the sidewalks or the beach. It feels like a ghost town. I pull out the little note card from my pocket and start to memorize today's quote. I'm really getting a lot in my head—a place Mom can't steal them from.

"Not I—not anyone else, can travel that road for you, You must travel it for yourself."—Walt Whitman

I run to the dock and slow down to a walk. I spot Will's boat. The *Lucky Lady* is all tied up and empty. He's already done for the day. Of course. My hands are turning blue. I tug my sleeves down over them and run on through town, wondering where Will lives.

I turn and head down the street to the church. I love

running down this street on the edge of the ocean, with all its gated houses, tennis courts, turrets and gazebos. Though I've run down it dozens of times now, I still feel like I'm entering a fairy world. So much beauty. So much land. So much wealth. And in the midst of it sits the old stone church with its big red door. The church parking lot is empty except for one car. Mr. Riggs's patrol car. Why would he be at the church now? I think back to what Mom told me about Mr. Riggs not wanting to hire Pastor Browning. Why? Everyone likes Pastor Browning. What is it like at the Riggs home? Why does Mom's church sounds good to Mrs. Riggs? And what about Douglas and Chelsea? That time I rode with them they both acted like they were in the presence of a military leader or something.

Distant voices break through the *thud, thud, thud* of my feet hitting the pavement. I stop, and my feet freeze on the ground. I back up and attempt to slither into the shadow of the pine trees when I spot Richard with both hands in his pockets, slouching against the huge stone entrance of his family's estate. He's talking with Pastor Browning. I can't exactly make out the words, but Richard, Mr. Monosyllable, who never manages to say more than "Yes, Coach" or "No, Coach," except for when he told me about his fighter-jet computer game, is talking in whole sentences. Not just talking—words are rushing out of his mouth like they've been let loose after being dammed up for months. His face breaks into a grin at something Pastor Browning says. He chuckles, then laughs right out loud.

And just as I'm about to creep off through the trees and make my way back home along the shoreline, I step on a fallen branch. I cringe as it cracks loudly in the chilly afternoon air. Next I hear a familiar vo ice call out, "Kate? Kate is that you?"

I sigh. So much for blending in with the trees. I turn back toward them and lift my hand in a limp wave even though I'm dying inside.

Richard's happy face goes stiff. The smile is gone. Does he think I'm mad at him because he ruined our chances to win the trophy? Well, I am. I wish I'd never interviewed him or had that article printed. I was actually beginning to think he wasn't a total creep.

"Hi."

"What a trouper. Always running." Pastor Browning chuckles. And his laugh sounds jolly and happy like everyone here is best friends.

"It's in my blood, I guess."

"Well, good for you, Kate."

I kick at a small stone. How can I politely leave?

"You look horribly cold," Pastor Browning says, walking toward me.

"Nah, I'm fine." I try hard not to shiver and to act as warm as a freezing person can pretend to be.

"Here, take my coat," he says as he takes it off. "You

can return it some other time. I don't have far to go. I'm just walking down the road to the church."

"No, no, I couldn't. I'm fine."

"No, you aren't. You're shivering and almost blue. Now take it." Pastor Browning puts his huge coat around my shoulders.

So much for my acting ability. How do I get out of this one?

"Are you headed home?"

I nod.

"Well if you don't mind walking, instead of running, I'd enjoy the company."

I steal a glance at Richard, who is busy examining the bricks on his driveway. "Okay," I say, and slip my arms inside the coat. I have a hard time saying no to Pastor Browning for some reason, even though I'd love nothing more than just to run on home without his coat right now. It hangs several inches below the ends of my hands, but it is warm.

Pastor Browning waves to Richard as we leave. "Thanks for the early dinner. Tell your parents hello for me."

"Yeah," Richard mutters before he turns away from us.

Friendly, isn't he? I have an impulse to ask. But I don't say anything. Instead I fall into step with Pastor Browning, enjoying the comfort of his gray wool coat that smells musty and familiar, like the church.

"That coat has just about swallowed you up." He smiles

and meets my eyes straight on with all of his normal, care-free friendliness. What a nice guy. He's even friendly to Richard. I bet he feels sorry for him, since he's left up here alone so often. But Richard seems to feel comfortable around Pastor Browning. Everyone does. Even Jamie, who doesn't know if she believes in God, likes him.

"Did you know we're having a special service in a few weeks?"

"No."

"Just between you and me, a lot of high muckety-mucks are coming to check on me to see that I'm doing my job okay."

"You're doing a great job."

"Why, thank you, Kate. I wish I felt as confident. But, anyway, I decided we should have more youth participate in the service. That should keep people awake."

I cringe. Has he spotted me sleeping in service? It has happened more than once.

But he just talks on. "You know, a few special songs, a poem, scripture reading. And as luck would have it, I was talking to your aunt Katherine about it and she said you'd been in some big speech contest in Arizona. So what would you think about the chance to put your talents to use here in Puffin Cove?"

Talents? Don't you mean disaster? I stare ahead at the road, not wanting to meet his eyes. How does Aunt

Katherine know about my short-lived speech career? Dad? And how often does she talk to Pastor Browning?

"Um, well, actually, that contest didn't turn out so well. I forgot my scripture passage halfway through and had to go get my Bible." My already flushed cheeks burn at the memory.

"Oh, I'm sorry. Well, I would never try to make you feel uncomfortable."

"I know that." I look up at him and try to block out the horror of the speech contest. But I can still feel the sting, still hear the sound of Dad's voice, how he laughed at me for fasting. "You thought going without food and water for so long that you became light-headed would actually help you remember your speech better?"

Pastor Browning's voice breaks into my thoughts. "Well, if you feel up to it, you can volunteer at youth group next time. By the way, what was the passage?"

"First Corinthians chapter thirteen."

"Aha. The old 'seeing through a glass darkly' passage. We've discussed that before, I believe."

I nod.

"I remember something else we talked about that evening on the beach," Pastor Browning says, and then stops walking and looks me straight in the eyes. "Remember how you asked me if our church allowed people to be cremated?"

"Yes."

"Well, it's been on my mind. I just want you to know

that if you'd like to have a service for your father, I'd be honored to help you."

I feel a lump growing in my throat, and my eyes begin to sting. I do want to do something with Dad's ashes. Maybe it's too many years of church, but it seems wrong to keep them hidden in my closet. But then I'd have to tell Aunt Katherine we never even had a service. I'd have to tell her everything. How I snuck out on my bike and picked up his ashes. How things ended between Dad and me. How I wish I could rewrite that last day, get a second chance. Oh, how I wish I could at least pretend it all happened with a nicer ending. Since it had to end. Did end. Could I really do it? Tell her? I blink back the tears. "Thank you," I say.

We walk on in a comfortable silence for a while, and then Pastor Browning asks me about school and what I am reading. I end up telling him how much I like *To Kill a Mockingbird*, and even how Mom took away all Dad's books.

"What a shame. But there is the library. . . ." He winks.

"I know." I grin.

Pastor Browning's long, steady stride slows. I look up to see his eyes fixed on Mr. Riggs's patrol car in the church parking lot. He sighs, a deep sigh, the kind doctors want you to take before they put their stethoscope up to your chest. "Well, well. Looks like I've got company." He turns to me and takes my hand in his and pats it. "Good-bye, dear Kate."

When he lets go, I start to take off his coat. "No. No.

You keep it. Return it tonight at youth group or some other time. I've got two other winter coats. My mother thinks ministers should be well dressed. She gets me a new coat every Christmas whether I need one or not."

"Thank you. It's really warm. I'll bring it back tonight then."

Pastor Browning turns, and his shoulders slump more with each step he takes toward the church. It seems I'm not the only one hoping to avoid Chelsea's father. I always leave early for youth group now so I don't have to ride in that morgue of a car with Chelsea, Douglas, and him. Even Mom prays he's not parked in his famous speed trap when she's in a hurry to drive through town. And now Pastor Browning, who likes everyone and even makes Richard smile, does not seem one bit happy about this visitor.

On my way back home I spot Aunt Katherine. She's bundled up in a sky-blue fake-fur coat, with a knit hat, matching scarf, and mittens. With her short, curly white hair, she looks like a jolly elf. "Hello, love. Oh, I'm glad you're wearing a coat. Isn't it a little big for you, though?"

I wave my arms back and forth, flapping the inches of empty sleeve at the bottom. "Just a bit." I grin. "It's Pastor Browning's. I was out running and saw him. He insisted I borrow it." I pause, then confess, "I was pretty cold. And what about you, did you walk all the way here?"

"Yes. I'll have to stop when the roads and sidewalks

get icy, but until then, when I'm up to it, I do like to walk to town. I hate being totally dependent on others." Aunt Katherine sighs and pats my arm. "That was very nice of Pastor Browning to loan you his coat. He's such a thoughtful young man, isn't he?"

"Yes, he is."

"I had such a nice chat with him earlier today. Now, you come right into the drugstore with me and we'll see if we can get you a bit more warmed up. I was just heading in to buy a little get-well card for Mr. Lane."

"Will's grandfather? What's the matter with him?"

"Pneumonia. He's in the hospital in Ellsworth."

"Oh, how sad. So that's why Will hasn't been at school. He's probably doing all the lobstering himself."

"Yes, he is. Poor boy."

And as I follow Aunt Katherine to the card section, a plan forms in my head. A plan that will help Will and also allow me to see more of him.

chapter twenty-one

AT YOUTH GROUP Chelsea stands in front of the window, gazing outside like there's something so interesting she can't keep her eyes off it. Which might make sense if it weren't pitch-dark. But who does she have to talk to? I'm sitting by Jamie, who glares at Chelsea every time she sees her. When Pastor Browning enters, he spots Chelsea and joins her at the window. "Pretty dark out there, isn't it?"

She nods.

"Come sit with me." He pats her hand.

After they're seated, he greets the rest of us. "Some special church leaders are coming to visit our congregation in a few weeks. I'm hoping the youth group can help present the service. It would be great if we had a few younger faces to do a couple of scripture readings, maybe a song. Or maybe even one of you could read a poem? Any suggestions?"

Silence.

Pastor Browning chuckles. "I keep forgetting how *eager* you all are to participate. Chelsea, your brother tells me you spend quite a lot of time on the computer. Would you mind designing the program?"

Chelsea blushes. I happen to know she does spend a lot of time on the computer, but it isn't doing things like designing church programs. "Sure," she says.

"Okay. Great. How about it, anyone willing to read a poem or scripture?"

After a long pause, Douglas, who now stays long enough to hear the announcements and Chelsea's scripture reading before he heads for the computer says, "Oh, why not? I will."

That's nice of him. And very nice that he stays to hear Chelsea's scripture. He seems like a nice brother, considering whom he has to put up with.

Then Pastor Browning convinces the two juniors who are friends to sing a duet.

Pastor Browning glances at me. But I shake my head no.

He nods. "On to our next topic. The big youth weekend retreat in Bangor on December ninth."

That's my birthday. My ears perk up.

"We're going to have a panel discussion on dating, and even a local film director giving a lecture on current teen movies, and, of course, a big dance."

"Can we invite guests?" Chelsea asks.

"Of course. And there will be youth groups from all over the Northeast attending. A great opportunity to meet new people."

I'm thinking of Will. Could I get him to come? Dance with me on my birthday? Maybe talk Mom into letting me go to the mall and get a new outfit? I'm daydreaming away when Chelsea stands to give her scripture reading.

Then Pastor Browning starts our lesson. "Tonight I'm going to talk about a man named Saul. Anyone heard of him?"

I have, of course. But I stay quiet.

"Well, Saul was a man in the New Testament who persecuted Jesus Christ . . ."

As Pastor Browning talks on about how Saul later regretted what he had done and changed his name to Paul and brought the Christian faith to Rome, I can almost see Saul/Paul, almost feel his regrets. Pastor Browning, seems to make written words come to life.

"Now let's talk about a modern-day Saul. Have any of you heard of Malcolm X?"

Jamie nods.

"Jamie, can you tell us about him?"

"Malcolm X was a young black man who sold drugs. I guess you could say he was basically into the crime scene."

Chelsea raises her hand.

"Yes, Chelsea?"

"Do you think we should really be talking about someone not in the Bible at church? I mean, a drug dealer?"

Jamie rolls her eyes.

And I really want to know who Malcolm X is now.

"I think it will be okay," Pastor Browning says. "Go on, Jamie."

Jamie sighs. "Malcolm X went to prison to pay for his crimes. And while he was there, he began reading and *educating* himself." She emphasizes the word *educating* and glares right at Chelsea.

"That's right." Pastor Browning nods.

Jamie continues, "And I think it was with the influence of his siblings that he discovered religion. Eventually he changed his name. He swore off his old life and became a strong advocate for black people during the Civil Rights Movement."

"Yes. Thank you, Jamie," Pastor Browning says. "Both of these men did things early in their lives for which they were later ashamed. I guess the moral to their stories is that people can change and that everyone deserves a second chance." He glances at Chelsea and his eyes grow wide and sad. She's rummaging through her purse. Pastor Browning smiles. "Both of these men went on to be strong leaders and important men of history."

After the lesson, we gather in Pastor Browning's office

for sodas and cookies one of the juniors brought. Douglas joins us. Richard never showed up, so if his dad really forces him to attend in order to have driving privileges, it looks like Richard may be doing some serious walking this week. Chelsea's standing all alone again, up against a shelf filled with plants. I catch my breath. On the top row, between a fern and a ceramic pot of African violets, is a huge, healthy Christmas cactus. The stems hang down around the other plants. It's so alive. So green.

Pastor Browning's words haunt me. "Everyone deserves a second chance." Dad didn't get a second chance. One massive heart attack stole him away from me. I didn't get a second chance with my Christmas cactus. I neglected it and it died. Sometimes there are no second chances. But Pastor Browning meant Chelsea. I know that. And really, she doesn't seem so awful, standing alone and quiet, with nothing to say or at least no one to say it to. And it hits me that maybe Chelsea and I aren't so different. She obviously is scared of her dad. And hides things from him, like the way she dresses. Not that I'm scared of Mom, but I do hide things and I don't exactly want to do what she wants me to do. If Pastor Browning can be nice, I guess I can try, too. Besides, I need someone to help me with my plan, and I have a feeling the way Chelsea's been talking about Andy, her new love, she just might agree.

I walk up to her. "Um, Chelsea?"

"What?"

"Did you know Will's grandfather is sick and now Will's doing all the lobstering alone, and it takes him so long he's missing school?"

"No." Her eyes look dull, bored.

"Well, I was wondering if you'd like to go with me tomorrow and help him on the boat, so maybe he'd be done in time for school?"

"You mean get up at dawn and get all wet and dirty and have to touch dead fish?" She scrunches up her little freckled nose.

"Yep."

"No, thanks!"

"Oh, I just thought, you know, Andy might be impressed if you knew more about his career," I say like it's any old sentence—not like the bait I hope it is.

Chelsea's eyes light up. Her forehead wrinkles in thought. "Hmm. Interesting, Kate."

I wait. Patient and quiet, like any good fisherwoman.

Seconds later, "Sure, why not? Besides, I haven't studied for tomorrow's biology test yet, and if we go, I won't have to take it."

"So, you'll meet me at the dock at five?"

Chelsea yawns. "Five a.m.?"

I nod.

"Okay."

"Good. See you tomorrow."

At four thirty a.m., I yawn as I shut off my alarm. I throw on warm clothes, grab my rain slicker, and head upstairs in the dark. Mom is actually letting me go. I told her since Chelsea and I both have study hall first period, we really won't be missing anything important. Aunt Katherine was there, and she confirmed that Will's grandfather really was sick and it was keeping Will out of school. "As long as Chelsea is along, I guess it will be all right." She even smiles at me, like she thinks I'm taking her up on her suggestion to be better friends with Chelsea. She probably envisions us all in white robes singing in some Heavenly choir.

I jog down Main Street under the streetlights. When I'm almost to the dock, I hear someone behind me call, "Wait up, Kate." It's Chelsea. She's running, too. I can't believe she actually got up. She's yawning, isn't wearing any makeup, and from the looks of her hair, she didn't even take the time to run a brush through it.

The dock is busy, full of lobster workers. We make our way through, searching for Will. Chelsea spots him first. "Will," she calls out. He turns. The overhead lights shine on his puzzled face.

"What are you two doing here?"

"We've come to help," I say, and try to act normal, like

my heart isn't dancing, like I haven't been spending every moment of the past several days hoping and waiting and wishing to look into Will's happy, friendly eyes again.

"Help?"

"Well, we want to try," I say. "We can measure the lobsters and bait the traps."

Will shakes his head. "Right, I can just see you two picking up lobsters with your bare hands."

"Please let us try?" I beg as Chelsea stands mute beside me.

"Suit yourself," he says as he hefts buckets of bait onto the boat.

"How is your grandpa?" I ask as we follow him in.

"About the same."

"Oh. I'm sorry, Will."

"Yeah."

"Me, too." Chelsea yawns.

It's still pretty dark as we head out. "You can really make a great living if you work hard trapping lobster," Chelsea shouts as Will pulls the boat close to one of his buoys. The icy air seems to have awakened the normal chatty Chelsea.

Will uses the pulley to lift the trap. When he pulls out a live lobster, all brown and very alive, its claws moving in attack mode, Chelsea screams.

"See?" Will says.

"I'll help you with the lobsters and Chelsea can bait the traps," I offer.

"You're stubborn, Kate. Anyone ever told you that?"

"No." But I love that he thinks I am. I love him noticing anything about me. As I pull a lobster out of the trap, I want to scream, too.

"Fish, I love you and respect you very much. But I will kill you dead before the day ends." The Old Man and the Sea—*Ernest Hemingway.*

I bite down hard on my lip and try my best to copy whatever I see Will do with the lobster he picked up. I check to make sure it's not a notched female. Then Will hands me a ruler to measure it. Determined not to be clawed, I hold it carefully away from me. "A keeper," I say, trying to sound brave. Next I have to rubber-band the claws. When I'm done, Will whistles. "Well, I never knew you had it in you. I'm going to change your name from City Girl to Lobster Girl."

I beam. Our eyes meet and it's like we're having our own secret telepathic conversation right in front of Chelsea.

While Will drives to the next batch of buoys, I show Chelsea how to fill up the bait bags.

"Eeew," she says, scrunching up her nose as I pick up a handful of the sardines and put them in the net bag.

I, too, have to make an effort not to gag at the strong smell and the slimy, slippery feel of them in my hand. I find a pair of rubber gloves and hand them to her.

She nods and puts them on.

"Maybe you could close your eyes when you pick them up," I suggest.

"Good idea."

As we work, she goes on and on about Andy. "Did I tell you he's studying marine biology?"

"Yes." Only every day.

"He says he's going to stay and work in Portland after he graduates. He says it's way better than living out here. There's tons to do, clubs, shopping, movie theaters, good restaurants—everything. I'm probably going down there this weekend. Someone at school said they might be able to give me a ride. Now I just have to convince my dad."

Chelsea and I fall into a pattern. I'm surprised she is sticking with this. I hope we might really be helping.

After a few hours, Will turns to us, keeping his hands on the pulley. "So is this a plot to get me back to school?" The attached trap begins to fall toward the water. "Or am I the Keyette Club's service project of the month?"

"The first," I say, meeting his eyes again and feeling my insides flutter like I somehow swallowed a butterfly. Trying to act nonchalant, I add, "But now that you mention it, maybe Chelsea and I could count this as community service. I'm still working on my ten hours."

As the trap disappears into the dark water, I ask, "So, is it working?"

"The pulley?"

"No, our plot."

He grins. "Oh, I don't think school is for me."

"Why not?"

He sighs.

"What does your mom think?" I ask, remembering how Mr. Lane had used his mother to get Will to go to school with me that first time I'd been on the boat.

"Uh, she wants me to go to school."

I nod. "So?"

Will looks at his watch and I do, too. It's almost nine a.m. He looks out at the ocean. He seems to be calculating how much work we've done. "Okay," he says, "I'll go. I can just work extra long Saturday and Sunday."

Chelsea says, "Don't worry, I'll stay out with you so you won't have to work longer on the weekend. I don't mind missing school."

Will chuckles. "I bet you don't."

"It's just that I have this stupid biology test."

Will shakes his head. "And I thought you had my best interest at heart."

"Oh, I do, Will. But couldn't we work hard today and all go to school tomorrow?"

"Let's go today," I say, "before he changes his mind."

"Fine. If I fail this test, I'll blame you two." She sticks out her lower lip in a pout.

Will rolls his eyes and whistles as he heads to the cabin

to pilot us back to shore. We stand in the cabin with him and chat about school.

Chelsea mentions trying to get to Portland this weekend. "My dad is so involved in those stupid local elections that he'll be so preoccupied I can slip away without many questions."

Jamie has told me all about the elections. Aunt Katherine reads the local paper every week and has made her decisions already on how she's going to vote on every issue. But Will's only comment is, "Elections? Shit. That means the pool hall will be turned into a voting place again. Didn't they just have elections last year?"

At the dock he drops us off and says he'll see us at lunch.

"But don't you need help taking the lobster in?" I ask.

"I can get them; I don't have class until eleven. Don't want Chelsea to miss biology."

chapter twenty-two

INSTEAD OF CHELSEA at the dock the next morning, I see Douglas. "Chelsea has a cold," he says when I reach him. "So I'm going to help." He has both hands stuffed in the pockets of his army-green coat. Even while he's standing his left leg jiggles back and forth. Is he cold? Nervous? Why is he here? This has nothing to do with Latin. He can't use this morning as volunteer work on his college applications, can he? Douglas never even talks to Will. Mom isn't exactly thrilled about me missing English today, and given Douglas's focus on grades, I can't imagine him wanting to miss a single class.

As if reading my thoughts, he says, "It's a decent thing of you to do, Kate. Helping Will. You shouldn't have to do it alone."

Wow. I'm blown away by his words. My cheeks turn warm.

Will's even more surprised than I am when he sees Douglas. "Hey, you guys don't have to take me on as a charity case."

"We know," I say, patting him on the shoulder. "You were doing absolutely fine without us. Think of this as a tiny gift to your mom. So she can have her wish come true and you will graduate from high school. And besides, now your grandpa won't have to worry so much, and it'll probably speed up his recovery."

"Hey"—Will shakes his head—"I can't just let you work for nothing. I'll have to pay you."

"Okay. Fine. How about if you pay us by giving each of us one lobster?" I suggest. "If we had to pay for one at a restaurant, that would be way above minimum wage."

Will sighs. "Okay. Okay."

Douglas and Will look at each other in awkward silence. But the three of us set in to work, and go at it hard all morning. Douglas hauls the trap up after Will pulls up to the buoy. I keep busy filling bait bags, while Will shows Douglas the difference between keepers and ones you have to throw back. Skinny, no muscle, Douglas is stronger than he looks. He lifts the trap off the pulley almost as easily as Will does. I've tried lifting it and it's heavy. I hate it that Will and he can lift it so easily and I can't. I make a goal on the spot to start working out in the weight room after school.

As always when I'm out on Will's boat, the time flies by. Sooner than I want, Will is pulling up to the dock. I wave to Will as I climb out of the boat with Douglas. Will has forgotten about giving us the lobster, which is just as well. I have a feeling he needs every lobster he can catch to pay the bills at home. "See you at lunch," I holler.

"Right," Will yells back. "How would I dare to miss school now? Have you ever considered a life in blackmail, Lobster Girl?"

I might, if it means I get to be with you every day and you'll call me Lobster Girl. I grin like a plotting schemer.

Douglas clears his throat. "Would you like a ride to school, Kate?"

"Oh, thanks, that would be great," I say.

As we drive, Douglas says, "We can't keep this up for long. It could take a few weeks for Will's grandfather to be well enough to help again."

I nod. "But we can't just let him drop out, can we?"

"Let's ask the youth group to help," Douglas suggests. "I'm sure Pastor Browning will think it's a great idea."

"Okay," I say, surprised by his interest. But then as I think about it, a youth group service project could go on his college résumé.

"Um . . . also, Kate?"

"Yes?"

"Well, Pastor Browning said you might have an idea about a good scripture selection I could read for that church service."

I smile. Tricky Pastor Browning. He's going to get me involved one way or the other. "Well, I happen to like First Corinthians chapter thirteen a lot."

"Great. Thanks. I mean I know I help out at church and I work on the Latin Bible, but honestly, I don't know much about the actual Bible. I've kind of tuned out church most of my life."

I'm about to ask why he helps out at church, but I think I know. His dad. "I've tuned a lot out, too." I giggle. "But I like Pastor Browning."

"Yeah, he's great, isn't he?"

At lunch, Douglas, who still has on his same clothes and smells like he spent the morning on a lobster boat, shares his plan with Jamie.

"Help kill lobster?" Jamie scrunches her nose.

"We wouldn't want you to do anything against your precious principles," Douglas retorts. Jamie's wearing her *Shoot the breeze, not Bambi* T-shirt today.

Jamie's eyebrows arch at Douglas like she's trying to read his mind, like she, too, wonders what's in it for him. She turns to me, puzzled.

I shrug and try to make my eyes say, I know, I can't figure out why he is so persistent about this, either. "It is killing animals," I agree. "But Will is going to have to drop out of school otherwise." I know how important it is to Jamie for people to get an education and hope my argument will persuade her.

She doesn't answer but looks past us out the window to the bare trees and the gray sky. Finally, she looks back at the table and us. "Okay. I'll help." She sighs, like she's just been asked to sacrifice her only child to save the world.

That night Douglas calls Pastor Browning and then calls all of us with our assigned days to help Will. Pastor Browning is going to help in the mornings, too. At lunch the new topic is lobsters.

Douglas points out three rather deep gashes on his left hand. "The thing just grabbed on to me and I couldn't get it off. Fortunately Will and his pliers took care of it. It was nearly five inches. Biggest catch of the day." Douglas sits up straighter, pushing out his chest in mock pride. Becoming an apprentice lobster worker seems to have given him something besides Latin and college to talk about.

"Wow, you could have really hurt yourself." Jamie traces her finger over his fresh wounds in pretend sympathy.

Douglas smiles. "Oh, it's not so bad. You'll see."

Jamie's eyes turn serious. "That's right. I will," she murmurs, like she regrets agreeing to help.

Will strides up to our table and takes a seat. His lunch tray is loaded with fries, a huge hamburger, and a large Coke. "That pastor dude knows a lot about lobstering."

"I think he knows a lot about everything," Douglas says with admiration.

I sit back and listen as Douglas and Will talk about traps, pulleys, and boats. Who would have thought these two could talk together about anything? Who would have thought Will would be sitting at our table. I glance across the room and see Candy eating with her girlfriends and smile.

On my next assigned day to help on the boat, it's icy cold. Even with long johns and several layers under my heavy rain slicker, I feel chilled to the bone. But I've grown to love the fishy smell and every creak and crack of Will's old boat. This is Jamie's first time and I said I'd come with her. I'd go out every morning if Mom would let me. And we've had good news. Will's grandfather came home yesterday. He's too weak to come out on the boat, but Pastor Browning says if we can hang on for a few more weeks, most of the lobsters will have gone too deep to catch, and the lobstering in general pretty much dies down until after the new year.

This morning, Pastor Browning, Jamie, and I fill bait bags while Will drives from buoy to buoy. Jamie closes her eyes after one look at the dead fish eyes. She swallows hard, turns her head, puts her hand in the bait bucket, and doesn't say a word.

I don't know if any of the rest of us are really helping Will, but I know Pastor Browning is. He doesn't have to ask Will a single question. I'm surprised at how many more traps we're able to get to in the same amount of time.

Besides, unlike us, he doesn't have to hurry off to school. He and Will can drop us off at the dock and then go out for two more hours to do the other side of the waterfront before Will's eleven o'clock class. He and Will could probably do it all and maybe even do it better without the rest of us "helping out." But I think Pastor Browning likes us working with him; he likes watching his little flock perform service as a group.

After a while Jamie heads into the cabin. I hear her yelling to be heard above the roar of the engine. "How much gas does this thing guzzle?" Poor Will.

"So how is *To Kill a Mockingbird*? Have you finished it yet?" Pastor Browning asks.

"I did."

"And?"

"And I think Harper Lee was very brave."

"Really? Why?"

How do I explain? How do I say in words how I felt when I finished the book? How I thought about last year, sitting in my room alone, no longer feeling I belonged with the community of believers that I had been raised with. "Because she was from the South," I answer Pastor Browning, "and even though she was white, she exposed the prejudice all around her. It's hard to see things that most people in your community can't see. It must have been lonely for her."

"It sounds like you're making that observation from personal experience." Pastor Browning raises his eyebrow and looks straight into my eyes.

I shrug my shoulders and toss another bait bag into the bucket. "Maybe. I wonder what all the people from her real hometown thought of her when the book was published."

Pastor Browning nods. "Yes, that did take courage. It's hard to imagine all the hate of that time period, isn't it, Kate?"

I nod, but I think of how Mom and her church hate homosexuals and think Jews and Muslims and all non-members are on their way to Hell. Maybe things really haven't changed that much.

The water is choppy now, and the sky is wild and gray. Will drops the trap I've just baited back into the water. His eyes catch mine. He smiles at me.

Everything melts. I don't feel cold anymore, or sad. I watch him as he heads back to the cabin to show Jamie more about the engine or something. It isn't as if we've gone out together, or even spent any real time alone. But from time to time we catch each other's eye at the lunch table or here on the boat, and when our eyes lock, my in-sides get all squirmy and warm and I feel like I could live on that feeling for hours.

The boat sways back and forth. As it begins to speed through the rough ocean, water sprays my face. I hold on to the side of the boat to keep from slipping on the watery deck and steal a glimpse at Pastor Browning. He's examining the stormy clouds like he sees more than just the angry mists of black and gray.

Suddenly, two dolphins pop up. They swim right alongside the boat. They dive down deep and then explode out of the water, nodding their heads at us, almost like they are waving.

I laugh and clap.

Pastor Browning chuckles. "They make life look so easy, don't they?"

"Yes."

Once, when Dad and Mom were having a rare talk about the taboo subject of religion, Dad said to her, "I'll admit I have moments I can't explain. Times when I am so moved by the world that my heart is full of awe. But that doesn't mean I have to call that feeling God." Whatever this is, whether it's God or awe, I like it out here. Everything seems simple. Jamie probably encouraging Will to alter his engine to use French-fry oil. Pastor Browning smiling at the gray clouds. The dolphins as they dive and swim.

As the boat stops, I smile, watching Jamie and Will join Pastor Browning at the pulley.

"'There ain't no sin and there ain't no virtue. There's just stuff people do. It's all part of the same thing.' . . . I says,

'It's love. I love people so much I'm fit to bust.'" The Grapes of Wrath —*John Steinbeck.*

It's hard to believe, but even Mom is proud of us. At the kitchen table tonight, eating with Aunt Katherine, she says, "It's you who brought all of your friends together, Kate."

Aunt Katherine smiles at me. "I know Will's mother is very thankful that he's in school."

I'm surprised at Mom. Can she really see that I don't have to go to her church to do something good? Max isn't even around to remind her to not be so strict with me, and she still seems okay. If this feeling could last forever, I'd be so happy.

Mom clears her throat. "Kate." She pauses. "I—that is, *we're* having a special choral group from out west provide the music for us at Sunday service this week. Would you like to come?"

I drop my fork, and it makes a big clink as it hits my plate. Although we haven't shut down the inn officially, since November first we've only had two guests, so Mom has been going to church on Sundays for the past few weeks. But this Sunday, Douglas is going to read 1 Corinthians 13 for the bigwig visitors. I feel like I should be there to support him. "Um, Douglas is doing a special reading at Aunt Katherine's church this Sunday," I say, grabbing for my dropped fork. "And I promised him I'd be there."

I stare at the prongs of my fork, avoiding Mom's eyes. I feel guilty calling it Aunt Katherine's church instead of Pastor Browning's church or even my church. But I know Mom's not going to argue about me attending with Aunt Katherine sitting at the table.

When I meet her glance, her eyes are sad. It's become so quiet I'm aware of the chewing sounds I'm making as I eat my salad. I close my lips tighter, trying to muffle it.

"We've really got to think about how we want to decorate the inn for Christmas, don't we, Rebekah?" Aunt Katherine pipes up in her cheeriest voice.

Mom turns to her. "Yes."

"Do you think we should have a big tree in the front parlor, or would it look better in the foyer?"

Soon Mom is deep in discussion. Aunt Katherine's eyes flicker and meet mine for just a second. I swear she is winking. How can she always be so jolly?

chapter twenty-three

AUNT KATHERINE DECIDES it's too cold for us to walk to church, and Mom has already left for hers. "We'll just drive my car."

I have never seen Aunt Katherine drive before. In the garage I head toward the passenger side of her big, old Lincoln, but she hands me the keys. "Why don't you drive us, Kate?"

"What?" I protest. "I don't know how to drive. I can't do this!"

"Well, then, it's a good thing the snows haven't started."

"But I don't even have my learner's permit yet. What if Mr. Riggs sees me?"

"With all those big, important out-of-town visitors at church today? You think Douglas is going to be out on the street checking for underage drivers? No, no, love. I'm sure he's already inside the church doing a lot of hand shaking." She winks at me.

So I get in and put the key in the ignition. Dad did let

me drive a few times in the church parking lot in Arizona when it was empty. "I knew this church property
would come in handy for something!" he said. But driving straight forward in an empty, flat parking lot didn't
prepare me for backing out of Aunt Katherine's garage.
It takes me nearly five minutes of inching forward and
backward to make it out onto the driveway. I'm lucky
it's a big garage. Now I have to face the steep drive and
am grateful that Aunt Katherine has so much patience.
Forward is easier, but I slam on the brakes three times
while we're going down the hill, I'm so afraid I'll drive
right into the highway. Aunt Katherine giggles like she's
my teenage friend instead of my great-aunt.

We have to turn two corners to get to the church. The
first time I turn, I end up on the sidewalk. But Aunt Katherine sits calmly like she's being driven by a professional
limo driver.

When we get to the chapel, I'm surprised to see it's
already almost full. Two unfamiliar men are greeting
everyone at the door. "Bigwig visitors," Aunt Katherine
whispers to me. But her whisper is so loud I'm sure both
men hear her. They frown at us. I take Aunt Katherine by
the arm and walk up toward the front to our regular pew,
which, thankfully, still has two empty seats. The whole
church smells like a florist shop. And no wonder. Baskets
of lilies, vases of roses, stands of carnations and gladiolas

overload both sides of the pulpit. It looks like a funeral. I'm about to sit down when Mr. Riggs, dressed in a very nice suit, taps me on the shoulder. "I'm sorry, these seats are reserved for our guests."

"Oh," Aunt Katherine says cheerfully. "Hello, Douglas. Don't you look nice?"

"Hello, Mrs. Stone." Mr. Riggs looks so formal, like a wax model of himself.

"New suit?" she asks.

"Fairly new," he murmurs.

"What's that?" Aunt Katherine cups her hand around her ear.

"Yes." He speaks louder, looking uncomfortable.

Aunt Katherine leans toward him, like she's going to ask about Michelle and the kids. But I can tell he wants us to be gone and wants Aunt Katherine to keep her loud whispers to herself.

I tug at Aunt Katherine. "Come on." I pull her away before she can say anything else, scanning the room for a place to sit. Richard and his parents are sitting in their regular pew right across from ours. Apparently they're on the VIP list. One of the big-shot visitors stops at their row to say hello. Mrs. Penrose stands and kisses the well-dressed man on both cheeks like she's French or something. Like Mr. Penrose, he also smells strongly of cologne. They chat and she laughs about something.

"Her voice is full of money." The Great Gatsby —*F. Scott Fitzgerald.*

I bite my lip and guide Aunt Katherine toward the back, but every seat is taken.

Aunt Katherine pats me. "Let's just stand at the back to hear Douglas recite."

"But you won't be able to hear back here."

"It's okay, love. For the most part, I don't mind it that I can't hear. I like watching the people. I find it much more interesting, and this is a perfect spot."

But I want her to hear Douglas. I want him to see us there, smiling up at him.

Mr. Riggs leads the two men who were greeting people at the door to our pew, and they sit in our places. I want to scream.

An older gentleman comes up to us and sets up a folding chair. He leads Aunt Katherine to it. "Why, thank you, William." She smiles at him.

"I'm sorry I can't find another chair for you, miss."

"That's okay. I'm fine," I say.

The choir stands now and begins singing the opening hymn.

I'm so upset. I want to ask why the VIPs, who can obviously hear fine, deserve to sit up front? What about the hearing impaired? Aren't they important, too?

I scan through the program Chelsea designed. It is pretty. She has a cornucopia on the front and a border of autumn leaves around the edges. Douglas's name is near the beginning. Good. But his reading selection is the Beatitudes, from the New Testament. I'm shocked. Why isn't he reading 1 Corinthians 13? He told me he thought it was one of the better parts of the Bible he'd read.

Pastor Browning stands at the podium. "Welcome." His voice sounds stiff, lacking his normal conversational ring. His brow is wrinkled, like his white collar is on too tight. Weighted down with responsibility, worry, or nerves, I'm not sure which. He reads through the announcements, including another reminder to the youth and their parents that the Bangor retreat weekend is coming up on December 9. My birthday.

As the congregation begins the opening song, Aunt Katherine joins in, and as usual, she makes up about half of the words. Douglas is next. "Blessed are the poor in spirit: for theirs is the kingdom of Heaven. Blessed are they that mourn: for they shall be comforted." His voice is strong and clear. The reading is fine. But it isn't about seeing through a glass darkly. I bite my lip hard. "Let's go," I say to Aunt Katherine. "I want to go home."

I don't know what I thought would happen if Douglas had read 1 Corinthians 13. Did I hope it would erase that embarrassing day in my life? Or something even more? Did I hope it would somehow have changed Dad's reaction? Make everything all better? Pretend I had given my piece perfectly from memory, pretend Dad was proud of me, pretend he never laughed? Pretend that our last night together hadn't gone how it really had?

When we get home, Aunt Katherine says she needs a nap. My driving on the way home didn't improve much. Maybe I wore her out. But I try to lose myself as I dust, clean, and vacuum the main floor and my bedroom. I sweep every ash out of the fireplace in the parlor we've started sitting around at nights, now that we rarely have guests. But still the heaviness in my heart weighs me down. So, in the evening, when Mom leaves for a church Bible study in Ellsworth, I nestle up on my bed and reread parts of *To Kill a Mockingbird*. I sigh, put it on my nightstand, and then thumb through the brown leather scrapbook Aunt Katherine kept on Dad, hoping to find comfort. I haven't looked beyond the place where Aunt Katherine and I stopped. I was afraid of the pain and tears it might bring.

After the page with the wedding picture, there are photos of Dad and me, all pictures taken by Mom and mailed by Mom. She even sent Aunt Katherine some of my early drawings and pictures I'd colored. Aunt Katherine pasted them in the album. Blue skies, red flowers, green grass, and a big happy smile on my yellow sunshine. Everything was easy back then. Color inside the lines, follow the rules, say your prayers, go to church, and you're a good girl.

I still want to be that good girl. I swallow hard and flip through more pages. Why doesn't it surprise me that there are no pictures of me after age ten? Mom and Dad were divorced. Mom must have given up on trying to keep in touch with Dad's side of the family. That's why I am surprised we ended up here with Aunt Katherine. She must have really been persuasive or offered Mom a lot of money. When I asked Mom about it, she just said, "I think it's time for us to have a change." Why? Did Dad's death bother Mom more than she let on? Had she had a fight with Aunt Deborah? Weren't things going well at her work? I never asked. We hardly spoke then.

I turn to the next page and see copies of my class pictures from the last few years, pictures that Dad must have sent. He even sent her a copy of an essay that I got an A-plus on. She's centered the lined loose-leaf paper page and pasted it carefully on the heavy scrapbook paper. *Why I Like to Run.* I had no idea Dad was sending her things. I turn the page and find a familiar program, one I would like to forget about. *The Church of the Holy Divine's Annual Youth Speech Festival*, the title reads. So that's how Aunt Katherine knew I had participated in a speech program. Dad had to have sent it that last week, the last week of his life.

I open the program and find my name and my selection, 1 Corinthians 13. And it all floods back. Everything.

It was a Thursday night, my regular evening to spend with Dad, and right after I arrived, he asked how my speech had gone. I told him how I had frozen midway through the chapter. I'd actually picked that chapter hoping Dad would come. He said once he'd always liked it. But he didn't come. I told him how I had to walk to my seat, get my Bible, return to the podium, and finish reading the piece.

"That's too bad," he said. "And one of the few fine passages of scripture."

"I can't understand it. I said it perfectly yesterday at home. And today, I fasted and everything. I guess I just don't have enough faith."

I can still hear his laugh. That deep chuckle of his. He was amused. I'd been humiliated in front of an entire auditorium and his response was to laugh? "Kate, Kate," he'd said between chuckles. "Don't you realize that going without food and water probably made you light-headed? Your fasting was probably the very thing that kept you from reciting well."

"No, I don't see it!" I wouldn't speak to him the rest of the night. I did my homework, but every time I tried to work on algebra equations, my head kept echoing Dad's words. *"Your fasting was probably the very thing that kept you from reciting well."* I think I was mad at him because part of me knew he was right. It was then, that night, that I began to doubt fasting and all the other things I had been taught. But instead of agreeing with Dad, I resented him for mocking me. But I know now it was more than that—I resented him for not stopping

Mom from teaching me about fasting in the first place.

When he dropped me off at Mom's later that night, he chuckled again. "So, you're starting this sulking thing, like your mom, eh? Well, maybe in a few days your steam will wear down and you'll get off your high horse and consider talking to your old, unbelieving dad again." I opened the car door. Did I say good-bye? No. I slammed the door and stomped up to our house. Without turning back. Without a single wave. Without anything.

When Sunday morning came, instead of skipping breakfast like I had done for years and fasting that Dad would accept the true Gospel, I ate a bowl of Cheerios and had a big glass of apple juice. I'd show him. Fine. If he thought fasting was stupid, why should I go to church with my stomach growling? When we stopped by his place after church to drop me off, the door to his apartment was locked and no one answered. I climbed through the back window and let Mom in and we found him. Dead. In his chair with two books open on his lap. I vomited up the Cheerios and apple juice. I haven't touched either since.

The doctors said Dad had a heart attack, which is rare for someone of his age and for someone in such good shape. He ran every day of the week. But Dad's father died young of a heart attack. And Aunt Katherine takes heart medication. So bad hearts kind of run in the family.

For a long time, despite my new doubts about the

power of fasting, part of me believed Dad died because I didn't fast. But now it seems that if I fasted for years and Dad never had a change of heart, and I fasted to run better and fainted instead, and fasted to remember 1 Corinthians 13 and then forgot it, maybe fasting doesn't really work. And besides, now fasting seems wrong, sort of like trying to manipulate the natural flow of things. It's like assuming God is this big, powerful being in the sky controlling every little thing that happens on earth, like God has a big chess-board and if you have faith, pray, and fast long enough, then God will move the pieces in your favor. Do I really want to believe in a being who is that manipulative, who plays favorites? Then that God becomes no better than Mr. Riggs saving a bench for his special visitors. I don't like the idea of a God like that, a God who saves some people from hurricanes and bombs and holocausts but lets others die without a chance or a clear reason. Why does anyone want to believe in that kind of God?

My dad never did.

If only I'd said good-bye. If only I'd waved. New tears stream down my face. Then my fists clench. But I was the child. I'm still the child. Damn it. Damn it! Didn't Dad have some responsibility, too? Didn't he have a moral ob-ligation to keep me from believing what he knew was not true? "Didn't you, Dad?" I shout toward the closet where his ashes are hidden. "You could have stopped her. You could have. You could have told me she was wrong. But no, instead you always answered, 'It's up to your mother,' when I came complaining to you."

I swing open the closet door and dig through my box of old clothes. I pick up the urn of ashes. The ashes I've never opened. I shake them. How could you sit by all those years and let her brainwash me? I could have had a normal life, like Jamie. I could have gone to dances and shopped at malls like Chelsea. I could have read books, the ones you wanted me to read. Don't you see how stupid I am? How ignorant? How little of the world I've seen?

I crumple to the ground. The urn rolls out of my hands. The lid pops open. I stare at the plastic seal for a long time. Then I open it. I run my hands through the ashes. Gray, weightless flakes sift through my hands. So ordinary, just like the remains I cleaned out of the parlor fireplace today.

chapter twenty-four

I WAKE UP from a dead sleep to the sound of my alarm. Four thirty. It takes me a minute to remember why I've set the clock. It's Monday. My day to help Will. I turn on my light and start to dress. I step over the scrapbook and the urn. I don't want to think about any of it. Dad. Fasting. Nothing. For now I have Will. Will and the ocean. And I'm glad.

At the dock, Will and I wait ten minutes for Pastor Browning. "It's not like him to be late," I say, shivering. Will looks worried. I know he counts on Pastor Browning's help. "Do you think we should call?" I ask.

"I guess."

I hurry to the pay phone at the end of the dock and look up the rectory number. The phone rings four times and then the answering machine picks up: "This is Pastor Browning, sorry I can't take your call. Please leave a message after the tone."

"Pastor Browning," I say into the receiver, "are you there?"

Nothing.

"This is Kate," I finally say. "Will and I were wondering if you were coming out this morning." I pause and wait. "Okay. Bye."

I run back to Will. "Just his answering machine."

Will nods. He looks at his watch. "Maybe I better skip school today and go out alone."

I nod, then say, "But I can at least help until school-time."

"Sure. Great idea. I wouldn't want to miss a morning with my favorite Lobster Girl."

My heart flutters as I follow him toward the end of the dock, where the boat is tied up. He does a little dance and clicks his heels in the air. "No school for me today. Yippee!"

"You don't have to be so happy about it." I wish Will cared more about school. "I think you better go, or Jamie will think she's helping you for nothing."

"Oh, shit. All right, I'll go, if you insist." He grins. Will seems extra jovial this morning. But I can't help being a little worried about Pastor Browning. It's so not like him not to show up. What if he's sick? What if he's too sick to pick up his phone? Who would find him? He could die—like Dad, all alone. I shiver. Calm down, I tell myself. It's sunny out, with no wind, and somehow that makes everything seem extra quiet, like the earth is on pause. Except for Will, who's humming and pulling in two or three lobsters from every trap. We are really doing well today. He looks over at me. "You are such good luck, Lobster Girl. You're going to make me a rich man today."

By seven thirty I'm beat, my arms are pulsing from helping lift the traps, I'm splattered with fish bait and salt water, and my back hurts from bending over. Will is heading the boat back toward shore to let me off, when the engine starts to make a strange sound. It struggles, then chugs, then stops. "Damn!" Will shouts.

"What?" I run up into the cab.

"We're out of gas."

"Oh." I look at my watch. Mom is going to kill me if I'm late. I told her I'd be back in time to take the bus to school. "What do we do?"

"Call the coast guard. But they could be a while."

"Oh."

After Will radios in, I ask him, "Will they come in a boat or a helicopter?"

"A boat, of course."

"But doesn't the coast guard have pilots, too?"

"I think so. I really try to stay clear of those guys with all their rules and regulations. But they do come in handy when you're out of gas."

I sit down on the bench at the back of the boat to wait. Will follows me and sits down next to me. He takes off my knit hat and strokes my hair. He kisses me on the cheek.

He puts his arm around me and pulls me in close and really kisses me on the lips.

Keep yourself pure. Let your first kiss be with your chosen mate over the marriage altar.

I open my mouth to protest, but any words are interrupted by Will's warm kiss. And I know I should feel bad. But it feels so nice. I want to lean into his arms, rest my head against his chest forever. Maybe the coast guard won't find us very quickly.

But they do. Will jumps up at the sound of their engine. "Great timing." He sighs.

And I want to sigh, too. Is this how it feels to be in love?

After they leave, Will turns on the engine and heads for land and I stand close to him and let him put his arm around me. "I'm sorry I'm getting you back so late," Will says as he pulls up to the dock. "I know you *like* school. But I'm not sorry we had some free time." He winks.

I smile back and kiss him on the cheek. "See you," I manage to say even though my heart's pounding so loudly I can hardly hear my own voice.

Mom's on the phone when I come in. "No, no, never mind, Douglas. Here she is. Just a minute and I'll see."

Mom puts one hand over the phone and frowns at me. "Where have you been, young lady?"

"Out with Will," I say. "His boat ran out of gas."

Mom rolls her eyes. "Do you actually expect me to believe that?"

"You can call the coast guard if you want. They brought us more gas."

She stands waiting for me to say something more. When I don't, she finally gets back on the phone. "Listen, Douglas, she says she was out with Will and the boat ran out of gas."

Silence.

"Yes, yes. I agree."

Silence.

"Okay. I'll talk to you later then. Thank you."

Mom hangs up the phone. "Do you have any idea what you have put me through?"

"I'm sorry, Mom. Really. But I have a test in half an hour. Do you think you could drive me to school?"

She sighs. But nods her head. As soon as we're driving down the street, she says, "Kate," in that tone of voice that lets me know a lecture is coming.

"Mom"—I open my history book—"I really need to study, can the lecture wait?"

She slows for a stop sign. "Lecture? I think you're missing or dead, and you're worried about a little lecture?"

I ignore her and keep my eyes focused on my book, but in my head I'm back in the boat and in Will's arms. We drive in silence the rest of the way to school.

My history test goes better than I expect. I'm almost skipping down the hall. But when I see what's ahead, I freeze. It's Will. He's come up behind Candy, and he's got his arms around her waist and he's whispering things in her ear and she's giggling. I turn and walk the long way to the cafeteria, wishing with all my heart that my eyes were playing tricks on me. How can he kiss me this morning and touch her like that now? No. No. He can't be touching her. Can he?

In a sad daze, I find my way to our lunch table. It takes me a few moments to realize there's none of the usual chatter at the table—at least, Douglas and Jamie are dead silent. And Chelsea's sitting here. She only comes by when she's desperate for company or has some good gossip to share.

"Has anybody heard anything about Pastor Browning?" I ask. My voice is weak and shaky. "He didn't show up to help on the boat this morning."

Chelsea, who's flipping through a *Glamour* magazine, says, "Maybe you should have phoned the county jail. But that's right—prisoners are only allowed one phone call."

I sit up straight and glare at her, wondering why anyone, even Chelsea, would say something so horrible. I wait for Jamie to call her on it. But she doesn't. Douglas hasn't even opened his lunch and he usually inhales it in the first five minutes. No one but Chelsea seems to be able to speak. I don't get it. Is she right? "What?" I ask. "What happened? Tell me!"

Jamie scoots toward me and puts her hand on mine,

but before she can open her mouth to speak, Chelsea blurts it all out. "Pastor Browning is gay. It seems like he forgot to tell Mr. Penrose and my dad that when he was hired. And last night Dad arrested him for exposing minors to pornography. The church computer is full of totally sick sites." She actually looks proud, like she's so cool to be in on the big news. "Anyway, he's so fired."

I stand up. I can't understand why she's talking like this. It has to be a nightmare. Maybe all the cold air has made me delirious. Maybe Will didn't really have his arms around Candy. I look across the table and see Richard Penrose standing a few feet away, listening to every word. His eyes catch mine and he instantly hangs his head. Richard Penrose, who has a father who took him out of school because he was afraid he might go gay like his older brother. And then I notice Douglas is gone. He stood when Chelsea began talking, and I guess he took off. Douglas who used the church computer to look up porn sites.

No. No. No! Suddenly the cafeteria smells horrible— the fries, the meat loaf, all of it makes me want to gag. My legs stumble over the bench. I stagger, pushing my way through the cafeteria door. I run down the hall and outside. I pound down the steps, down the street, running and running and running. My lungs burn with the cold air. Houses, cars, everything blurs as I pass. All I can see is Pastor Browning, staring up at the storm clouds on Will's

boat. Will's boat. Will's boat where I got my first real kiss.
Just today. But now I hear Pastor Browning's voice, "If you
ever want a service for your father, Kate, I'd be honored to
help you." I leap over the curb onto the next street. I hear
a car screech on its brakes. I don't even turn. I keep running and running. Everything looks gray, like ashes. Like
Dad's ashes. If I run faster, maybe I'll escape it all. I'll be
back on the boat with Will and Pastor Browning and Will
won't be with Candy. I push harder and harder and harder
until I can't think or feel. I trip. My hands reach out to
break the fall. I'm on the sidewalk. I try to use my hands
to get on my knees. They're red and numb. Shouldn't they
be hurting? My palms are red with blood mixed with tiny
fragments of gravel. I try to wipe it all off on my jeans. I
stare at what I tripped over. A broken toy strewn over the
sidewalk in front of me. Some sort of superhero action figure. First I see its legs. Then an arm. Then the other arm.
And finally the head. I pick them all up. I clench them in
my bleeding hands and hug them to my chest. My stomach aches so badly. I can't breathe. I hear footsteps. They
sound far away, like an echo. Like in a dream.

I hear a voice. "Kate?"

I turn. It's Jamie. And Richard. He's right behind her.
Why is he here? They're both huffing and puffing and gasp-
ing for breath. Richard's eyes meet mine, then flicker away.
Jamie kneels down beside me and puts her arms around

me. Still clenching the broken toy, I choke out words. "I don't believe her. Chelsea is lying, isn't she?" I plead.

Jamie just pats me. "Yes. Well, at least in part. We can all guess he didn't download porn sites on the church computer."

Richard crouches down by me.

"I'm so sorry," he says.

No, no, I shake my head. It can't be true.

"Is he really in jail?" I finally ask Jamie.

"Not anymore," Jamie answers.

"But Mr. Riggs, did he really put him in jail?"

Jamie turns and looks up at Richard. She wants him to talk. He stares at his knees. "Pastor Browning, he never told me he was . . ." Richard looks so uncomfortable. Worse than I've ever seen him. "I never knew. All we ever did was talk and play computer games." He shakes his head.

No one speaks. What is Richard trying to say?

Finally, Jamie says, "Can you tell us what happened, Richard?"

He looks at her. He nods. "We were playing this game on the computer. The Rev, I mean, Pastor Browning, likes the same fighter-pilot game I do—nothing to do with porn sites," he adds in a strong voice. "He comes over for dinner a lot, and afterward sometimes I play against my school buddies back in California and he gives me tips." Then Richard's eyebrows close in. It's a look I've never seen. I mean he frowns a lot. But this is different. It's like he wants to punch someone. Hit them hard.

"That's all we have ever done. How was I supposed to know Mr. Riggs has been trailing us? He thought Pastor Browning was hitting on me, like I was gay or something. Just because my brother's gay doesn't mean I am."

"Right," Jamie agrees. "So, Mr. Riggs came in last night?" Jamie asks.

"Yep. Marches right in past Betty, our housekeeper. He actually had his gun drawn."

"And then what?" she prompts Richard.

"He arrests Pastor Browning for exposing minors to pornography, takes him away in handcuffs."

"And that's when you called your dad?"

Richard nods. "And he flew in first thing this morning with his lawyer. Apparently Mr. Riggs didn't have a shred of proof. All he could show was that porn sites had been downloaded using the church computer. Gay porn sites," he adds.

"But . . ." I start.

Richard continues. "So my dad, big damn homophobe that he is"—he spits out the words—"he asked Pastor Browning point-blank if he is gay."

"And?" I ask.

"And he said he was. Dad asked him to quit on the spot."

"Is Pastor Browning—" I choke on the words. "Is he really fired?"

Richard nods his head. "Sorry, Kate."

Kate. He called me by my name. He's never called me by my name. I look up at him and see kindness and pain in his eyes. He likes Pastor Browning, too. He stayed for the lessons when he didn't have to. He laughed and talked nonstop to him. His dad and my mom should be dropped off on a deserted island together. Just the two of them.

"But Pastor Browning didn't download those sites," I say.

"Of course he didn't download them," Jamie says, patting my shoulder.

"But if he's homo—" I stop myself, not wanting to say the word out loud.

"—sexual," Jamie finishes for me.

"What about the candy bars and the Scouts? He helped the Scouts."

Jamie says, "Yeah, I thought about that this morning, too. He really is a saint, isn't he?"

"But I could tell Mr. Riggs. I could tell Mr. Penrose."

"Kate. We can all guess who did it. Who else had access to the computer every week? And you should have seen his face at lunch today. Guilt. Guilt. Guilt."

"It wouldn't matter," Richard says. "My dad hates, with a capital *H*, gays. He has enough power with the church to have him fired and never hired again as a minister."

Richard is staring at specks of my blood that have stained the cement. A plane is flying overhead; Richard looks up at it. After it's gone, he turns back and says, "I'm really sorry. I like him, too."

Jamie shakes her head. "What a mess. He's a nice guy, isn't he? What other adult in this crummy town stood up to help Will Lane when his grandfather was sick?"

"Or checked on me when my parents basically dumped me here?" Richard asks.

"It's days like today that make me want to leave Puffin Cove and never, ever come back." Jamie sighs. "Did you know Mr. Riggs even made Douglas change his scripture reading? He said the one you suggested was too depressing. Come on." She puts her arm out to help me up. "We better get you to the nurse to clean up your hands."

chapter twenty-five

CHELSEA AND DOUGLAS are both on the afternoon bus. Douglas has his head buried deeper in his books than usual. He has to know about the accusations his dad made against Pastor Browning. And what would his dad do to him if he found out? Something so horrible that he doesn't have the courage to admit what he did. I'd hide in my books, too, hide for the rest of my life. Chelsea, though, seems to want to tell the story over and over to anyone on the bus who will hear it. She acts like her dad is a hero for uncovering the fact that Pastor Browning is gay. "Isn't it gross?" I hear her saying to a couple of other girls. "I can't imagine ever liking a girl."

"Sick," one of the other girls agrees.

Lately Chelsea and I had almost been getting along. Is she just doing this to score points with her dad? Is she covering for Douglas? I have a feeling she knows what really happened.

I'm not at all eager to get home. As Will says, news travels fast in Puffin Cove.

Mom is pacing back and forth in the hallway when I arrive, as if she's been waiting for me. "Kate," she hisses.

"I know," I say. "Pastor Browning is gay. You don't want me to go to that church. Don't worry, Mom. I won't." I want to add that I'm done with church period. All churches. But I don't.

"Yes, that is part of it, but right now it can keep. You and I have other things to discuss." She pauses.

I look at her, puzzled. No one is around. We haven't had a guest all week. No fresh cookies are baking in the kitchen. The house smells empty, dead. Is she worried about finances? Do we have to move back to Arizona? Whatever it is, it's big. The worry lines on her forehead are almost pulsing. Then it hits me. She's been in my room. The urn. Dad's book. *To Kill a Mockingbird*. I left it out on the nightstand.

"I went in your room today," she starts.

If I ever felt like running away from home, now is the time. Go, I tell my feet. Leave. But they stay. Stuck in place. I study the wood floor, the uneven cracks and the blackened nail heads. Guilt floods through my veins. But as quickly as it comes, I fight it. Why should I be ashamed? I haven't done anything wrong. I look at her in defiance. "And?" I ask.

"I think you know what I found. An urn of ashes and one of your father's books."

"My father's ashes, you mean? The ones you were just going to leave at the crematorium?"

"Kate. Don't speak to me in that tone of voice. I'm your mother. I deserve respect."

"Why?" I ask. I'm not about to let her pounce on me. I sneak around almost all the time to keep her from getting upset. Why? Why should I have to hide such simple things as my dad's ashes and the one book she didn't manage to steal?

"Kate!"

"I'm serious, Mother." She hates it when I call her Mother. "Why should I treat someone who is heartless enough to deny a funeral for my father with any respect?"

"But Kate, you know." Her angry tone turns into something I hate worse. Her religious voice. Sweet and strong and so damn, damn sure. "You know it's against church doctrine to be cremated. How could I have a funeral? How could I allow his ashes to be in our home? To desecrate it like that?"

I shake my head at her. It's so pointless. How do you reason with a fanatic? Someone should write a book about it. Like those how-to guide books. *The Idiot's Guide to Reasoning with a Fanatic.*

"You don't comprehend at all what I'm trying to say, do you, Kate?"

"Me?" I ask in disbelief. "Comprehend what? I comprehend things. I comprehend that you are more afraid of desecrating your sacred home than doing anything about Dad's ashes. Mother, you were married to him once. You had me together. I'm half his blood. Don't you have any feelings for me? My father died."

"He died in sin and he influenced you to become like this," she hisses. Her eyes are wild now. "If your father was someone like Max, we wouldn't be having this discussion. You wouldn't be the dishonest kind of person who reads books I forbid behind my back. Besides, I told your teacher you couldn't read that book."

"Well, I told her you changed your mind." I feel like my eyes are just as wild as hers. I throw my backpack and it crashes against the wall of the hallway. The picture hanging above it, the one with the two little children chasing after a kite, falls right on top of my backpack.

Mom slaps my face. "How dare you lie about me!"

As I'm touching my hot cheek, she leans over and picks up the picture and carefully places it on the hook, tilting it back and forth until it's perfectly straight. Now she turns to me. Her eyes are on fire. "Don't you see what your father stirs up in you? I don't want you reading his books, for your own sake. Can't you see how out of control you become? So full of Satan that you would lie to your teacher?"

"Dad is dead, Mom. D-E-A-D." I spell it out. "All I have left are his ashes and the one book you didn't already steal from me. What about that commandment, 'Thou shalt not steal?' Who is really full of Satan? Those books weren't yours to take. They're all I have. His books, some pictures, and his ashes. How can you rob me of these few memories? What about charity, Mom, your famous motto? Don't you have any charity at all for me? Is slapping me really a loving thing to do? Why can't you let go of it? He's gone. He's not around to influence me."

She turns red. She has never slapped me before. Even as far gone as she is, she knows she's wrong on that one.

"But he did influence you." Her voice is softer now. Like a teacher trying to explain simple math to a child. "Don't you see? Because of him, you'll never be like your cousins, or like the church girls at your school. Never." She starts sobbing. "Charity would never go to a false church where they have a gay minister. Gay. You know homosexuals pervert the whole godly form of procreation and threaten the very foundation of the traditional family unit." She shakes her head and continues crying, like I've disgraced her beyond repair.

Mom falls into a chair, sobbing. And she says I'm out of control. What is this? Not exactly perfect composure. I can't muster up one tear. I can't bear hearing such horrible accusations hurled at Pastor Browning. I walk away like a zombie.

I don't snap out of it until I'm sitting inside Aunt Katherine's cottage, next to her on her couch. Her arms are around me and now the tears come.

chapter twenty-six

THE URN OF ASHES was still sitting where I left it on the floor, but *To Kill a Mockingbird* was missing. This morning it's cold and snowing. It's also a teacher workday—a holiday for me. Mom and I didn't speak at breakfast, and now she's on errands in Ellsworth for the day. So Aunt Katherine and I have a secret date, a date we planned last night. One Mom wouldn't approve of for a lot of reasons. I put the container in the backseat of Aunt Katherine's car, start the engine, and sit, waiting for the heater to warm the car.

I take off the brake and pull out of the garage. I do it on the first try. I skid a little on the inch of freshly fallen snow as I steer over to the front of Aunt Katherine's cottage. She's standing, waiting for me, dressed all in blue— her fake-fur coat and a knitted cap, scarf, and gloves. I brake and she gets in. "How are you, love?" she asks.

"Okay." I feel the corners of my mouth form a slight smile.

"Still want to do this?" she asks.

I nod emphatically.

I drive slowly when we get to the highway and look behind the trees to the crossroad, praying Mr. Riggs isn't in his usual place.

"Don't worry, Kate," Aunt Katherine says, reading my mind. "If he's there and has the gall to stop us, I'll gladly give him a piece of my mind. What he has done is beyond shame, and if I know him at all, he'll be lying low, doing office work for a few weeks, before he attempts his next big arrest."

"Good."

"Turn left here. Now right. I hope I checked the tide chart correctly. It's got to be low tide, you know."

We're heading to a place I've never been. It's an island, Aunt Katherine explained, but one that you can walk out to when it's low tide. She and Dad used to watch the tide charts and made trips out to it when he was a boy. It seems like the right place to have Dad's long overdue funeral service.

As I suspected, Aunt Katherine had no idea about the ashes. She knew Dad was cremated but assumed we'd had a service. She didn't want to pry and ask. I also told her about Mom taking all his books. Last night as we made our plans, I thought of inviting Pastor Browning, since he'd offered to help give a funeral, but now it doesn't seem right with all his own problems. Besides, I like the idea of just the two of us having a funeral, with no church at all. And I've had time to think about Will. And Aunt Katherine's words keep haunting me. Friendship first. Then love. I like the sound of Will's voice. I like the way I feel when he touches me. But what about his likes and dislikes? His interests? And mine? Do they mesh? Do we have enough in common?

"You're doing an excellent job driving, love." She pats my leg. "We should find a place to park, just to the left. There." She points.

I pull over and stop the engine. I can't believe I've driven this far. And I did okay.

I reach into the backseat and pull out one of the two photos of Dad and me at the race. I tuck it into my coat pocket and pick up the urn. I hand it to Aunt Katherine. She holds it. She sucks in her breath like a wind has just ripped by us.

"So small," she says. Her eyes get that faraway look like they did last night when I first told her, and fill with tears again.

"I know. That's what I thought, too."

"And you really biked all that way to pick up your father's ashes and never told your mother?"

I nod.

The corners of Aunt Katherine's mouth turn up. "I think your parents were right to name you after me."

As we walk, Aunt Katherine carries the urn close to her chest, like it's a newborn baby. I link my arm through hers and together we cross over to the island on mud. Without any ocean water to insulate it, the mud is quickly freezing in the cold air, but some still sticks to the bottom of our boots. The salty, fishy smell is pungent. Once we get to the island, Aunt Katherine heads to a clump of pine trees right at the shore. At the edge of the firs is a huge rock. Big and flat enough for three people to sit on. But we stand. It's too cold to sit. Aunt Katherine sets the ashes on the rock and opens her purse. She pulls out a book, *Where the Wild Things Are.*

She opens it and begins reading. Her voice is strong and sweet and dances along the wind out into the water. She shows me the pictures before she turns each page. A boy in his bedroom, a boy off on wild adventures, a boy returning to his mother, and finally, a boy going to sleep.

When she's done, I swallow hard. "Okay. My turn." I pick up the ashes and hug them tightly against my chest. I stare far out into the ocean and begin to recite from memory.

"Though I speak with the tongues of men and of angels, and have not charity, I am become as sounding brass, or a tinkling cymbal.

"And though I have the gift of prophecy, and understand

all mysteries, and all knowledge; and though I have all faith, so that I could remove mountains, and have not charity, I am nothing.

"*And though I bestow all my goods to feed the poor, and though I give my body to be burned, and have not charity, it profiteth me nothing.*

"*Charity suffereth long, and is kind; charity envieth not; charity vaunteth not itself, is not puffed up,*

"*Doth not behave itself unseemly, seeketh not her own, is not easily provoked, thinketh no evil;*

"*Rejoiceth not in iniquity, but rejoiceth in the truth;*

"*Beareth all things, believeth all things, hopeth all things, endureth all things.*"

My eyes sting. Aunt Katherine puts her arm around me and pats my shoulder. I continue and the words tumble out effortlessly.

"*Charity never faileth: but whether there be prophecies, they shall fail; whether there be tongues, they shall cease; whether there be knowledge, it shall vanish away.*

"*For we know in part, and we prophesy in part.*

"*But when that which is perfect is come, then that which is in part shall be done away.*

"*When I was a child, I spake as a child, I understood as a child, I thought as a child: but when I became a man, I put away childish things.*

"*For now we see through a glass, darkly; but then face*

to face: now I know in part; but then shall I know even as also I am known.

"*And now abideth faith, hope, charity, these three; but the greatest of these is charity.*"

I open the lid of the urn and shake the container on its side. The ashes blow with the wind. I'm glad the ashes of my father end up here among the trees and the wind and the water. Aunt Katherine scoops some up and they disappear easily in the wind. Soon the urn is empty. We stand there, silent, and I know something. Mom is right. I'm not like Charity or the church girls at school or even Mom. And it *is* because of Dad. Maybe he didn't stand up for me like I wished he had, but he managed to poke a hole in Mom's perfect world of black and white. He allowed doubt to seep in. He chose not to join my mother in her beliefs. That alone let me know that there was a different way—a better and more charitable way to think.

Before we leave, I take the picture out of my pocket. I take one last look at us with our arms around each other, both with medals around our sweaty necks. I place the picture under the big rock.

"Good-bye, Dad."

chapter twenty-seven

I'M STANDING AT the dock, shivering and nervous. After Aunt Katherine and I got home from the island, Jamie called. We had to rearrange our morning lobstering schedule for this week. Mr. Riggs won't let Douglas or Chelsea come. So I'm on duty again this morning. And if Pastor Browning wasn't going to be there, I wouldn't go, either. I can't erase that picture of Will with his arms around Candy or the sound of her giggles.

"Kate." Pastor Browning approaches me with a wave, sounding as cheerful as ever.

"Hello." I don't know what else to say.

"So, have you heard the good news?"

"Is there any good news? All I've heard is bad news."

"The doctor says Will's grandfather is well enough to start back on the boat next week. And there are still a few good weeks of lobstering left before the season is over, so it's great timing, since it appears my days around Puffin Cove are numbered."

"I'm so sorry, Pastor Browning." I kick at a pebble on the dock, avoiding his eyes.

"Ah, well. Having an agnostic as a minister probably isn't the best thing anyway, and add being gay, well . . ." He doesn't finish.

My cheeks burn. "But Pastor Browning, I know you didn't download . . ." I slowly lift my eyes to his. "Well, that stuff you were accused of. I mean, I know who did."

"Oh, you do?" He rubs his mittened hands together. "Well, can you do me a favor?"

"Of course."

"Let's keep that information between you and me."

"But . . ."

"At this point it wouldn't matter, anyway. They're going to get rid of me regardless, and it would only mean more trouble for that person at home."

I nod and then we walk down the dock together. "But what will you do?"

"Well, let's see. I'm going to use the rest of this week to transition church matters to an interim pastor, pack up, and then next week, I'll head down to Boston. A friend of mine is Latin department chair for one of the universities there. He needs a full-time research assistant."

"Oh."

"I'm just sorry we can't continue having youth group. And so close to our big weekend retreat. That would have been fun. I'm also sorry about the change in the church program. I know you and I were really looking forward to Douglas reading our favorite passage, in First Corinthians."

"Well, it seems not everyone shares our passion for that selection."

"No, sadly not. I guess I didn't do a lot of things right. I guess I was stupid to think the Don't Ask—Don't Tell theory would ever work."

"Well, it can't work if the Don't Ask party asks."

Pastor Browning grins. His eyes are bright and carefree. He looks happier than the last few times I've seen him. I can relate. It's hard to hide things, things you know people wouldn't approve of. I feel happier today, now that I don't have to hide Dad's ashes.

"We'll miss you," I say, and bite down on my lip to keep it from quivering.

"Yes, I'll miss all of you. And to tell you the truth, I worry about Richard. He doesn't have many friends, and now he's even more angry with his father. And he's left alone so much. It's one of the reasons I went over so often. He's going to need some good friends, Kate."

I nod and think, I could do it for Pastor Browning. Richard isn't turning out to be such a snob after all.

Will joins us, carrying his usual two buckets. "Hey, Lobster Girl. Hey, Pastor." Will waves at us. "Looks like a storm may be coming. Think we can beat it?"

"We can sure try." Pastor Browning relieves Will of one of the buckets.

Will acts as if nothing is different between us. Like he didn't kiss me and then flirt with Candy on the same day. But on the other hand, he must have heard all about Pastor Browning. At least he's not prejudiced; that's something we have in common.

The three of us head to the boat, and we work like everything is the same. I fill the bait bags, Pastor Browning and Will unload the traps, and we work in peaceful silence, with the waves lapping around us.

I wake up to my alarm. I dash off a note to Mom. *"Gone out on Will's boat,"* I write. It was Jamie's turn today, but at the last minute her father convinced her to come to Boston for the Thanksgiving weekend and spend some time with him. When she called, I was happy to cover for her, knowing Pastor Browning would be there again. It's probably the last time I'll see him. He's grown to be such a part of my life. My heart feels like it's ripping every time I think of him being gone. And why he's going.

As I stand waiting on the dock, I think about my strange Thanksgiving yesterday. Aunt Katherine was sick with a bad cold, probably from our trip out to the island. Mom had assumed, stupidly, that we would both go with her to the Thanksgiving dinner at her church. When she asked again Thanksgiving morning, I stared at her like she was crazy and wondered if she will ever stop trying. So she sulked and went without us. Can you believe it? On Thanksgiving?

I made toast and fresh orange juice for myself and Aunt Katherine. Then we watched the Macy's Thanksgiving Day Parade, my first time ever. For lunch I opened a can of chicken noodle soup and we watched the movie *Miracle on 34th Street* and afterward *The Simpsons*, also firsts for me. Of course, I've watched TV before. I used to watch old black-and-white movies with Dad and lots of the Discovery Channel and History Channel, his two favorites. But he wasn't really into parades, Christmas movies, or cartoons. I didn't even miss the big traditional feast we usually had with Charity's family. I don't really like turkey or dressing anyway.

And now today, of course, there's no school because of Thanksgiving. In the half dark I spot someone heading toward me, but it isn't Pastor Browning. Is it Will? Then the shadow gets nearer and I see that it isn't Will at all. It's Richard.

He has a half smile on his face. "I'm here to help in Pastor Browning's place."

"He's gone?" I ask. It's the first time I've seen Richard since Monday, when he ran after me.

Richard nods. "They made him move out two days early. I stopped by last night just as he was packing up his car to leave."

"But . . . but I didn't even get to say good-bye," I burst out.

"I know. I'm sorry. He said to say good-bye to you and the others." Richard sounds sincere.

"Hey, Kate," Will calls out. "Hey." He pauses, flustered at seeing Richard, too.

Richard doesn't look like himself in a green rain slicker and a thick blue knit cap. With both Will and me watching him, he seems embarrassed and lowers his head.

"Pastor Browning had to leave early," I explain. "I guess he asked Richard to take his place."

Richard nods.

Will rolls his eyes. I think he's had it with all this neighborliness. It must be one thing to take it from us, his friends, but I'm almost sure he and Richard have never even talked.

The silence grows tense. Richard breaks it by saying, "Hey, if I'm in the way, I mean . . ." He doesn't finish his sentence.

Will doesn't say anything.

Poor Richard. He must really like Pastor Browning, or really feel guilty for what his dad did, to get up this early and come over and face us.

But I want him to stay. I don't want to be alone with Will. What if he kisses me again? What if I let him? What does that say about me? My insides start to churn. Think fast. "Oh, I think it would be great to have the help, right Will?" I blurt out in the most cheerful, carefree voice I can muster. "Besides, I have a feeling Richard is just here for the payment you offer. I'm sure he's heard about the lobster deal," I tease.

Will's eyes meet mine and he smiles back. "So you like lobster, Penrose?"

"Doesn't everyone?" Richard jokes back.

"Don't ask." Will sighs.

With the ice broken, we head onto the boat. Richard learns fast. And, of course, he's much stronger than me at pulling the traps off of the pulley. When I struggle with the first one, he says, "Here, let me help." I don't want him to. I continue to struggle without answering, and so finally he just reaches out and helps me.

We stay out the whole day, but we're done early because there are so few lobsters in the traps. It's too cold for them now.

"Um, thanks. Really." Will puts out his hand to shake Richard's after we've unloaded the boat. But he doesn't thank me. I realize he never has.

"No problem." Richard returns his half of the shake. And when Will hands both Richard and me Styrofoam containers with our lobsters, Richard takes his and says, "Thanks."

"See ya, Lobster Girl," Will says to me. "You're going to miss getting up early with me, aren't you?"

I manage a half smile. And yes, I'm going to miss him. But maybe it's a good thing.

Will heads off to the lobster pound to settle his account.

Richard and I walk down the dock together. "Um, I have my car," Richard says. "Would you like a ride home?"

"Nah," I say, wrapping my arms around my lobster container. "That's okay. I like the walk."

"Oh. Okay." He doesn't look at me but instead stares out at the edge of the dock, watching the waves lap against the wood.

I guess that sounded rude. And a stab of guilt pricks at my heart, remembering Pastor Browning's words, about how Richard would need friends. But I'd die if Jamie saw me riding in the Penrose tank, and even though she's in Boston, I think I would rather walk.

chapter twenty-eight

"So, how is it having Max back?" Aunt Katherine asks me a few days later, between coughs that are deep and rattle in her congested chest.

"Good. He and Mom are having some interesting discussions. He said he'll read some of her church books if she reads some of his philosophy books." I put fresh logs on the smoldering coals.

"And?"

"Well, she took them, but I doubt she'll open them. That should keep things stirred up for a while. Anyway, he keeps her too busy to constantly be harping on me. And he's okay, even though I don't like his smelly cologne." I scrunch up my nose in disgust. "But he asks me about things. Like why I've been taking the late bus home from school."

"You mean your mother has no idea you're working out at the gym?"

"No. She's never asked."

"Hmm."

"I don't see how you can get along with her, Aunt Katherine. If I were you, I would have never invited her out here to manage the inn."

Aunt Katherine tries to talk but instead chokes and coughs. I run to her side.

"I'm okay," she sputters. She pats the couch next to her. "Sit down, Kate. I don't think what I have is contagious."

I sit and smell the VapoRub Aunt Katherine has on her chest and around her nose.

"First of all. You have to remember I haven't lived around your mother for years and years like you have. I can imagine how frustrating it is for you, but your mother is rather charming and she is doing a wonderful job keeping the inn in good working order. Now, I'm not sure I understand the other part of your comment. I didn't invite your mother out here. She phoned me and asked if I had any sort of a job. You had to know that, didn't you, love?"

I sit up straight. My eyes widen. "You didn't invite her?"

"No. I never dreamed she would come back east. Your mother left the East Coast after she married Steven because she felt she was losing her faith. She said she needed the support of her family and church friends."

"But why?" I shake my head, still puzzled. "I mean,

she had a good job in Arizona, and all her friends and her sister who lived close by."

"For you, Kate. She said she was worried about you."

I stare at her in shock.

Aunt Katherine sighs. "I've never brought it up because from what she described, you were having a pretty rough time of it, and I didn't want to mention unpleasant memories."

"But what did she say?"

"She said you wouldn't come out of your room, you were barely eating, and she was worried she was going to lose you, too. She thought a new start, leaving the sad memories behind, might help."

I move to adjust a log on the fire, then pace back and forth, trying to let all this sink in.

Mom asked Aunt Katherine.

Mom asked Aunt Katherine.

"But she's so angry at me most of the time," I say, turning back to Aunt Katherine. "And hiding every one of Dad's books from me is the cruelest thing in the world. I mean, does she really think she can keep me from reading?" I sweep my hand in front of Aunt Katherine's well-stocked floor-to-ceiling bookcase.

"No. I think she realizes, at least on some level, that you're going to do what you're going to do. But maybe it's just too hard seeing Steven's books in your room. It's like a constant reminder of her failure to keep you in her church."

"Oh, Aunt Katherine, I can't believe it. Why would she do this for me? She's not that nice. She's heartless. Unless I do things her way, she hates me."

"She doesn't hate you, Kate. It's going to take time for her. I'm sure in her plan, you would have this new start, begin running again, make new friends, and go back to church. And it mostly worked."

"She'll never give up. Never!"

"Well, maybe that's a good thing."

I stop pacing and stare at Aunt Katherine. "Why?"

"Well, love, she did give up on trying to convert your father. And when she did, she also gave up loving him. What you're saying is that in her own way, your mother is never going to stop loving you. You know I loved your father like he was my own son. But I can tell you, Steven was one of the most passive people I've ever known, especially toward your mom. He never liked standing up to people. You certainly didn't inherit all this fire and gumption that's such a wonderful part of you from him. Your mother may be many things that you don't like, but she doesn't lack courage. She doesn't sit around and let things happen to her, now does she?"

"Oh, Aunt Katherine." I sit beside her and hug her. "You see the good in everyone."

"Not everyone." She chuckles and it brings on another coughing spell.

"I better let you rest." I kiss her forehead and wonder why it's so easy to be affectionate with her.

"Okay, love. I'll see you tomorrow."

Now it's Friday. My birthday. Mom and Max lit a candle in a muffin for me when I came into the kitchen for breakfast. That was nice. So what if no one at school knows? As I trudge through the cafeteria doors, I feel a familiar tug at my ponytail.

I turn. "Hi, Will," I say even as my insides recoil. I've seen him twice more walking with Candy in the halls. Once, he had his arm around her shoulder.

"I sure miss you on the boat in the mornings. Pop isn't nearly as fun."

"So, you're still going out?"

"For another week or two."

I've been careful to avoid Will. The day he kissed me, I thought we were boyfriend and girlfriend. How dumb was I? Kissing me seems to mean nothing to him, and he doesn't act any differently toward me. Worse, he doesn't notice that I'm not exactly all smiles.

"So, are you going this afternoon to that big dance thing in Bangor?"

I look at him, puzzled. "What?"

"Oh you know, the one with Chelsea's church. Some dance. Movies. I don't know everything."

"Are you?" My mouth drops open in disbelief.

"It sounds fun. Well, the dance and movie, anyway. Chelsea invited me." He grins and his eyes tease like he's trying to make me jealous.

Ha. Little does he know. Fine! Go with Chelsea. Go ahead. Leave. Kiss Chelsea. Kiss Candy.

"That's nice of Chelsea." But by the way, what happened to her mature boyfriend, Andy, and her vow to stay away from stupid high-school guys?

"But are you going?" Will asks.

"No."

"Why not?"

"Because that church fired our friend, Pastor Browning."

"Huh?"

"You remember, Pastor Browning, that guy who helped you keep in business while Pop was so sick? Well, the church sponsoring this Bangor retreat fired him, or didn't you hear?"

"Oh, Kate, you know me. I don't get into politics or religion. Too much hassle. I wish you'd come. We could dance." Will tugs at my ponytail.

I look at him. He doesn't even say anything about Pastor Browning. He just grins, so carefree. "What about Candy? Is she coming, too? That way, you can have more than one girl on your arm. That's the way you operate, right?" Did I just say that?

Will almost blushes. "Uh, Candy? She just can't keep her hands off me."

"It seems like the feeling is mutual."

"Don't be jealous. She's just a friend, really."

"Just a friend?" Not Aunt Katherine's kind of friend. I haven't been that kind of friend with Will, either. I sort of skipped that part. I realize we really don't have much in common, Will and I. I can imagine his arms around me again. Only now, my insides don't warm. My heart feels like one of Will's lobster traps, sinking deeper and deeper into the darkest part of the ocean. He doesn't care about the things I do—the goodness of Pastor Browning, learning more about the world, or reading books. And I guess I don't care that much about lobsters, the music he listens to, or going to the pool hall.

"Ah, City Girl, it'll be fun." His eyes light up with mischief.

But the look in his eyes that I always thought was so magical no longer makes me smile.

Chelsea interrupts us. "Hey, Will, so be at the church at four, okay?"

"Sure." He grins.

I turn to go. "Hope you change your mind, City Girl," he says.

✻　✻　✻

City Girl, Lobster Girl, my head repeats over and over as I add ten more pounds than my usual amount to the machine in the school weight room. I want this workout to kill. I want the pain to tear into my muscles. I don't want to think about Will or anything else. After about ten minutes, when I'm dripping with sweat, the guys' basketball team tromps by, joking and poking roughly at one another. Richard is one of them. He's laughing with one of his teammates. I find myself smiling, happy that Richard is making friends. Even Jamie talks to him now, like he's a decent human being.

When the bus lets me off, it's already dark. Instead of climbing the hill to the inn, I walk in a foggy haze down Main Street. Christmas lights shine out from every store. My mind keeps going back to Will. Why should it bother me so much that he's going to the church dance? He admitted he's not into religion or politics. It's not like he's mean to people, or avoids them because they are gay or religious or different from him. He likes everyone. But he isn't the guy I thought he was. And I think Aunt Katherine's right. I want someone who shares more of my values, not just someone I want to touch me. But still it rips at my heart. Will.

The bakery windows are decked with pine boughs, and the drugstore has a tiny train, which even now, after the store is closed, chugs around a miniature Christmas village. I walk until I'm standing in front of the old stone church with the new brass plate giving it historic status. So Mr. Penrose was right. He does know how to get things to happen in a hurry. I stare at it in the shadows, huge pines surrounding it. I tug at the big red door and find it's open. It's as cold inside as out. I guess they don't turn on the heat during the weekdays. I've heard the new minister is a woman. Mom would die. Still, I bet she is an avowed heterosexual, or signed a contract of celibacy. They aren't going to mess with any more problems like they've just been through.

Two small lamps light the chapel. As always, the wood rafters above smell like my grandparents' cabin. And even though it and my grandparents are so far away and Dad is gone, the memory swells sweetly inside of me. I sigh. I still have Mom. And Mom is still Mom. But now that I know she asked Aunt Katherine if she could come here—well, things are different.

I stroke the stained glass of the nearest window. I look out through the colors to the muted glare of the streetlamp. *"Now I see through a glass, darkly."* Pastor Browning was right. As I peer out through this darkened glass, the car on the street, the house across the way, even the trees are fuzzy, less distinct. Maybe peace does come in not having a crystal-clear view of life, not having all the answers, not having everything right and wrong, black and white. All I know is that tonight, standing here on my sixteenth birth-day, looking out through an ancient stained-glass window, I can't hate this church.

I've barely headed down the road again when I hear footsteps behind me. I stop. The footsteps stop. I start. The footsteps start. My heart clutches, but still I spin and face my stalker.

It's Richard. I recognize that blue knit hat he wore on the boat.

"Kate?" he calls out.

"Yes." I let out my breath and a cloud of fog forms.

"I didn't want to scare you," he says, walking closer.

"Well, you didn't," I say, stuffing my trembling hands in my pockets. "Can I help you?" I ask, trying to sound irritated, but instead I find myself more curious that he called me by my name again.

Richard clears his throat. "Well, to be honest, when I came home from basketball practice, I saw you walk-ing into the church. I was hoping to catch you before you left."

I stare at him, too curious to even be embarrassed that he's been following me.

"Pastor Browning gave me a book to give to you," Rich-ard explains. "It's never seemed like a good time."

"Oh?"

"Could I bring it over to your house later?"

Boy, that takes me off guard. And then I realize Richard is here in Puffin Cove. He didn't meet with all the others for the big Bangor weekend retreat. His father is still a VIP at church, but Richard didn't go. I wonder if he's grounded from driving for not going on the youth outing. "You're not going to the youth weekend in Bangor?" The words burst out of me before I think them through.

"No!" Richard frowns. "I'm never stepping inside that church again after what they did to Pastor Browning. Besides, I have a basketball game tomorrow night."

"But what about your parents? What about your 'wheels'?"

"What?" Richard looks confused.

I feel my cheeks burn, but I continue. "You said to Pastor Browning, 'No church, no car.'"

"Oh, right. Well, I hear walking is good exercise. Remember, I told you I liked to walk and hike—hobbies of mine." He smiles again. "So, is it okay to drop by in a while?" he asks again.

Shocked, I answer, "Sure."

"Cool, I'll be by in about half an hour." Then he turns around and heads back toward his house, waving like we're good friends.

I shake my head as I walk home. Richard is taking a stand against his parents' church. And Will? Will is going to the dance because "it sounds fun."

Aunt Katherine's cottage is dark. The inn is quiet and lacking its usual smell of cooking soup or freshly baked bread. I find a scrawled note attached to the front of the fridge.

Kate, Aunt Katherine is worse. Max and I have taken her to the hospital."

Hospital? What if it's pneumonia? The word haunts me. I pace back and forth on the narrow strip of hardwood flooring in front of the living-room fireplace. I can't lose her, too. I can't. I try Mom's cell phone. Nothing, only voice mail. I pace so long I'm sure I've worn the stain off the wood floor. I open and shut my fists. I count to ten over and over. When someone knocks at the front door, I freeze, then run, hoping it's them.

But when I open the door, it's Richard. I stare at him like he's part of a dream.

"Um. I'm sorry," he says. "Are you on your way out?"

"What?"

He eyes my coat.

"Oh. No." I pull at my collar. I guess I never took it off. "It's my aunt Katherine. She's sick. My mother took her to the hospital."

"Oh. Sorry. Should I come back another time?" Richard asks, holding a book and a brown paper bag.

"No. No. It's okay. Come in." I lead him to the parlor, to the couch where Mom sits with Max. I offer him the couch and then sit in the chair next to it.

He hands me the book. *Through a Glass Darkly*, the book cover reads in faded gold letters. Behind it is a painting of a huge church stained-glass window. The corners are ragged, and one is torn off. I touch the cover, rub my hands over it, and as I do, the trance I've been in seems to lift.

I open it. *"To Kate, who knows the power of charity and can see through a glass darkly. With admiration, Pastor Browning."*

"It's a good book," Richard says.

"You read it?"

He nods.

"You read my book?"

He looks sheepish. "Sorry, it's pretty worn, I didn't think you'd mind."

I realize how stupid I sound. "No, I don't mind." I carefully turn the pages, and as I do, my heart warms. It's the whole chapter—1 Corinthians 13—one verse to a page, with beautiful illustrations on the opposite page.

Richard sits quietly while I look through the book. As I close it, I look up at him.

Richard takes a small package from out of his pocket. "I ran into Jamie on my way here and she asked me to give you this. She said she'd have come over herself, but she was already late for work."

I open it. It's a paperback copy of *To Kill a Mockingbird*. Inside the cover is Jamie's familiar scrawl. "*To Kate on her sixteenth birthday. Hide this, girl, okay? Love, Jamie.*" Then below it she's copied a quote. "*Out beyond the ideas of right-doing and wrong-doing there is a field. I'll meet you there.*" —*Rumi, Ancient poet*

I bite my lip to keep tears from coming.

Richard's rustling the brown bag and looking really uncomfortable. He stammers. "I just . . . well, Jamie mentioned it was your . . . oh, shit. I mean, uh, shoot, it's for you." He hands me the bag.

I look inside. I pull out a Christmas cactus, all in bloom, pink blossoms bursting from the waxy green stems. I stare at it for the longest time, trying to absorb this surreal moment. Something else is in the bag. I peek. It's a pack of Jelly Bellys.

"But . . . h-how? Why?" Now it's my turn to stammer.

"I saw you buy Jelly Bellys once at the mall," he explains.

My cheeks flush. He remembered me buying them at the mall? I play with one of the blooms on the cactus. "And why the cactus?"

"Um, I don't know. It's almost Christmas. You're from Arizona. I—I hoped you'd like it."

I nod. "Thank you. It's very sweet. Really." As I touch the little pink blossoms, I can't help but wonder if there is some cosmic force at work. "I used to have a Christmas cactus, but it died." And Dad died. And Aunt Katherine? I feel close to tears again. Talk fast, I tell myself. "So, why did you decide to come here for school?" I blurt out, before I realize how stupid my questions sound.

"My dad. I told you he's homophobic. My older brother is gay. He blames the private school we went to. So he shipped me off here, where guys are rough and tough." His voice lowers to a deep bass.

So Jamie was right.

"I admit I was pretty pissed at first. But it's okay now."

"Yeah, I like it."

"Listen, Kate, I'm sorry about all the mess with Pastor Browning. We both really liked him. Can we be friends?"

I look at him, about to say "Sure." But then I remember the Super Sports Weekend.

"Why did you break curfew on the Sports Weekend? We could have won that trophy if you'd have run."

Richard sighs. "I don't know if you'll believe me. The school officials didn't."

"Try me."

"I was dead asleep in my room. Then there was all this pounding on my door. Whoever it was, they were singing and shouting and obviously drunk. I opened the door and stepped out so I wouldn't wake up my roommate. While I was leaning against the door, trying to get Chelsea and her two friends to go back to their rooms, two chaperones spotted us. Before I knew it, about five coaches and all the adults on the trip were around us. I had taken this six-pack away from Chelsea, and told her to not drink any more. That girl is so much trouble. What my dad sees in her I'll never know."

My eyes are wide. "Your dad?"

"Yeah. You don't think I'm dumb enough to fall for someone like her, do you? He was so eager for me to have a girlfriend, he invited her over all the time."

I'm silent. And I'm relieved. I do believe Richard. "I'm sorry." I say. "I just listened to what everyone else said."

"Yeah, well, there's a lot of that going on around here."

I chuckle.

Richard smiles back at me. I've never been this close to him before. He has a kind look in his dark green eyes. Serious, too. I don't know why I've never seen it before. Maybe because I never bothered to look that closely.

"I've wanted to be your friend for a long time," he admits.

"You have? You always ignore me."

"Well, you're always with Will."

"Oh." I gulp.

A car pulls up. I jump.

Max steps into the hallway just as Richard and I get there. He's carrying balloons in one hand and a cake in the other. "She's okay," he says when his eyes meet mine. "Walking pneumonia, several prescriptions, but she's here. Your mom is helping her right now."

Mom, with Aunt Katherine on her arm, enters behind Max. Mom's eyes meet mine. And I see something I know is in my own eyes. Worry and relief. We do have that in common. We both love her.

Aunt Katherine sees me, and her eyes, unusually dull and tired, brighten slightly. I realize suddenly it feels like I've been holding my breath underwater and now I can finally breathe again. I want to run and hug her and bury my head in her arms. But instead I just smile back and whisper, "Thank you"—to God, to the cosmic force, to Mother Earth, to anyone who might be listening. "Are you okay?" I ask.

"I'll live," she says in a raspy voice that turns into a cough. She coughs and coughs. "As long as I don't take many more winter adventures out to certain islands." She winks at me. Mom looks puzzled. But she'll forget. And something tells me it will be like this again and again. Aunt Katherine and me knowing things we don't always share with Mom. Things Mom really doesn't want to know about anyway. And that makes me feel safe, like warm fires and snuggling on soft sofas and feeling my neck tingle every time I hear Aunt Katherine call me "love."

I become aware again of Richard standing right behind me.

Aunt Katherine and Mom are both peering at him.

"Oh, Mom, Max, Aunt Katherine." I step aside and Richard moves forward. Richard, whose dad was friends with my dad. Richard, who watched me go into the church tonight. Richard, who loved Pastor Browning, too. As he steps beside me, I smell the scent of fresh soap. Clean and nice. "This is Richard Penrose." I look at him and smile, then add, "A friend of mine."

author's note

To the best of my knowledge, there is no Church of the Holy Divine. But Kate's fictional story is dear to my heart, because like her, I broke away from a church that dictated what I thought, drank, wore, read, and saw. Our church maintained an insulated community that kept us busy by design. As an adult I spent twenty to thirty hours a week attending services and doing "church work," in addition to raising my three children. Even if I had been tempted to doubt my religion, I wouldn't have had the time.

Kate was almost sixteen when she broke away. I was forty. And my father hadn't just died—my twelve-year-old daughter had. As I grieved for her, I began thinking a lot about life after death. I discovered I was no longer comfortable with the answers my church gave me. I did the unthinkable. Consumed with my deep sadness, I began to question and doubt other aspects of my conservative religion, including the limited, demeaning role of women and the ostracizing of homosexuals.

I began to read books and explore other ideas. As my eyes slowly opened to the larger world outside my church, I realized there were many other churches like mine that claimed to be the one and only true church and kept their members obedient through strict rules and limited outside influences. They were also most often governed by a male hierarchy. Many limited women to the roles of homemakers and mothers and instilled this philosophy in girls from a young age.

Admitting to my church community and family members that I no longer had faith in the doctrines I was raised with was very difficult. However, not even the deep sorrow of being considered "the black sheep" by those I love could convince me to go back. Waking each morning free to decide what to do with my day, what to wear, and what to think and read is too liberating. The wonder of it feels magical every single day.

I'm still not sure about what happens after we die. Is there a Heaven? A Hell? I don't know. And I'm finally at peace with that.

Beckie Weinheimer
March 2007